The Last Summer

To Lisa
I hope you enjoy
reading Margaret's story
as much as I did
writing it

Lorna Shaw

The Last Summer

The first novel of the New Lancastrian series

LORNA J. SHAW

authorHOUSE®

AuthorHouse™ LLC
1663 Liberty Drive
Bloomington, IN 47403
www.authorhouse.com
Phone: 1-800-839-8640

Published by AuthorHouse 07/11/2014

ISBN: 978-1-4918-5284-2 (sc)
ISBN: 978-1-4918-5286-6 (hc)
ISBN: 978-1-4918-5285-9 (e)

Library of Congress Control Number: 2014901008

Dedication

I would like to dedicate this book to my two older sisters, Mildred Austin and Blanche McLean, whose husbands each died of Alzheimer's from whom many of the anecdotes of the heroine's vicissitudes were taken by permission.

Frightened from a frail sleep, Murgit sat up quickly, gnarled hands clasping her hollow chest as the haunting dream faded into the foggy dome of the snow hut. She hunched on her couch of tattered hides, rocking slowly, keening softly into the folds of her worn parka.

Insulated from the howling blizzard, the frigid room lay in murky silence. The flame from the seal oil lamp cast weak shadows toward the wide family bed of bracken and bearskins. Murgit's son sprawled naked between layers of soft caribou pelts, the warm bodies of his two wives and their children beside him. Murgit listened to their sounds of sleep. Sighing, she fed the lamp a chunk of blubber and turned to her sewing basket. The leggings for her oldest grandson were almost finished. She tied the last of the knots and gnawed the sinew threads with the stub in her shrunken gums. Replacing the leggings in the basket, she rose and smoothed the ragged covers of her couch. Then she undressed slowly, methodically folding each garment. Finally, clad only in a thin vest, the shriveled woman pushed the wisps of stringy hair from her face, and glancing at her sleeping family, she brushed past the bearskin curtain to crawl up the tunnel into the Arctic night. The wind blasted her shivering frame. Gazing up at the vast sky Murgit prayed to the Great Spirit for deliverance to death before the village scavengers awoke. And then amidst the blinding snow, she stumbled away toward the endless world.

No man is an island, it continues on of itself; any man's death diminishes Me because I am involved in mankind: And therefore never send to know for whom the bell tolls; it tolls for thee . . . .
John Donne 1624

Chapter One

MARGARET DARWIN GLANCED AT HER wrist watch again and sighed, resigned to the certainty she would now be very late for an appointment with her accountant, Bill Davidson. A telephone summons that morning to meet with her doctor the same afternoon had caused some little concern but her apprehensive mood was now rapidly changing to one of irritation instead. Thirty minutes ago, a crisply efficient nurse had ushered her to an examining room to await the arrival of Dr. Joel Green. And here, she had sat, patiently viewing the sepia prints on the pale green walls, a lumpy sort of a woman with fading brown hair pulled into a knot at the back of her head. She picked at a frayed thread on the cuff of her white polyester blouse, and to relieve her boredom, stood up to fold her blue raincoat over the back of the wooden chair and then sat down again, smoothing the wrinkles in her gray flannel skirt.

Her frustration eased as Dr. Green entered and closed the door quietly. She watched his friendly freckled face as he crossed the room to lay her chart on the desk. "Well, Mrs. Darwin. And how are you feeling today?"

She shifted her frame on the hard chair. "About the same, I guess."

The nurse pushed the door open and held out a portable phone. "It's urgent."

He reached for it. "Green here . . . Yes . . . When?" Turning toward the door, he walked out into the hall with a marked tone of gravity in his voice as he asked, "Is Dr. Fairfax in the hospital?"

Margaret heaved a sigh and rose to walk over to the window. A garbage truck was hoisting a large dumpster and she watched as the jowls of the monstrous machine devoured the trash. The truck beeped its way back down the alley as she looked at her watch again. At this rate I'll never make it to the travel office either! Walking back to the chair she noticed her chart on the desk and casually lifted the cover of the folder to scan the page ". . ." ovarian cancer, stage IV. Prognosis, terminal." Her vision blurred and she leaned forward to steady herself on the desk and read the words again. A freckled hand closed the file.

Margaret raised her stricken eyes to Dr. Green's and saw a compassionate misery. "Cancer?" she whispered. "I'm going to die?"

He lay his hand on her shoulder.

She shuddered violently.

"I'm sorry," he said quietly taking her hand. "Let's sit down." He rolled his chair in front of hers. "There's never an easy way to say this, to soften the truth . . ."

"How long do I have?" she asked dully.

"It all depends . . ."

She raised her eyebrows.

He opened the chart. "You came to see me almost three weeks ago with symptoms of abdominal pain, fatigue, malaise. Upon examination I found some tenderness in your lower left quadrant. The ultra sound confirmed a small mass in the ovary. That's when I consulted Dr. Carson, an oncologist, and he agreed we should run the full battery of tests."

"Dr. Carson. He's the one who examined me at the hospital, before the barium enema." She still remembered the intense prodding before undergoing the horrendous procedure in the x-ray department.

"Yes." He held Dr. Carson's report. "You have a small palpable mass in the left ovary, anomalies in the large bowel, an inconclusive mammogram because of fibrous tissue and cysts. The most damaging evidence is in the blood test, a very high serum count indicating an advanced ovarian malignancy."

She closed her eyes. "So what do I do now?"

"You have few options, Mrs. Darwin. When Dr. Carson received the lab report he asked me to see you immediately. He advises, and I agree, that you have a total hysterectomy as soon as possible."

She opened her eyes. "When?"

He laid the report on the desk. "It's Friday afternoon. I've been trying to make arrangements for your surgery. You will possibly be admitted to hospital on Monday and we want to run some more tests, blood studies, a bone scan, a new type of mammogram . . . I hope the operation can be scheduled for Tuesday morning at the latest. We'll talk about chemotherapy and, or radiation later."

She pressed her lips tightly together and drew a deep breath.

He touched her arm. "Look, Mrs. Darwin. Go home and talk this over with your husband, your family . . . If they have any questions . . ."

"I'm a widow," she said quietly.

"Do you have children?"

"Two sons."

He nodded. "Well, I'll do everything I can to help you through this." He watched the top of her bowed head for a long moment before standing up to reach for her coat. "I must go now. My son's been in an accident and I've got to get to the hospital."

She rose woodenly and he helped her with the coat before they walked up the hall to an empty waiting room. "We'll be in touch with you on Monday morning," he said patting her shoulder. "Let's hope for the best . . ."

Margaret nodded and walked slowly out of the clinic. Reaching the busy street she threaded her way through the throngs of shoppers, her mind whirling as the reality of her illness set into the depths of her mind. Her pace quickened with each step and the brisk April wind dried the tears in her green eyes as she fled along Markdale Street, the rumbling sounds of traffic drowning the pounding of her heart. She was almost running by the time she reached the park, and out of breath, she slowed her stride and felt herself crumbling into little pieces. She collapsed on a bench, weeping.

A group of small children nearby stopped their play and watched. A young mother approached, her brows knit together, her lips drawn in a tight line. She touched Margaret's shoulder.

Looking up into the woman's anxious eyes, Margaret grabbed her purse and hurried away from the playground, stumbling across the rough grass toward a stand of bleachers beside a soccer field as hot tears coursed down her cheeks. "Oh God! I'm going to die!" she wailed, sinking down on a bench. "Why! Why? After all I've been through!" Years of pent-up grief burst from her heart, overwhelming this new anguish and she railed at the injustices of life as dreadful, soul-wrenching sobs exorcised the torments of bygone days. Finally, exhausted by the ordeal, she turned and lay her head down on her outstretched arm on the next tier, crying quietly.

Boisterous boys clad in team colours began appearing on the field, kicking soccer balls, running, dodging, shouting to their teammates.

Sighing, Margaret wiped her face and heaved herself to leaden feet to walk slowly back to Thornbury Village.

Long ago, Thornbury Village actually was a village, a crossroads in a rural hamlet some distance from the city of Toronto. As years passed, the church, the school, the smithy, the emporium and the inhabitants of a few houses were joined by retired farmers unwilling to leave their roots. Then Torontonians discovered the delightful countryside, and an insidious urban sprawl added a cosmopolitan flavour. A small hospital and retirement home was built to meet the needs of an aging population. As the city's burgeoning borders encroached steadily across the rural landscape, Thornbury disappeared into a busy commercial center, swallowed by industry and huge suburbs. A new hospital was built elsewhere and the old one became a large chronic care complex with an adjoining apartment building for family care-givers. A large gilt sign mounted on the red brick wall enclosing the facility indicated a reversion to the former name.

. The wrought iron gate clanged shut as Margaret crossed the wide expanse of lawn and gardens to enter her apartment. Hanging up her coat, she went into her small tidy kitchen and plugged in the tea kettle. By the time she had changed into her old pink chenille bathrobe the kettle was singing merrily. She carried a tray into the living room and sat in her rocking chair beside the window, sipping the tea, hoping in some way to fill up the dreadful gaping hole inside her chest. She rocked slowly for an eternity staring out at the Green as the twilight of an April evening crept across the neat rows of tulips now closing their sleepy heads. The shadows mounted the red brick wall opposite her apartment building and she watched as the lights in the nursing home came on, one by one.

How many months had she sat in the small room on the third floor of that building and looked out upon the same scene. How many weeks had she listened to the sounds of misery and wretchedness from the corridor. How many days had she watched the transformation of her husband into a vegetative state. How many hours had she contemplated the unfairness of God who allowed such dreadful things to happen to good people. And now it was happening to her!

She sat and rocked until the room was almost dark, her mind still numbed by the events of the afternoon. Automatically reaching for the lamp switch, she groped futilely, forgetting for a moment she had given her lamps to Bruce and his wife Jennie after they had driven her home from the family Easter dinner with Charles and Mavis. Easter dinner . . . Easter dinner . . .

A tear rolled down her cheek. Was it only two weeks ago? Two weeks of bright hope and planning for another future? Two weeks of happiness?

She closed her eyes remembering . . .

Her four grandsons had been excused and had gone to romp about in the basement while the adults remained at the table drinking their coffee. Margaret looked around the attractive room admiring the furniture that had once graced the dining room in her own home. Her eldest son, Charles, sat at one end of the table reminding her very much of John, her late husband. His dark hair and eyes, his straight nose and perfect teeth, his erect posture were mirrored by his wife Mavis who sat at the opposite end of the table. It had always been a topic of discussion with a sense of wonderment among friends and family how two people who looked so much alike could have found each other amid the thousands of students at the university and married. New acquaintances instantly marked the similarity, and even strangers in crowded places often turned their heads wondering if they were twin siblings. Mavis, a younger replica of her mother Gertrude who was seated next to Margaret, smiled and asked," Will you have some more coffee, Mother Darwin?"

"Please," replied Margaret passing her cup along to Gertrude. She folded her dinner napkin meticulously and glanced around the table. "By the way, I'm thinking of moving out of Thornbury Village."

Charles raised an eyebrow. "Oh?"

"Yes. I can't live there any longer now that your Dad's gone . . ."

Bruce glanced at Jennie. "Uh . . . Where are you planning to move?"

"I don't know yet."

Charles frowned. "You don't know?"

Mavis pressed her lips together.

Gertrude pushed back her chair. "I think we need some more coffee, Mavis. I'll go and make some."

Margaret watched the tall slender woman elegantly groomed in a mauve silk dress, her mauve hair expertly coiffed about her noble face, carry the silver server into the kitchen. She glanced down at the nubby brown tweed skirt and beige nylon blouse she was wearing and felt like a dowdy poor relation. Moments lapsed, and sensing an undercurrent of tension around the silent table, Margaret wondered if they were afraid she might be planning to move into one of their homes. She wiped her lips and decided to quickly set their fears at rest. "I've been thinking of putting the furniture into storage for several months. I . . . I'd like to go to England."

Charles raised both eyebrows. "England!"

"Yes. I've been reading about the different tours. The Elderhostel thing. I think I'd enjoy it. I mean, getting out with people my own age, making new friends . . . It's time to move on, make a change . . ."

Charles cocked his head. "Do you have enough money?"

"I don't expect it will cost very much. I'm not planning to stay in fancy hotels or anything like that . . . Just a bed and breakfast type of place. I've been talking to Bill Davidson. He's made some good investments with the money from the sale of the house. And when your father's insurance cheque comes through I should be all right."

"When will you go?" Jennie asked.

"In May. The weather should be nice then."

Charles cleared his throat. "Mavis and I are going on a holiday in Bermuda in about three weeks. We may be away when you leave . . ."

"And I have a convention in Vancouver," Bruce added.

Margaret shrugged. "I suppose I can manage to get myself to the airport without you." She grinned and said brightly, "No one's indispensable, you know."

Jennie chuckled. "I'll be here to help."

Margaret smiled at her blonde cherubic daughter-in-law. "Don't give it another thought. I'm glad to have something to do."

Later that evening as Bruce drove her back to Thornbury Village, she turned to her grandsons in the back seat. "Are you boys still bouncing balls in your living room?"

Mark grinned at her. "No, Grammaw. Mom's really cracking the whip these days."

"Then I'm going to trust my lamps to her tender loving care."

Jennie gasped. "Your Capodimonte lamps! The ones Dad bought for your silver anniversary?"

"Yes. I was admiring my dining suite tonight. Mavis has decorated her dining room very nicely, hasn't she. I want you to have something of value too, Jennie. They might as well be in your house as in a storage space."

"But you'll want them for later . . . After you come home from England."

"No. They're yours. They might get broken with all the moving."

"Well . . . Thank you very much . . . I'll try to take good care of them."

Bruce cleared his throat. "You don't owe us anything, Mom. You know that, don't you . . . I mean, when you and Dad moved into Thornbury, you gave us a lot of good stuff besides the car that was almost brand new."

Margaret patted his knee. "I know, dear."

When the family trooped into her apartment to bear away the precious lamps, she gave them her small television set and a clock radio too. After watching them drive off into the night, she walked back into the apartment and with a sudden unfamiliar rush of elation felt she was halfway to England already.

England! Margaret stopped rocking. I can't go to England after all . . . Oh what am I going to do . . . She began to rock again and watch the dying light outside in the garden as lines from a familiar poem came to mind . . . *"Rage, rage against the dying of the light."* She remembered Dylan Thomas had penned those lines to protest his father's mild acceptance of a pending death. Now her death was pending too and she had no rage left either. She rose to carry her tray back to the kitchen and grasped the edge of the sink in wretched misery. "What am I going to do?"

Tears streamed down her cheeks as she rinsed the dishes and replaced them in the cupboard. Her head was beginning to ache fiercely behind throbbing eyes and she went into the bathroom to splash cold water on her face. Staring at the pale, bloated reflection in the mirror she shivered. I look dead already. Oh God . . . What am I going to do?

A long black evening yawned ahead and Margaret reached into the cabinet for a full bottle of white tablets. The family doctor had prescribed them when John had first entered the hospital and she had been unable to sleep without him at her side. When the pharmacist had given her the pills with a warning that they were related to Valium, Margaret decided not to use them, fearing she might become addicted.

Now she looked at the bottle in her hand. It doesn't matter any more. I could take the whole bottle and it wouldn't matter at all.

She raised her eyes to the wretch in the mirror. "No. Don't even think about it."

She spilled one tablet into her palm, looked at it and added another before returning the bottle to the cabinet. Gulping them down, she went into the bedroom, crawled into bed and waited in lonely despair. Finally, she felt herself sinking into oblivion.

Drifting amid the tendrils of consciousness, floating upwards through the drowsy depths into the wan light of morning, Margaret remembered Charles and Bruce. The thought of the news she would have to share with them dragged her heart down to the murky bottom of despair. A pressing need to call them, to see them, to tell them of her illness weighed increasingly on her conscience and banished the veiled wisps of dreams. Finally, she rose from her bed to deal with the issue at hand and dialed Charles' number.

"Good morning, Mavis."

"Hello, Mother Darwin. Well . . . We haven't heard from you for ages. I suppose you're busy, getting ready to go to England."

Margaret bit her lip. "I haven't heard from you either," she replied, hoping a caustic note hadn't crept into the tone of her voice. "I imagine you're keeping busy too with the boys and all . . ."

"Yes, and with all the work getting ready for the addition on the house."

"Oh?"

"Charles did tell you about my mother moving in with us, didn't he?"

Margaret was about to say he hadn't when Mavis continued, "So when we build a granny flat on the garage for her, we're going to extend the second floor to make a master bedroom for us too. We're quite excited about it. It'll give us an extra bathroom upstairs as well as one in Mother's suite too."

"Oh?"

"Charles drew up the plans with the contractor. He's supposed to start work before we leave for Bermuda."

"Speaking of Charles, I'd like to talk to him. Is he at home?"

"No. He's at the office. It's tax time. We hardly see him any more."

"So he won't be home this afternoon . . ."

"I'm not sure he'll even be here for dinner. He says the clients are lined up at the door. Do you want to leave a message for him?"

"No. I guess not. I'll try to see him tomorrow. How are the boys?"

"They're fine. I'm taking them to soccer practice after lunch."

"Then I'd better let you go, Mavis. Give them my love."

"Sure. And I'll tell Charles you called."

Hanging up the receiver, Margaret sat quietly by the window, staring vacantly at the wheelchairs wheeling, the strollers strolling on the Green, her thoughts far removed from the scene. At last she sighed, picked up the phone again and dialed Bruce's number.

"Hello, Mom," her younger son said sprightly. "How are you today?"

"I was wondering if you were going to be home this afternoon, dear. I thought I'd stop by. There's something I'd like to speak to you about."

"Gosh, I'm sorry but I'm heading back to the plant right now. The lab called. They're having trouble pouring the resins. I'm liable to be there for quite a while. Can't you talk to me now?"

She blinked away sudden tears. "No. Not now. Perhaps I can see you tomorrow . . ."

"Okay, Mom. I'll catch you later."

Her maternal composure dissolved instantly upon hanging up the receiver and she flung herself across the bed, sobbing uncontrollably, awash in abysmal loneliness. Oh God! What am I going to do? What's going to become of me? Oh God, God, God . . . After some time she turned over and stared at the ceiling through brimming eyes. Unconsciously, her left hand began to massage her abdomen. She wiped her eyes with her sleeve and thought of how many months she had laid in this bed, feeling the pressure, the presence of something there. Too tired, too depressed to care, she had ignored it hoping it would go away. And it did, occasionally. But sometimes, in the dark of night, she would touch herself and find the presence had returned, quietly but steadily reminding her that all was not well. Only after John's funeral did she finally make an appointment at the clinic.

And now . . ." Oh I can't lie here all day!" She rose, pulled on a shirt and slacks, made her bed and went out to the kitchen to discover she had very little left in the kitchen to eat. I meant to shop on the way home yesterday . . . And I forgot about Bill Davidson! And ordering my tickets for England! Well, I can forget about that now. I'll have to call Bill first thing Monday morning. What a mess! And there's no point in shopping for groceries today if I'm going into the hospital on Monday.

Walking down the corridor to the cafeteria, Margaret stopped at her mailbox and found a note from the building superintendent reminding her that the tenant's agreement had expired at the time of John's death. There was a long waiting list for a vacancy and he would appreciate hearing from her soon. She stuffed the envelope into her pocket and walked into the empty cafeteria to select an egg salad sandwich, a carton of milk and a steaming bowl of vegetable soup. The tasty soup awakened her appetite and she had almost finished it when a woman approached carrying a coffee mug.

"Mrs. Darwin."

She studied this woman dressed modestly in a dark blue coat.

"You don't recognize me out of uniform, do you? I'm Shirley Martin. I used to care for your husband."

"Oh. Mrs. Martin. Yes, I didn't recognize you. Will you sit down?" She pushed her tray aside as Shirley took off her coat."

"So how are you, Mrs. Darwin? I never expected to see you again after, after Mr. Darwin passed on."

"I'm still here, but not for long. So . . . Mrs. Martin, Shirley . . . What are you doing here?"

"I've got some time to kill before I go on duty. I've just come from my cousin's funeral." Shirley reached for her purse and pulled out a pack of cigarettes. "Do you mind if I smoke?"

"I'd rather you didn't."

Shirley dropped the pack on the table and picked up her coffee mug instead. "It was awful," she sighed. "Thirty-five years old, two kids . . . She had a breast removed five or six years ago. She went through chemo-therapy and seemed to be fine. And then two years ago they found a lump in her other breast so they took that one off too. And after that, it seemed like it was just one dammed thing after another. She had a hysterectomy and more chemo. And then it was in the bowel and she had a colostomy. She just went through living hell. Excuse me, Mrs. Darwin. I really need a cigarette." Shirley rose and moved to a table some distance away, lit her cigarette and drew deeply. She exhaled slowly and a cloud of smoke circled her head.

Margaret watched for a moment, picked up her sandwich and milk and walked to the door stopping by the table. "I'm sorry," she said softly and reached out to touch the nurse's shoulder.

Shirley raised moist eyes. "I wish she'd never let them start hacking away at her. She was feeling okay. She should have stayed home with her kids and smelled the flowers."

After Margaret put her sandwich and milk in the refrigerator, she sat in her rocking chair and stared at the tulips. "She should have smelled the flowers," she mused." Maybe I should smell the flowers. Sometimes I feel sick and tired but it hasn't stopped me from planning to go to England. And I feel all right now . . . But after the surgery . . . And when they start chemo-therapy" . . . Jane had chemo and she lost all her hair. Oh God! I don't want to be bald! Not that on top of everything else . . . Oh vanity! Foolish, foolish vanity . . . What a price to pay for my life? But there's no guarantee . . . And when that fails what if they hack away at me too?

She began to rock more quickly. I won't think about it now. I've got to find a place to live when I come home from the hospital. I can't go to Bruce's. They don't have room for me. And I won't go to Charles' . . . Not when Gertrude is there too. I'll get a place near the hospital. And a moving company can move my stuff. I'll ask the boys to take care of it. That's not too much to ask of them.

Margaret walked back to the atrium and bought a newspaper in the tuck shop. Spreading the classified section on her kitchen table she circled several ads in the apartment rental column and called three listings, making appointments for the next morning. Snacking on her sandwich and milk she perused the rest of the paper and a full colour page caught her eye. A group of art students were drawing chalk murals on the floor of a mall. Their teacher at the local high school had suggested the project after watching the Mary Poppins movie video.

Margaret almost smiled. Mary Poppins . . . John and I took the children to see the Mary Poppins movie in New Lancaster.

Memories of a family vacation at a fishing lodge on the Montreal River brought respite to her troubled mind. After several fine days of boating and swimming in a pristine wilderness, they were now confined to a smoky lounge as a bout of cool rainy weather swept across northern Ontario. They had played Old Maid and Crazy Eights, read stories, worked jig-saw puzzles in front of a temperamental fire in the huge fireplace and grew bored as the rain drummed incessantly on the corrugated tin roof. The owner of the camp, fearing they might pack up and leave, suggested a movie. The forty mile ride to New Lancaster had seemed a small price to pay for the children's happiness. Almost twenty-five years had passed but Margaret still remembered the lovely town on the shore of a large lake, the tree lined streets, the old stately homes . . .

She shrugged her shoulders dismissing the memory and rubbed her face as the chore of packing and organizing herself pressed on her mind. She would have to ask the custodian for cartons to pack her dishes and linens. Retrieving her luggage from the storage space, she opened the doors to her bedroom closet and stood for a time, wondering where to start. Most of her clothing was so old she hated to even look at it. Winter clothing. Summer clothing. What should I take? What will I need? Will I live through another winter? Will this be my last summer? Despondent, she closed the doors, went into the bathroom, gulped down three pills and curled up on her bed, still fully dressed.

Her family watched from the bureau. A silver-haired man smiled serenely at her from a silver frame, the same smile he wore when all was well in his home and office, a handsome man with dark eyes, a firm chin. This picture had graced the financial page of the newspaper marking his promotion to manager of the district office of a large insurance company. Oh John . . .

A young dark-eyed serious woman watched from another frame. Her daughter wore the robe and hood of a university graduate. Oh Jane . . .

Charles and Mavis posed regally in their wedding portrait, the cathedral length train of Mavis' gown draped artfully to one side, his black tuxedo defining her satin brocade.

Bruce, the husky athlete, dwarfed his petite Jennie as they laughed for the photographer in the sunshine after their informal wedding in Darwins' rose garden.

You're all I have left now . . . And you're not much help to me, are you . . . You weren't much help with your father either, you know . . . And as he grew away from us into that little dark secret world, you grew away from him, and me too. It was my fault. I let it happen. Why did I think I had to protect you from your father's illness? I should have insisted you become more involved with his care . . . I know, you were afraid. And I was too. We all were . . . Did you think it was easier for me? To know I was losing your father a little more every day? To know there was no hope at all? Was it easy for me to give up my home, my life, to move here to be with him? To take care of him? And then the nightmare of Jane . . . Oh God! I can't think about Jane. Not now . . . Not now. But is it so terrible to die? To go gently into that good night . . . And what comes after night . . . Morning? Resurrection? I don't know. I don't know anything any more.

Sunlight shone through her eyelids and she struggled to open her eyes wondering lethargically why they wouldn't move. Her limbs seemed to lie apart from her body like a broken marionette, the strings in tangled disarray. She lay quietly and strangely unafraid as though she was watching from a great distance, high and lifted up, far removed and only waiting for her total self to come together and function again. She remembered Bruce telling her about a college friend who had drunk himself into an alcoholic coma. 'He looked like the lights were on but nobody was home when they carted him off to the hospital,' he had said.

I wonder if I look like nobody's home too. I'm not going to take any more of those pills . . . Unless . . . Now able to open her eyes she turned her head and looked at the family photographs for a long time and then around at the furnishings in the room. I'm not sorry to leave this place. It's never been home to me. It's memories that make a home . . . Good memories of happy times, love shared . . . laughter, and even tears . . . Well, I've had the tears . . .

She pushed herself to sit up dizzily on the side of the bed and eventually managed to make her way into the bathroom. Dropping her clothing on the floor she stood for a long time under a very warm shower, washing away the cobwebs of her mind. By the time she had dried her hair she was able to eat the last of the bread and cheese, wash it down with a mug of tea and walk out to the corner to catch a bus downtown.

A block from Main Street, Margaret entered a large brick house to inspect an apartment on the second floor. Mrs. Ryan, the owner of the house, caught her breath at the top of the stairs. "You'll like this place," she puffed. "It's big and bright and close to the center of town."

Margaret walked about the spacious living-room, fingering the drapes, opening a closet door. "Your previous tenant must have had a cat."

Mrs. Ryan frowned.

"Can't you smell it?" Margaret asked, walking toward the kitchen.

Mrs. Ryan sniffed the air.

She came back to look into the large bedroom. "It's a very nice apartment but I couldn't live here with that odour."

Mrs. Ryan raised her eyebrows. "I suppose I could have the carpets cleaned."

Margaret nodded. "I'll think about it. I'm having surgery this week and my two sons will have to supervise the move . . ."

"Well this is ideal for you then. It's close to the hospital."

"Yes," Margaret replied. "I'll let you know this afternoon."

She walked three blocks further down the same street to a white frame house with a clean bright apartment on the first floor. Quite pleased with the place, she was ready to make arrangements when the windows began to rattle and she heard a freight train rumbling nearby.

The landlord frowned.

"Does this happen often?" Margaret asked, raising her voice.

He leaned toward her as the noise grew louder. "Not really."

"I'll let you know if I want it," she shouted as the din became unbearable.

Leaving the house she came to a shiny set of double tracks and surmised she was looking at the main rail line for southern Ontario. Several blocks away she found the third apartment building, a huge warren of corridors filled with stale odours of curries and old clothing. She shrank from the noise of crying children and said to the manager, "I'm looking for something quiet."

Mrs. Ryan was happy to see her, and happier still when Margaret gave her a post-dated cheque for two month's rent. She assured her new tenant that the rugs would be cleaned immediately and she could move in before the end of the week.

Relieved that she now had a roof over her head, Margaret walked back to Main Street and entered a coffee shop crowded with Sunday morning regular adherents. Sitting on an uncomfortable stool she munched on a doughnut and pondered whether to return to Thornbury Village and pack, or visit her sons' homes and reveal her uncertain future. Deciding to face the dreaded task, she drank the dregs of her coffee and went outside to hail a cab. Next door, a florist was carrying pots of azaleas outside to a sidewalk display. On impulse she bought two plants heavy with rosy blooms and took a cab to Bruce's house. The driveway was empty. No one was home. Frustrated, she continued on to Charles' house. Finding no one home there either, she came back to sit in the taxi, disappointed, perplexed, relieved.

"Where to now, Lady?" the cabby asked at last.

Biting the tip of her little finger, she hesitated. "Fairlawn Cemetery," she said at last, certain the remaining members of her family had not left their home. She paid the driver at the entrance and walked almost a quarter of a mile along the rows of headstones until she came to her own. Her husband and her daughter lay beneath her feet, their names engraved above and below her own name in the rose marble. The date of her own death would complete the epitaph.

The grass on Jane's grave resisted her attempts to dig a hole with the plastic pots. The fresh sod on John's grave was easier so she planted both azaleas there. She stood up and leaned against another headstone to view her work. So this is where it ends . . . Oh my dears . . . I don't think I'm afraid any more. Fear has been my constant companion for such a long time. My fear for you, John. Fear for our future. Fear of losing all we had shared together over the years. Fear of being alone . . . And I was afraid for you too, Jane. So afraid for your suffering, for your loneliness and the loss of all your dreams . . . Well, my life is drawing to a close now too, and some day soon I'll enter the valley of death and journey on to meet you . . . Are you in heaven? Is there really such a place? You didn't hear the story the rector told us at your funeral, John . . . Or did you? He stood there and said, 'Mr Darwin has begun a voyage. Imagine this, my friends. Your loved one is aboard a ship. It is leaving the pier. And you, his family and friends, have come to say farewell. You are saddened by his departure. You have a sense of loss because you will not see him again in this life. You wave goodbye as the ship leaves the harbour. You watch and wait. And as the ship slips beneath the horizon you cry, "There he goes!'

"'But my friends, remember this. There is another horizon. And there is another shore. And as John Darwin disappears from your sight, there are people on that other shore who see the ship coming toward them. And among those people are his other loved ones who have gone before, his parents, his daughter, his friends. And they cry out, 'Here he comes!'

"Is it true, John? Is there another shore? And will you and Jane be standing there waiting for me as my ship pulls in? Is there really a place called Heaven? Is this life just a testing ground to see if we're worthy to enter into our Valhalla or Nirvana or Heaven or those Elysian Fields? And what if we're not worthy? . . .

As Margaret mused on the poignant truth of her mortality a sudden sadness filled her heart and tears streamed afresh down her cheeks. She picked up the plastic pots and walked toward the entrance depositing them in a trash container near the gate before beginning the long trek back to Thornbury Village. She trod slowly along the path by the road, unaware of the beauty and clarity of the bright April afternoon; the pale green buds on branches reaching their gloved fingers toward the sun; the lush grass along the trickling ditch; quarrelsome sparrows twittering in the shrubs and hedgerows; crocus blossoms bright against the moist dark earth in the flower beds of the occasional bungalow. She walked pensively, burdened by the knowledge that less than a day of freedom remained. Invading cancerous demons had already seized control of her life, shaping her future, altering her plans. And tomorrow she would surrender her being to the exorcising rituals of the priestly servants in the temple of medicine; there her body would be sacrificed on the altar by the hands of the high-priest surgeon. No longer would she, or could she consider herself to be the master of her fate, the captain of her soul.

After walking for an hour, Margaret reached the suburbs and entered a busy fast-food restaurant, tired and hungry. After devouring the standard fare of burger, fries and a 'shake', she called Charles' and Bruce's numbers from a pay telephone. When answering machines requested a message, she hung up and caught a bus back to Thornbury Village.

Frustrated that her time was growing short, she busied herself sorting clothing and packed a small bag to take to the hospital. When there was still no answer at her sons' homes she groaned aloud in despair." They never have time for me. I might as well be dead." That sobering thought pierced her soul and she lay down on the bed to wallow in self pity. It's always something else. I think they mean well but there's never enough time. I don't expect that much. What's the matter with us? With me? Am I some sort of a pariah? I don't bother them with my affairs. They're always so busy with their lives. And they never had time for their father either. But now, when I need them, really, need them . . . Will they have time to come and see me at the hospital? Will they have time to take care of all this moving? Oh God . . . What am I going to do? She wiped her eyes on the sheet. We're a family and families are supposed to care for each other . . . But we're more like polite strangers passing on the street . . . I don't think they care about me, not really care . . . Oh God . . . If I could just go to sleep and never wake up again . . .

Unaccustomed to the exercise and fresh air, a weary Margaret closed her eyes to rest for an hour. Waking much later in total darkness with a terrible nausea, she rushed to the bathroom and vomited her last meal. She looked at her trembling, perspiring reflection and said, "That's it. The sooner I die, the better. I'm not going to the hospital tomorrow. I won't have the surgery or chemo-therapy or anything else. I can't go through with it. I can't and I won't!"

She wiped her face and sat on the edge of the bed. I'll move to Mrs. Ryans' and stay there 'til I die. That thought brought her no comfort and she looked across the room to her sons' pictures. And will you come to see me there? Or will you still be too busy? She brushed away a tear. I don't want to be a burden to you but there's nothing I can do about it now. She lay back on the bed. I won't have to tell them right away. She sat up again. They think I'm going to England, and when I don't go they'll wonder why. I'll have to tell them . . . She began to pace the apartment. I can't go to England but maybe I can go someplace else . . . Not too far away . . . But where?

The newspaper lay on the table, the chalk drawings exposed. She stopped pacing". New Lancaster! I could go to New Lancaster for the summer. I could stay there 'til I die. Or when I start to get sick, really sick, then, then that's when I'll come home . . . That's when I'll tell them."

She felt a great weight had dropped from her shoulders as she sat down at the kitchen table with a pen and paper to make a list of things to do, to plan her course. An hour later she rose, made a cup of tea and ate the last of a box of soda crackers, knowing she had reached another milestone in her life and she would not turn back.

Shoving the pills to the back of the cabinet, Margaret drew a hot tub and lay in the scented water until she felt drowsy enough to return to bed. She awoke before dawn and forced herself to stay in bed until the hands of the clock pointed to seven. Dressing for the day she walked to the cafeteria for breakfast and stopped at the superintendent's office door on her return.

"I received your note. I'll be leaving before the end of the week."

The balding bespectacled man rose from his desk. "That's quite all right, Mrs. Darwin. Where are you moving?"

She swallowed. "I'm not actually moving. I've decided to go away and I'm sending my furniture to an auction house."

He stroked his chin thoughtfully. "Have you got a minute?"

She stepped inside the office, wondering.

"This isn't common knowledge but my wife and I have separated. I'm living in a motel room and just found an apartment yesterday. Now I need furniture. Would you let me have a look at what you're selling? Perhaps we could save each other a lot of bother?"

An hour later, Margaret had disposed of the contents of her apartment except for her personal treasures. She put his cheque in her purse and called Mrs. Ryan.

"It's Margaret Darwin calling," she said. "I've had a change in my plans and I won't be taking the apartment after all. Will you tear up my cheque?"

A long silence ensued.

"Mrs. Ryan? You do understand I won't be moving into your apartment."

"But you said you'd take it . . ."

"I know I did but I've changed my mind. I never signed a lease. And the cheque is post-dated . . ."

Another long silence.

"Mrs. Ryan?"

"Yes . . ."

"I can call the bank and put a stop payment on the cheque . . ."

"All right, Mrs. Darwin. I'll tear it up."

After Margaret hung up the receiver, she thought for a moment and then called the bank and put a stop payment notice on the cheque anyway.

She was about to dial her doctor's office when the telephone rang.

"Mrs. Darwin? It's Betty at Dr. Green's office. I'm calling to confirm your admission to hospital this morning. You're booked for x-rays this afternoon and surgery at ten o'clock Tuesday morning."

"Is Dr. Green there now, Betty?"

"No."

"Could you give him a message please? Tell him I've decided not to have the x-rays or the operation."

"But Mrs. Darwin! You can't do that . . ."

"Yes I can. Will you give him the message? He can call me here at home this morning but I'll be out for awhile this afternoon."

"I'd better connect you to his nurse. Will you hold for a minute?"

Seconds later she heard, "Mrs. Waters here, Mrs. Darwin. Betty tells me you've decided not to have the surgery."

"Yes."

"You can't do that. You mustn't . . ."

"I can do it, Mrs. Waters. I've already made up my mind . . ."

"But you don't understand. We can help you. They're getting wonderful results with the new platinum chemo-therapy . . ."

"You don't understand, Mrs. Waters. I don't want to spend the next year or two in the hospital recovering from operations, undergoing tests and treatments. I don't want to do that. If I can have a few more good months then I'm willing to face whatever happens next . . ."

"But Dr. Green? He's made all these arrangements . . ."

"I appreciate all he's done for me . . ."

"But what do I tell him? What do I say?"

"I'd like to thank himself myself if I could. Tell him . . . Tell him I've decided to go away and smell the flowers."

"Very well, Mrs. Darwin," the nurse said abruptly and hung up.

Margaret looked at the receiver and sighed. "I'm certainly burning my bridges behind me, aren't I."

Bill Davidson, John's old friend, rose slowly to greet her.

"Thanks for seeing me on such short notice, Bill. I know it's a busy time of year for all you tax people."

He smiled fondly. "That's all right, Margaret. I'm not handling as many of the tax cases now. The young fellows are taking on most of the clients these days. It's time for us old racehorses to leave the barn and head for the pasture." He leaned back in his chair and said, "I ran into Charles the other day at the bank. He said something about you going to England for the summer. Jean and I were over there a couple of years ago. I never saw so many rhododendrons and rose bushes in my life."

Hoping to deflect his interest in her plans for the summer, Margaret asked for more details of their trip abroad and eventually led the conversation around to her investments. ". . . And I should assign you my power of attorney, Bill. There's still John's life insurance policy. I know I can count on you to do what's best."

He handed her the papers and called for his secretary to witness her signature. "You're going to be a wealthy woman, Margaret. Be careful you don't meet up with some fortune hunter on your travels. They're always on the lookout for rich widows, you know."

She pushed herself out of the comfortable chair and smiled wryly, "You won't have to worry about that, Bill." She picked up her purse. "I can't thank you enough for all your help."

He shrugged. "I get my commission, Margaret. And you were John's wife. I know he would have looked out for Jean if the shoe was on the other foot." He accompanied her to the door. "Have a good vacation and be sure to take your raincoat and an umbrella."

She kissed his warm dry cheek and sudden tears came to her eyes. "Goodbye Bill. Thanks again, for everything."

Margaret went into her bank downstairs in the same building to cash a cheque and get a bank draft for five thousand dollars. Clutching her purse, she walked three blocks along Markdale Street to Charles' office on the tenth floor of a new building. An attractive receptionist looked up from her desk. "May I help you?"

"I'd like to see Charles, Mr. Darwin, please."

"Do you have an appointment?"

"No. I'm his mother. I just want to see him for a minute."

The girl raised her eyebrows and leaned over to push a button. "Mr. Darwin's mother is here to see him."

The office door opened and an impeccably groomed secretary emerged. "Please come in, Mrs. Darwin," she said quietly. "He's with a client but he won't be long." She ushered Margaret to an easy chair by the window and returned to her desk smoothing the lapels of her dark blue suit.

Mindlessly twisting the strap on her purse, Margaret surveyed the attractive reception area, becoming increasingly aware of her shabby old raincoat. The office door opened finally and Charles appeared with his client. He noticed his haggard mother and turned quickly to shake the client's hand, smiling, nodding, and laying his hand on the man's shoulder to usher him out the door. Speaking briefly to his secretary, Charles turned to greet his mother. She watched her slim, handsome elder son cross the thick carpet, smiling as he bent down to kiss her cheek.

"Well, Mother. What brings you to town?" He sat down in the chair across from hers.

"I wanted to say goodbye to you. And I had a few things to finish up with Bill Davidson."

"I'd forgotten you were going to England so soon."

"Well this is the first of May, dear."

He nodded.

"So I'm leaving on Thursday."

"Can Bruce take you to the airport? This is such a busy time for me."

"I know. Mavis mentioned that she hardly sees you these days. She's looking forward to Bermuda."

"So am I. Have you seen the boys lately?"

"I've got some boxes to leave at your house tomorrow, some pictures and ornaments, keepsakes that might get broken . . . I'll see them then."

Charles stood up and held out his hand to his faded grey mother. "Well you have a nice holiday. You've earned a good long rest." He laid his hand on her shoulder and walked her to the door. "Be sure to send us a postcard now and then."

The office phones were ringing as he bent to kiss her cheek. "We'll see you when you get back."

"Goodbye Charles."

"Goodbye."

Dismissed, she watched him walk away toward the telephone and felt very much like another of his clients. As the doors to the elevator closed, a sudden wave of loneliness swept over her and she leaned her head against the wall and closed her eyes. I've been alone for such a long time and so nothing's changed. But now everything's changed! And I can't do anything about it.

Her dark mood persisted on the bus ride back to Thornbury Village and she decided to call Bruce's home.

"Hello Jennie. It's Margaret."

"Hello. How are you?"

"Busy. I was wondering if I could come over now. I'm getting myself organized and have a few things I want to leave with you."

"Of course. And stay for supper."

When the taxi pulled into the driveway, Jennie came out to greet her and carried in a large carton while Margaret paid the driver and brought two framed paintings inside. As Jennie admired the watercolours, Margaret said, "You might want to find a place for them. They'll be safer hanging on the wall than stowed in the back of the closet."

"They'll look nice over the sofa," Jennie mused. "We have a starving artist oil there now. These will add a touch of class along with the lamps. Come out to the kitchen and tell me all about your trip while I cook supper."

Her two grandsons returned from school at that moment and led her out to the garage to see the puppy they had purchased yesterday at a kennel. She became involved in their play and later, when Bruce came home, he found his mother in the basement recreation room engrossed in a game of checkers with his youngest son, Tim. "Hi Mom," he said coming down the stairs to kiss her.

She smiled up at her tall sturdy son. "Hello dear. I'm getting beaten by this boy of yours."

"Just you wait. I'm teaching Mark to play chess."

She turned to her older grandson. "Good for you. Your grandfather liked chess but I wasn't very good at it so he taught your dad and uncle to play the game instead. They used to beat him once in a while."

Bruce laughed. "Only when he let us, Mom. Jennie tells me you're leaving this week."

She stared at the board. "Yes." She moved a checker."

Tim clapped his hands. "There Gramma! I gotcha!" He marched his king rapidly across the board as his little freckled face beamed.

"Supper's ready," Jennie called. "Come and get it."

They crowded around the table with the puppy under their feet. "This kitchen's getting too small," Bruce said as he passed his mother the bowl of mashed potatoes.

"And now we've added a dog to the family," Jennie snorted.

"It won't be long before we can put an addition on the house like Charles," he said. "Or maybe we'll just buy a bigger house."

Margaret smiled. "It's about time you started to reap the rewards for all the money and energy you've poured into that business of yours."

He nodded. "This new product looks like a winner and the trade show in Vancouver should prove it. If all goes well then I can start to give Jennie and the boys some of the things we've been dreaming about."

Margaret looked around the table. "You've got each other, and your health, and even a puppy. What more do you need to be happy?"

As they finished the meal, Bruce said, "I'm going to drop the boys off at their Cubs' meeting tonight and go on to the office for an hour. Would you like me to take you home now, Mom?"

"And leave Jennie with the dishes?"

"It's okay," Jennie said. "If they're all out of the house it won't take me long to clean these up."

As Margaret waited in the car while Bruce took Mark and Tim into their meeting she pondered whether to share the news of her illness with her son. *I know he's busy . . . But he's got to know sometime . . . And perhaps this awful heartache would go away if I could just talk to someone . . .*

Bruce hurried to the car and glanced at his watch as he turned on the ignition. "Are you really pressed for time, dear?" she asked.

"I don't know when I've ever had so much to do. And meeting the deadline for Vancouver . . ." He shook his head. "I don't sleep well these nights, Mom. I wake up in the middle of the night making mental lists."

She nodded and folded her hands on her purse as he backed out into the street.

"You're awfully quiet," he said as they finally approached Thornbury Village. "Is anything wrong?"

She swallowed. "I'm going to miss you."

"No you won't. You'll have a wonderful time and meet a lot of people and come back feeling like a new woman."

She grimaced in the dull light. "Well I'll be different, that's for sure," she said, at the same time considering the improbability she would ever come back at all.

He pulled up at the gate. "Don't change too much, Mom. We love you just the way you are."

She kissed him and quickly got out of the car before the dam burst behind her eyes. He drove away as she stumbled blindly into the building, stifling her sobs until she reached the sanctuary of her bedroom. "Oh what am I going to do!"

"Only two more days," Margaret said to her worn reflection as she readied herself for a meeting with Mavis. She had forced herself to eat lunch in the cafeteria although her stomach gnawed constantly, and bouts of diarrhea were an added affliction. "If I can just get away from here and living this lie, I know I'll feel better."

Later that afternoon, she drank tea in the cheery breakfast nook with Mavis and her mother as they showed her the plans for the house and their selections of carpet, drapery, paint and wallpaper. The trip to England had occupied only a fragment of the conversation, and Margaret was relieved to sip and smile and approve the entire building project.

John and James breezed through the back door, dropping their books on the kitchen counter. "Hi Gramma."

Margaret rose and went over to give each of them a hug. "My goodness," she said. "Both of you will soon be as tall as your father."

They grinned and shuffled their feet. "Can we go out to play, Mom?"

"Don't you want to visit with Grandmother Darwin?" Mavis asked.

Margaret reached for her purse. "It's all right. I've got a couple of errands to do on my way home and I should be going now. I'll just call a cab."

As Mavis accompanied her to the front door, Margaret nodded to an oil painting leaning against a carton in the foyer. "Perhaps you'll have room on one of your new walls for that," she said. "And there's a couple of figurines in the carton along with some books and family pictures. They might as well be used as stored in a closet."

Mavis was admiring the painting as Margaret said," Here's my cab already." She kissed her daughter-in-law goodbye, waved to her grandsons embroiled in a street hockey game and drove away from the last of her obligations. A sense of relief that bordered on dismay filled her heart; relief that no one had pressed her for details on her destination and where or how they could reach her should a need arise; dismay that no cared enough to ask for details on her destination and where or how they could reach her to show their concern for her health and safety and happiness.

Thursday afternoon, Margaret locked the last of her suitcases and looked about the apartment. She had vacuumed and scrubbed every corner. Her dishes, pots and pans were stacked on the kitchen counter; her linens, laundered and folded on the table. Four green garbage bags, filled with old clothes, old condiments, and old contents of cupboards and closets, waited in the corridor for the custodian. "It's all trash," she mused as she piled another bag on top. "If only I could get rid of the trash inside my head as easily."

She picked up her purse and went out to wait for the cab at the gate. Seven days had passed since her visit to Dr. Green's office; one week in which her life had changed irrevocably. As the iron gate banged shut behind her she had a sense that she was burning her bridges and there was no turning back. Only the tulips waved goodbye.

Chapter Two

THE TAXI SLOWED SUDDENLY AND Margaret leaned forward to see a phalanx of red lights flashing across the south-bound lanes of the Don Valley Parkway. "What's happening?" she asked.

The cabby glanced in the rear-view mirror at the anxious face of his passenger, a frumpy sort of a woman with mousy hair pulled into a bushy knot. "Dunno," he muttered. "It must be something big." He watched as she looked at her wrist watch, sighed and slumped back in the seat, her lips drawn into a thin line. When her troubled green eyes met his in the mirror he quickly turned his attention to the road. Earlier, when she had assisted him loading the mound of luggage into the cab, he had noted a gentle shabbiness about her person, the worn leather purse and the scuffed walking shoes. Even the baggy blue raincoat had seen better days. Stealing another glimpse of the plain, pleasant face, he wondered if she had been in a rehabilitation center, or perhaps even in custody. That place where she had been living looked like some kind of an institution with the tall brick wall around it but the name Thornbury Village on the gilded sign at the gate gave him no clue to its purpose or function.

He had spent his years behind the wheel of the cab observing the occupants of the rear seat and now he noticed this passenger's pallor, the modest green dress beneath the coat, the small pearl earrings. Everything about her appearance suggested that she had been out of circulation for some time. Even the large round sunglasses she now donned as a shield against the glare of the bright spring sunshine seemed antiquated.

Inching his car forward he surreptitiously watched her gazing out the window at the city sky-line above the forested hillsides while the north-bound traffic drifted monotonously along the opposite side of the valley. Her anxiety level seemed to be rising as he noticed her frequently consulting her watch, biting her lip, chewing the tip of her little finger. The thought occurred to him that Thornbury Village might be some sort of an asylum. "Uh . . . what time does your train leave, Ma'am?"

She leaned forward again. "Six-thirty."

He nodded. "You'll be all right. I see some patrol cars up ahead now. We should be outa this soon."

She gazed through the windshield at the distant flashing lights. "It looks kind of hazy . . . maybe smoky. Something's on fire . . ."

Soon, a faint pungent odour of burning grass permeated the interior of the taxi. Now, police were on each side of the roadway monitoring the flow of traffic, and as the cab crested a knoll Margaret saw a fire creeping down the west side of the blackened valley from a wooded ravine amid drifting billows of smoke. The driver turned his head. "Look at that! And the bridge is on fire too," he mused. They drew closer. "Yeah, the old wooden bridge on Coach Road . . . There's been a bad accident up there. It looks like a gas truck."

From afar Margaret watched the profusion of vehicles' flashing lights as sporadic flames continued to lick the charred timbers, and yellow-coated figures scattered across the scrubby slopes to quench the blazing grass.

The driver tilted his cap. "Yeah. The old bridge is gone. Good riddance . . ." He glanced in the mirror again and said reassuringly, "We'll be outa this in a few minutes."

Passing the last police car, the taxi regained momentum and Margaret looked back at the smoking scene. Another burning bridge, literally this time . . .

The finality of all the decisions of recent days became more real as she watched the cabby pile all of her worldly possessions on the curb outside Union Station. Vestiges of doubt surfaced briefly and she lagged behind the porter's creaking hand cart entering the terminal. Banishing her fears permanently she hurried to catch up to the redcap as her footsteps echoed beneath the cavernous dome of the concourse. He was moving rapidly toward the baggage counter. "I have to buy my ticket," she called.

He swerved quickly and stopped at the long brass grill in front of an agent.

She drew a deep breath. "A ticket to New Lancaster on the Northland this evening."

"Return? Or one way?"

She opened her purse and hesitated, as another bridge flared. "One way."

The porter lifted her heavy suitcases onto the low baggage counter at the head of a long queue. His shiny face smiled broadly as she pressed a generous tip into his hand. "Thank you, Ma'am," he said. She nodded at her fellow passengers and took her place at the end of the line.

Her decision to travel by train had come as a result of the accumulation of her possessions, three large suitcases, a garment bag and several smaller cases. Upon learning she would have to change buses halfway to her destination and cope with her luggage as well, Margaret had decided to take the Ontario Northland instead.

At first she had wondered if leaving the city of her home would be a poignant departure, but as her plans formalized, she decided it would not be difficult at all. Apart from her two sons and their families she had no ties in Toronto or anywhere else for that matter. As an only child, she had no close living relative. Her isolation at Thornbury Village and the passage of time had severed old associations and she had had neither the time nor inclination to make new ones. Her bridge club had disbanded. The Ladies' Guild at the church managed to hold the bazaars and teas without her. Her old rector Jim Pearson had retired and moved away, and the new priest didn't recognize her name when she had called the office several weeks ago to make John's funeral arrangements. She wasn't surprised since she hadn't attended the church for almost seven years. One couple of her former circle of friends had retired and moved to Australia. Another friend had died and her husband remarried. As Margaret stared blindly out the window of the coach at the people passing by on the platform, she wasn't surprised she could calmly say goodbye to all she had known for the last fifty-seven years. Somewhere deep within, she felt as though a part of herself had already shriveled and died and it was only a matter of time before the process was complete.

The train was already gliding out of the station before she became aware they were moving. Young people occupied most of the seats in the coach, chattering, laughing, shifting places. She watched their antics and surmised they were university students starting their summer vacations. Outside, soot-covered empty factories crept backward. Commuters jammed the expressways with the evening traffic. She watched the myriad of little boxes in the suburbs as red lights flashed at crossings with bells clanging. The long muffled wail of the diesel horn echoed across the newer smaller factories and industrial malls that had mushroomed among the ruins of old neighbourhoods. The white-coated steward pushed his food cart along the aisle and Margaret took a styrofoam cup of tea and a muffin. She leaned her head against the cool pane and closed her eyes, suddenly aware for the first time of how truly tired she was. The multitude of preparations for departure had gone so smoothly and yet now she was exhausted, almost too weary to lift the cup and drink the tea.

The conductor moved slowly along the aisle collecting tickets and she looked at her watch, surprised the evening sun still shone so brightly on the lush rolling hills north of the city. She watched the pretentious country estates of the nouveau riche, the split rail fences bordering brick drives leading to colonial mansions; clipped hedges and terraced gardens surrounding brick and stucco Tudor manor houses; endless white rails lining the pastures and paddocks behind sprawling fieldstone bungalows and barns.

The train stopped momentarily to discharge a number of grey homogenous middle-aged men carrying briefcases, and Margaret watched them hurry to waiting cars. A soft mist settled across the gathering dusk as farms and fields and forests blended in the shadows. After a while the glittering lights of towns in the lake district shone through the darkness and more passengers, many of the students, disembarked at intervals. She had gleaned from the gabble flowing along the aisle that most of the young people were employed at the multitude of resorts in Muskoka. She watched them stumble out onto the platform dragging an assortment of backpacks, duffle bags and suitcases, milling about looking for directions to their destinations Much to her surprise, she spied her former pastor among a group of clergymen on the platform, Jim Pearson noticed her watching from the train window and shortly appeared in the aisle beside her in the company of another man of the cloth,

"Mrs. Darwin, What a surprise to see you I was sorry to hear that John had passed away."

She nodded slightly and murmured. "It was for the best. Now he is at peace,"

"Ah, yes, I'd like to introduce you to a friend of mine, Peter Spencer. He is heading north to do some fishing. Where are you going?"

Margaret smiled brightly, "Did you ever hear of a place called New Lancaster?"

A wide grin displayed Peter Spencer's large yellow teeth. "That's where I'm going," he said.

Margaret regarded his equine features and the grey wisps of hair straggling out from under a greasy trilby hat and thought of an old English character actor in a British comedy series.

"May I join you, Mrs. Darwin?" he asked, nodding to the empty seat on the aisle.

Jim Pearson who had been holding an ice chest said to his friend, "I'll set this on this seat. Perhaps you would like to see our fish. Margaret?" He raised the lid and she stood to gaze upon two shiny rainbow trout lying on a bed of crushed ice.

"My, goodness! They are beautiful,"

"Peter's taking them along to convince our friend John that he would be happy to join us at the Chapel Lake retirement home for priests. Our peers at the seminary used to call us the apostles, Peter, James and John because we always wanted to go fishing in Ash Bridges Bay in Lake Ontario;" Jim Pearson laughed. "We never caught anything like this then. Did we, Pete?"

Margaret sat down "What are you going to do with these?"

"John and I will have them for breakfast," Peter Spencer grinned. "These will make up his mind in a hurry. He seems to think he should retire at his son's home in Ottawa but I know that won't work out for him. His son and his family don't even go to church!"

Jim Pearson shook his head sadly and nodded to Margaret as they heard the conductor's "All aboard!" He squeezed Peter's shoulder as he closed the chest lid and left them to continue their journey.

The lights dimmed after they left the last station and the coach grew quiet except for Peter Spencer's sibilant snoring. As the train gathered speed, Margaret gazed out the window and listened to the wheels clacking rhythmically through the silent woods and beside log-lined lakes. She caught snatches of conversation from the seats across the aisle. The two young men were heading north to work on the natural gas pipeline from western Canada; the two girls were employed at a tourist camp near Temagami. She listened to the camaraderie, the coquetry, the laughter, and felt as old as Methuselah's wife.

Watching one of the young men, blond and muscular, return to his seat from a trip to the lavatory she was reminded of Bruce. Dear Bruce . . . He said I'd come back from England feeling like a new woman . . .

Margaret opened her eyes as a peal of laughter across the aisle trickled down into soft snickers. Drawing a deep breath, she sighed. And now I'm not going to England after all . . . All the plans of mice and men . . . She wiped traces of tears from her eyes and settled back in the corner of the seat wishing so desperately that her circumstances were changed and she was indeed on a plane heading across the Atlantic Ocean instead.

The train stopped after midnight to shunt cars onto a siding by the transcontinental line and then headed north again, the diesel engine's lonely horn wailing across the granite rocks of the Canadian Shield. Resting her cheek in her palm, her finger tip between her teeth, Margaret gazed at the darkness outside as though looking into the emptiness of her own soul. A black loneliness accompanied by an overwhelming sense of loss hovered close by, about to reduce her to a quivering lump of flesh. She sat up, smoothed the folds in her green knit polyester dress and focused on the wall at the end of the car, determined to remain dry-eyed for the rest of her journey.

The blond fellow was joking with the girls again. He even sounds like Bruce. Dear Bruce . . . And Charles . . . How can two brothers be so different? Charles . . . You're like your father in so many ways but I don't remember him being so, so, such a stuffed shirt! Oh I don't know. Is that what your father was? I don't think so. But then I can hardly remember what your father was before . . . No. I won't blame your father for you, Charles. But why couldn't you tell me that Gertrude was going to move into your house? You couldn't keep that a secret forever. Did you think I'd be jealous? Or did you feel guilty? Did you think I'd even want to live with you and Mavis?

She turned to look out the window and caught her reflection staring back at her. Oh God. I look like such an old hag . . . No wonder the family's glad to see me go . . . I've got to get on with my life, what's left of it. I've got to find myself again. I've been a wife and a mother too long. Now I'm a widow and that's like being a nobody . . . Well, almost a nobody . . . I've got to be me again . . . But who am I? What am I? What's left of the old Margaret . . . Oh God, I want to laugh again . . . I can't remember what it's like to laugh, to be happy. These young people . . . They don't seem to have a care in the world. At least they don't show it if they do . . . But perhaps they share their troubles with their friends. That's it. They have friends . . . And I don't. I don't have a single friend in the whole wide world . . . And now I don't have the time or the opportunity to make a real friendship work. Her musings ended as the two fellows helped the girls with their luggage when the train stopped in the sleepy hamlet of Temagami. Peter Spencer stirred sleepily and smacked his lips. Hoping he didn't waken. She rubbed her cheeks wearily and read a decrepit sign for a Lone Wolf Lodge leaning among a clump of small spruce. As the train left the station the boys came back to their seats and slumped down into a quick sleep while Margaret watched a sliver of a silver moon rising through the trees along the lake. The diesel horn howled across the rugged emptiness and she wondered if somewhere in that wilderness there really was a lonely wolf, as alone and lonely as she, baying at the moon too.

Chapter Three

SHORTLY AFTER TWO O'CLOCK IN the morning Margaret pulled on her raincoat and stepped down to the station platform of New Lancaster. She shivered in the chilly air and looked around at the dark red clapboard building with its small smoke coated windows. Two girls got off another coach and were met by an older man. They hustled over to a small car nearby and drove off into the night, Peter Spencer said 'good-bye', walked to a waiting car and it roared out of the parking lot in white plumes of exhaust fumes and a spattering of gravel. As an ancient baggage wagon with iron wheels lumbered by, Margaret recognized her luggage and followed the bald spindly man pushing the cart.

"Are these yours, Lady?"

The train was pulling out of the station and she had to raise her voice. "Yes. I'll need to call a cab."

"Walt's probably sleeping in his car around back. You wake him up and get him to drive over here and we'll load your stuff."

Margaret walked along the side of the station and came to another parking lot with a solitary taxi. Seeing a large lump behind the wheel she tapped gently on the window.

The fellow stirred, and tipping his hat backward, he rolled down the pane. "Yeah?"

"The agent said you'd drive around the other side and pick up my bags."

"Okay."

Margaret slid into the back seat as the bags were thumped into the trunk. Walt, a smaller version of a sumo wrestler, opened the door and heaved her garment bag onto the seat. "You sure have a lot of stuff! Are you movin' into town to stay?" Without awaiting an answer he slammed the door and waddled around to get into his seat. "So where are we goin' to, Lady?"

"I don't know. Is there a hotel downtown? Not too expensive?"

"The Beachside is kinda pricey . . . But the Wellington Arms? Well I guess it ain't too bad."

"I'll try it then."

Grunting to shift gears, Walt drove the taxi out onto the main street. The darkened windows of houses gazed upon the pale pools beneath the streetlights as New Lancaster slumbered peacefully in the calm of a crisp spring night. After driving several blocks in silence, Walt turned the cab onto a side street and stopped in front of a three storey red brick building with two chipped white pillars at the entrance and a green neon sign 'Wellington Arms' overhead. "Here we are," he said.

Margaret pushed open the grubby glass door into the dimly lit lobby where a small television set flickered in the corner. The desk clerk raised his head and put on his glasses as she crossed the black and grey tiled floor to lay her purse on the counter.

"What are your room rates?"

"By the night or the week?"

"Is there much of a difference?"

"The room is cleaned and the linen changed once a week for a hundred and fifty. Or it's thirty-five a night, plus tax of course."

"I'll take a week then."

The short swarthy clerk was watching Walt pile her luggage in the lobby. "I'll give you a room on the third floor right across from the elevator. You'll have to unload your bags yourself because I can't leave the desk."

She signed the register as Walt came over to say, "That'll be five bucks."

She gave him a ten dollar bill and said, "Keep the change."

He smiled and loaded the bags on the elevator. The clerk handed her a large key and said, "Your room's 307. You can't miss it. And the coffee shop opens at six in the morning."

The cage gate of the elevator clanged shut and the whole contraption rattled and shook as it slowly ascended to the third floor and stopped before a heavy wooden door. Margaret propped it open with one of the suitcases and crossed the hall to open the door of 307. Switching on the single light bulb in the high ceiling, she found herself in a long narrow room with a green covered double bed against the wall. A metal bedside table and lamp with a faded silk shade stood next to the tall window overlooking the street. Green light from the neon sign glared against the glass. A roll-up blind was half drawn, and two green sateen panels, faded along the middle edges flanked the window. A wash basin with a towel rack stood beside a wooden table and chair along the opposite wall, and a wooden clothes closet leaned against the wall next to the door. The linoleum floor creaked as she walked over to lay her purse on the table and hang up her coat. Returning to the elevator, she began to carry in her luggage. On the second trip, the door to 306 opened and a young slim woman wearing a T-shirt and jeans emerged and quietly closed the door. She turned and came face to face with Margaret. Pushing her long dark hair over her shoulder and pulling on a denim jacket, the girl walked down the hall, came to the red exit sign over a door and disappeared. Margaret raised her eyebrows, and carrying the last suitcase into her room, she locked the door and went over to sit on the bed.

"Well I'm here," she said to a snow scene on an old calendar hanging on the wall above the table. "Now what . . ." The silence seemed ominous and she sat there several minutes thinking that for the first time in her life she had nothing left to do. Nothing to do but die.

At last, she rose wearily to prepare for bed and realized the toilet was elsewhere. Key in hand, she opened her door and looked up and down the gloomy corridor. Setting off in one direction across squeaking floors, she discovered the Men's room and had to retrace her steps to the opposite end to find the Ladies'. Back in her room, she undressed in semi-darkness because her blind was a foot short of the sill and there was another tall building across the street. Settling herself on the hard mattress and too weary to sleep she stared at the band of green light shining across the door and closet. Now every bone in her body seemed to ache and her head throbbed behind tired eyes. She found the aspirin bottle in her purse, gulped down three tablets and crawled back under the thin sheet and stiff blanket. Memories and apprehensions jumbled together as she lay stroking the tenderness in her side, hoping she hadn't strained herself carrying the luggage, and wondering what she would do on the morrow.

She had only been asleep a short time before footfalls on the creaking boards outside the door awoke her. More footsteps. Masculine voices. The elevator cage rattled several times and the hotel grew silent again. Daylight flowing through the gap in the window blind, and traffic sounds outside disturbed her rest too. She finally fell asleep and was then awakened by a key turning in her door lock. She raised her head to see the bulky outline of a woman who muttered, "Oh excuse me," and closed the door again quickly.

Feeling ill, she rose and took a long warm bath before returning to bed to sleep until noon. Hunger wakened her at last and sent her down to the empty coffee shop for a bowl of soup and a sandwich. The waitress who appeared to be the assistant cook as well, occupied herself in the kitchen, and judging from the aroma, Margaret guessed a hearty supper was being prepared for all those guests on the third floor who went to work so early in the morning. She drank a second cup of tea and decided to go for a walk.

Spring had arrived in New Lancaster. Warm sunshine streamed down upon the tranquil town, and smoke from a bonfire somewhere in the neighbourhood drifted along the quiet street. She turned right upon leaving the hotel and walked down Wellington Street toward the lake, crossed a parking lot beside a ball diamond and came to a boardwalk that stretched far to the west. Along the beach a muddy swath churned up by the waves from a south-west wind contrasted sharply to the rest of the deep blue lake. Two remote islands lay on an empty southern horizon while the shady western shore appeared dark and foreboding. She turned toward the east with the wind at her back and discovered this part of the lake was a large bay. Tiny cottages dotted the eastern shore toward a distant promontory. Farm buildings scattered across the pale green and grey mosaic of fields on the hills above the lake.

She walked slowly along the deserted beach, appreciating the beauty of lake and shore and sky, the rolling waves breaking monotonously beside the winter dunes, the giant blue dome overhead with puffy white clouds drifting off to the northern hills. She passed food concession booths boarded up for the season against the sand and wind. More playgrounds and ball fields lined the boardwalk. She came to another large parking lot next to a sprawling motel.

A long patio in front of the Beachside commanded a splendid view of the lake and marina and harbour. The table umbrellas remained closed but several groups of men were enjoying refreshments in the sunshine behind a waist high fence topped with boxes of yellow and purple pansies fluttering in the breeze. She walked on past the motel to the marina where a few boats were already in the water and a man was operating a crane to unload a sailboat from the storage racks. Reaching the end of the boardwalk she crossed the boatyard to a long concrete pier where a broad muddy river emptied into the lake. More docks lined the banks, and across the river, green lawns of homes ran down to the water's edge.

She walked up River Street, passing garages and maintenance shops with clanging irons, hissing pressure hoses and gas fumes, until she reached a busy thoroughfare where a large bridge spanned the river. She turned left onto Bridge Street away from the river, passing clothing shops, a hardware store, a butcher shop and discovered a theatre, the same theatre where she and John had taken their children on that rainy afternoon so many years ago. She got her bearings with that landmark and knew the next intersection would be Main Street. Turning to walk two blocks west, she came to Wellington Street. A branch of her bank occupied the corner and she regretted leaving her purse locked in a suitcase in her room. The business hours were posted on the glass door, and checking her watch, Margaret realized she would have to wait another day to open an account. A short distance down the street hung the green sign of her hotel.

A round, bespectacled man stood at the desk as Margaret entered the lobby. He raised his eyebrows but she nodded her head and proceeded to climb the wooden staircases to the third floor. Taking off her coat and shoes, she stood in front of the window and recognized the building across the street as the fire hall. An ancient bell tower added a quaint touch to the facade.

Footsteps creaked in the corridor. A door opened and closed. Bored by the empty street she threw back the bedspread and stretched out on her back to survey her dismal surroundings. The stark room reminded her of a cell. She imagined herself inside a convent and wondered how a nun could bear to live out her life in such a place. The pale green paint was peeling off the ceiling over the wardrobe and the discoloured plaster gave evidence of leaking water. She looked around at the drab walls and shoddy furniture in dismay. I can't stay here for long . . . I'll have to find something else.

Finances were not a real concern for her. The expenses at Thornbury Village had eaten up John's pension and some of their savings but she had no reason to think she would become penniless. In her present situation she estimated that she could live on a thousand dollars a month for food and rent and incidentals. Clothing could be a concern because she knew her supply of outfits was limited. Since moving to Thornbury she had had little time or need to shop. Her wardrobe had diminished over the years and most of it now seemed frumpish, but with an innate sense of frugality, she now reasoned it would be foolish to spend a lot of money on clothes when she had no occasion to wear them. If she should move to better accommodations then her expenses could escalate rapidly. I'll open a bank account tomorrow and live on a budget.

Sighing with boredom, Margaret turned over and noticed a Gideon Bible on the shelf of the bedside table. For want of something to read, she picked it up and began to turn the pages. She had never read much of the Bible. The stories were interesting but she equated them with Grecian myths or fairy tales. The account of Noah's ark and the flood seemed rather improbable and she had found the Homeric tales in the Odyssey much more exciting. David slaying Goliath seemed tantamount to Jupiter hurling his bolts to vanquish the Titans. The story of Delilah beguiling the long-haired Samson, cutting his mane, dooming him to a life of blindness among the Philistines, reminded her of a fairy tale she had read to her children long ago. The wicked witch had cut Rapunzel's locks to deceive the prince. He too was sentenced to wander blinded in the wilderness. The God of the Bible appeared to Margaret as a fearsome, fierce deity, wreaking vengeance on old and young alike, giving no thought to the innocent child or the unfortunate bystander. She found the religion of the Old Testament too bloody, too awful, too cruel for her own sensitive nature. The epistles read in Elizabethan English from the lectern stretched beyond her scope of interest, and the homilies delivered from the pulpit rarely seemed applicable to her own experiences. The Gospels were another matter. These stories seemed kinder and more appealing as a gentle Jesus went about Galilee teaching about love, and healing the sick and casting out demons. As she lay in the silence of the seedy room she contemplated her barren spiritual experience and the torment of her own demons. She finally tossed the Bible back onto the shelf with a sense of futile hopelessness.

Disturbed by creaking floorboards in the hall and banging doors, she irritably covered her head with a pillow and wondered what the room rates were at the Beachside. Her frustrations grew as late afternoon wore into evening and sounds of male laughter and loud voices drifted up the stairway and under her door. When she discovered the coffee shop adjoined the crowded saloon, she decided to look for another place for supper and walked back to Main Street to find a smoke-filled diner, a murky Chinese restaurant, the Hang Kow, and a donut shop. Hungry, she decided at last to go to the Beachside where there was sure to be a decent restaurant. Margaret soon found herself sitting at a candlelit, damask covered table for one in the corner of the dining room. The piano played softly in the other corner and she cringed at the damage this meal would do to her budget. Be nice to yourself for a change, Margaret. She picked up the leather bound menu and ordered without looking at the right column. Two hours later she paid her bill and casually asked the waitress the room rates at the hotel.

The girl smiled and lowered her voice. "Too much," she said. "I think they start at about one twenty-five."

"A night?" Margaret asked.

She nodded, wide-eyed, and turned to the next table.

Margaret walked slowly back to the Wellington Arms resigned to another restless night.

The revelry ended after midnight but she was still unable to sleep. Finally she went down the hall to the bathroom, and on her return, the door of 306 opened and the same girl emerged. She fumbled with her shoulder bag and hurried down to the fire exit stairway. Wondering, Margaret went back to bed.

Awakened by bright sunshine streaming through her window and facing the prospect of another long lonely day, she buried her head in the pillow and wept. What am I going to do . . . I can't go on like this. I need to talk to someone. I need to let someone know I'm here. Someone. Anyone . . . Maybe a priest. I'll find the Anglican church and speak to the rector. She reached for her watch and saw it was almost nine o'clock. Wondering, she then realized that it was Saturday, a plausible explanation for the peace and quiet in the hallway.

She dressed casually in a beige blouse and a brown and beige flowered skirt and walked downstairs for breakfast. As she lingered over toast and coffee an unusually handsome young man came in and sat at a table across the room. The waitress chatted and laughed with him as he ordered, and Margaret noticed his flashing smile, the dark curly hair and twinkling eyes. Finishing her coffee, she ambled out to the lobby to look for a telephone book to find the address of the church before going upstairs to brush her teeth. As she was entering the elevator to leave, the attractive man dashed up the stairs to open the door of room 306. A fleeting thought of the temptations of youth crossed Margaret's mind before she was distracted by the rattling descent to the lobby.

St. Jude's Anglican Church had been listed on Main Street. Margaret walked up a small hill past the post office, and several blocks further west, she came to an old red brick building with a slate roof and stained glass windows, set back from the street on a wide lawn. A yellow and white canopy ballooned above large round tables and stacks of white chairs on the lawn beside the church. A corps of those indefatigable church women were spreading pastel table cloths and organizing the seating. Margaret stopped in front of the sign and read the rector's name, one Reverend Harold J. Copse. The front doors of the church yawned widely and she entered the vestibule. A rotund woman carrying a tray of table napkins came up the centre aisle and smiled. "May I help you?"

"The rector, Mr. Copse. Is he here?"

"He's in the study. Just through that door." She turned and pointed toward the side of the pulpit.

Margaret walked slowly up the aisle of the beautiful old church. Oak beams supported the ceiling and walls of ivory stucco. A magnificent round stained glass window dominated the front wall above the altar; the figure of Christ with staff in hand and a lamb in his arm, glowed in the morning sunlight. Choir stalls lined the apse with the organ to one side. White ribbons decorated the pews and, with the canopy outside, Margaret surmised there was to be a wedding and reception here today. She hesitated at the front of the church and looked around the sanctuary.

A gentle voice at her elbow said, "You're not one of our ladies, are you."

She turned to see an elderly unshaven gentleman in a worn blue shirt, a thatch of white hair almost covering his ears. Dark brown eyes smiled at her from behind wire-rimmed glasses perched half-way down his big nose.

"Are you Reverend Copse?"

"Yes, but everyone calls me Harry. Are you here about the wedding?"

"No. I'm Margaret Darwin. I thought I should come and talk to you . . ."

"Come into the study."

He led her along the front row of pews, across a hall and into a book-filled room crowded with empty boxes. Lifting a carton off a chair he said, "Please sit down. As you can see, I'm in a terrible mess. I'm retiring. Tomorrow is my last Sunday service and I'm leaving next week to visit my son." He paused. "This is my last wedding. Now then, tell me what I can do for you."

"Well, I'm new in town and looking for a church home but I won't take up any more of your time. I can see you're very busy . . ."

He sighed. "Oh I can't seem to get anything done, with all the interruptions . . . The wedding . . . I wish my dear wife was still alive. She was such a wonderful help." He looked out the window and sighed again.

"Look," Margaret said suddenly. "I've nothing to do today. I can help. Do you want all these books packed in these boxes?"

His face brightened and, as he looked closely at this pleasant woman with a round face and green eyes, he thought for a moment she reminded him of his dear dead wife. "Could you? Would you mind?"

She smiled. "Of course not. Do you want them in any particular order?"

He shook his head and reached for an old tea-towel. "I've been using this to clean them . . ."

The books were so dusty Margaret supposed they hadn't been opened for years. Nevertheless, they seemed important to the old man and she carefully wiped and placed them in the cartons. The telephone rang several times as Mr. Copse attempted to clean out his desk. Each time, he had to descend into the nether regions of the church to deliver a message to one of the women preparing food for the reception. The florist arrived while he was away and Margaret was pressed into service as a consultant on the placement of candelabra and huge sprays of forsythia, cherry blossoms, tulips and daffodils. Returning to the study, she found Harry reading the papers from his drawers as he sorted through them.

He looked up as if he had never seen her before. When she picked up her duster again, he nodded and asked, "Where do you live?"

"Right now I'm staying at the Wellington Arms."

He stared at her. "My goodness! That's no place for you."

"It's all I can afford."

"But you're not going to actually live there . . ."

"I don't want to rent an apartment . . ."

"How about a boarding house? Mrs. MacPherson rents out rooms. You should look her up."

"Oh?"

"She's across the river. A big white clapboard house just past the bridge. You can't miss it."

"Thank you, Mr. Copse. I believe I will."

"Harry," he reminded her.

She smiled and went on with her packing. "By the way, what time is the wedding?"

He picked up his desk diary. "Three o'clock."

She glanced at her watch. "It's after one now. Do you have to go home to freshen up? Shave?"

He pulled out his watch. "Oh dear! Yes. I must go. Will you be all right here by yourself?"

She took his arm and guided him through the door. "Yes. I'll be fine. Don't worry about a thing."

She quickly returned to her packing, not bothering to dust any more of the books. She knew now this gentle old man bordering on senility would never open these cartons. They would lie in some attic or moldy basement until they ended up in a garage sale after he had died. One by one she piled the boxes along the wall, stopping to rub her aching side occasionally. "Better to burn out than rust out," she muttered as she turned to another row of shelves by the window. The study was beginning to look almost tidy when a middle-aged man stuck his balding head through the doorway. "Where's Harry?"

"At the rectory getting ready for the wedding, I hope."

He smiled and held out his hand. "Clyde Morrow, organist."

She offered hers. "Margaret Darwin, bookpacker."

He grinned. "I'm just checking in. I'll get along now."

Margaret resumed her task, listening to strains of familiar music wafting through the church as Clyde set his music in order. Harry returned looking much cleaner and groomed, and carrying his white surplice over his arm. "Why this is wonderful!" he cried, surveying the room. "You've done a miracle."

"I'll just finish these up," she said. "I'll leave the desk for you."

He looked at the clutter on his desk. "This is where they'll sign the certificates," he said. "Now where did I put all that stuff?"

She stepped down off the low stool and came over to help him clear away the mess. They found the license among the papers, his prayer book in the bottom drawer and the church register in the other bottom drawer under a single rubber galosh. She polished the top of the desk with the rag and said, "Perhaps I should leave some of the books on the shelves as background for the photographer."

Harry nodded. "That might be best."

Melodious hymns filtered into the room and he took out his watch again. "I do hope I can remember everything today."

Margaret carried his surplice over to him. "Here, let's get you ready and then we'll just sit down and listen to that lovely music."

After several selections, she glanced at her watch. "It's almost three. Shouldn't the bridegroom be here by now?"

He pulled out his watch and frowned. "Could you peek and see if his parents are here?"

"But Harry . . . I don't know these people."

"They'll be right there in the front row."

She raised her eyebrows and walked across the room as a young man in a grey tuxedo came to the door. "Reverend Copse?"

"Yes. He's right here."

The fellow brushed past her. "Reverend Copse . . . Do you remember me? I'm John Moore, Brian's best man. I was here last night."

Harry stood up slowly. "Yes. Where's Brian?"

"He's not coming. He's called the wedding off."

Harry sat down again. "Not coming! What do you mean?"

John handed him a folded piece of paper. "He wrote this. I . . . I think I'd better get back to Brian. He's waiting for me in the parking lot. He's pretty upset . . ."

As Harry read the note, Margaret took the young man's arm. "Are Brian's parents in the church?"

"I don't know. I guess they are."

"Well you slip in there through that door and bring them here right now."

She walked toward the window and could see the decorated wedding cars on the street. Harry was running his fingers through his thatch of hair.

"I've sent John to bring Brian's parents in here. They'll have to help you tell the bride and her family."

He groaned and continued to rub his head.

John returned leading a couple with concerned faces. The stocky well-dressed man with curly red hair graying around the temples said briskly, "What's going on here, Harry?"

Harry handed him the note, and the woman took her husband's arm as she read it too. Their puzzled faces turned to dismay.

"I'm sorry, Mr and Mrs. Haskett," said John. "I'd better go see Brian. He's out in the parking lot. He's awfully upset."

"You tell him to stay right there," Mr. Haskett said. "I'll be out in a minute."

Mrs. Haskett set her purse down on the desk and looked for a tissue. Margaret handed her a box from the windowsill and Mrs. Haskett dabbed at her eyes trying not to smudge her mascara. She was an attractive woman, slim in a stylish navy silk suit with a large white collar. Her dark hair curled around the white pillbox hat with a navy net and bow. Mr. Haskett took her arm. "Now look, Amy, I'm going out to talk to Brian, and you go along with the Reverend here to tell Midge and her family the whole deal is off. Show Deirdre the note, and if she puts up a fuss, tell her I'll be back in a few minutes."

The room seemed almost empty as the two men left.

Harry stood up slowly and said, "We'll have to go and get it over with, I suppose."

The organ seemed to be playing a little louder as he led Amy out into the hall. Margaret watched them exit the side door and turned back to the books. Amy Haskett's purse lay on the desk and she picked it up to hurry after them. Outside in the parking lot, she saw Mr. Haskett with an arm around his sturdy curly red-haired son talking earnestly to him. She continued on to the vestibule with the purse under her arm.

Three bridesmaids in pink floral gowns and wide straw hats clustered together at the door. The bride in a long white organza gown with tiers of ruffles was listening to Harry as her mother, a short, perky, bottle blonde, and wearing a rose crepe dress, held her around the waist and read the note. Margaret hurried to close the heavy oak doors to the sanctuary as Clyde pulled out all the stops on Handel's Largo. She turned and noticed the bride's father in a navy jacket leaning against the wall, his arms folded, a white boutonniere stuck in his lapel. He seemed detached from the crisis at hand, his weather-lined face a mask of serenity calmly surveying the chaos. The bride had turned to her mother and was crying, "I'll kill him! I'll kill him!"

Mr. Haskett joined the group, nodded to the bride's father and whispered to his wife as the hysterical bride raged up and down the vestibule crying, "Where is he? I'll kill him!"

Mr. Haskett replied calmly, "He's in the parking lot."

A squeal of tires and a splattering of gravel was heard as the bride turned around to tear open the door. Margaret caught sight of her face for the first time and blinked. Under the veiled white picture hat was the face of the young woman from room 306!

Deirdre threw her hands in the air. "Doug! You gotta to do something."

He shrugged and straightened up. "Whatever you say, Deirdre."

"Well . . . Go with her. Take her home. Do something!"

He ran his fingers over his face and smoothed his wiry salt and pepper hair. "Come on, girls," he said to the bridesmaids. "Let's go and save Midge from herself."

Margaret watched him lead the whispering young women from the church. *I just can't believe all this could happen. Why would any girl be so foolish? Why?*

She became aware that Harry was in the centre of an argument of what explanation should be given to the guests inside the church and which one of them should give it. "Well Reverend Copse will just have to go in there and tell everyone," Amy Haskett said as Margaret handed her the purse.

"Tell them what," Deirdre Landers snapped. "That my daughter's a tramp and your saint of a son found out about an affair before it was too late?"

"No, no," said Harry quickly. "I can't say that."

"And what about the reception? All the food?" Amy asked.

"The food can rot for all I care," Deirdre retorted.

"That's easy for you to say," Mr. Haskett interjected. "You aren't paying for it . . ."

"You just had to say that, didn't you!" Dierdre exploded. "You had to remind me that the Landers aren't in your class. It's just as well our kids aren't getting married. You'd never let us forget we come from the wrong side of the tracks!"

"Now, now," Harry said. "This isn't getting us anywhere."

They grew silent and finally Margaret drew Harry aside to whisper in his ear. He nodded and returned to say, "What if we tell them the wedding has been postponed for an hour or so and invite everyone outside to the reception? And after they've eaten, then we can announce that it's been cancelled. We don't want to deny them a nice meal, do we?"

They stared at the rector, amazed at his subterfuge.

Mr. Haskett said, "Makes sense to me."

Deirdre nodded. "Let's all go home and let Mr. Copse handle it then."

Harry frowned as the three parents left but he realized there was nothing else he could do. Margaret walked around to the side door with him and noticed his hand shaking as he opened the door to the sanctuary. It closed behind him and the organ stopped playing abruptly.

Margaret never saw Harry Copse again. She packed the rest of the books into the boxes and walked out through the empty church leaving the bouquets and candles and ribbons behind, reminders of an extraordinary afternoon. From the street, she could see guests milling about under the canopy and she knew somewhere in their midst was an aging gentle clergyman who would never perform another wedding ceremony.

The lobby of the Wellington Arms was surprisingly quiet. Too tired to climb the creaking stairs Margaret rattled her way to the third floor and discovered the doors to 306 were wide open. The handsome occupant had obviously flown away. She could see wire hangers strewn across the rumpled bed. A newspaper lay on the floor, an empty beer bottle on the bedside table, a can of shaving cream on the sink, a bath towel on the table. She shook her head at the foibles of youth and went into her own room to lie down.

Her left side ached and she lay down, quietly stroking her abdomen. *After all this I still need someone to listen to me . . . But I can't talk to a tired old man who's coming to the end of his journey . . . He's probably seen it all in his time, despair, infidelity, anger, bitterness. Where's his God now? Where are you, God? Where's all this love and joy and peace? I don't have any joy. And I'm not so sure about the love. I love my sons but do they love me? Where were they when their father and sister were dying? I needed their compassion and they couldn't give it to me. And I need peace . . . Oh how I need peace!*

She wiped her eyes with the back of her hand and lay there drowsing in the gloomy room. *So where are you, God? I can't find you. What did you do . . . Did you create this old ball of dirt and then go off to the outer universe and leave us to make our own way? Did I read somewhere that you were like a watchmaker who made the finest timepiece in the world, wound it up, and then left it to run down by itself? Is that what we're doing now? Just running down and one of these days everything will come to a dead stop? Science tells us that our sun only has enough energy to last another five million years. Oh God! Five million more years of all this misery! I don't want to even think about five more days . . . I need some peace God, and I need it now . . .*

The hotel bar grew noisy late in the afternoon and she stirred. "There's no peace here," she mused. "Maybe I'll check out that boarding house. Any place will be better than this."

She threw a sweater around her shoulders and set off toward the bridge. The white clap-board house, a large three storey structure, loomed over the sloping bank. Two wide bow windows faced the river, separated by a doorway opening onto a raised veranda. Margaret walked halfway up the hill along a cedar hedge before turning down Oak Terrace to find the entrance. A carpet of dandelions masqueraded as a lawn. On the far side of the house, a dilapidated wooden garage leaned precariously toward the river. She walked up the front steps to the porch and rang the doorbell. She heard footsteps approaching and then the door was opened by a tall, slim woman with frizzy strawberry blonde hair.

"Hello?"

"Are you Mrs. MacPherson?"

"Yes."

"My name is Margaret Darwin. Mr. Copse at St. Jude's told me you might have a room I could rent."

"You must be new in town." She studied Margaret's face. "How long are you planning to stay?"

"I'm not sure. Probably most of the summer."

"Come in then and I'll show you the room."

Margaret stepped into the front hall. A shadowy parlour brooded on her left and a sombre dining room, on her right. A wide staircase disappeared into the realms above. She followed Mrs. MacPherson along a wide hall past a bathroom under the stairs and turned into a large room dominated by a massive four poster bed. Light filtered through the venetian blinds on the huge bow window to reveal a bureau, a dressing table and an armoire, all a rich rosewood mahogany. Matching tables on either side of the bed held what Margaret was sure were Tiffany lamps. A large rocking chair stood in the bay of the window. She quickly decided the furniture in this room was worth a small fortune.

Mrs. MacPherson turned on one of the lamps. "Would this suit you?" she asked, her facial profile lengthened by the shadows. "I have a smaller room upstairs that will be available in another week. I charge four hundred a month for that one."

Margaret swallowed. "And how much for this?"

The woman hesitated. "Would five hundred be all right? You'll have to provide your own linens of course. And you can use the kitchen as long as you clean up after yourself." She led Margaret across the hall into a large kitchen with a table and chairs in front of the other bow window overlooking the river.

Margaret nodded.

She pointed to a series of cupboards with locks on them. "You'll keep your food in there but you'll have to label what you put in the 'frig. The college students on the second floor keep some stuff in here but they eat at the school cafeteria most of the time. They use the 'frig mostly for their beer."

Margaret nodded again.

"So what do you think?"

"I'll take it."

"Give me a cheque and you can move in any time."

"I'll have to go to the bank and open an account," Margaret said. "I can do that Monday morning."

"Where are you staying now?"

"The Wellington Arms."

Margaret's new landlady frowned. "What do you do for a living?" Her pale hazel eyes narrowed as she studied her prospective tenant.

"I'm a widow. My husband had Alzheimer's. He died a couple of months ago. So when I thought about moving out of Toronto, I remembered New Lancaster. We were here for a short time many years ago."

"Well you won't want to stay at the Wellington any longer than you have to. I'll get you your keys and you can move in tonight if you want."

"I'll have to buy some sheets and towels," Margaret said. "Perhaps Monday would be better."

"I'll lend you some to tide you over. I'll be right back." She returned in a few minutes with keys to the front door, the bedroom and the kitchen cupboard, and a stack of linen. "There you go."

"Thank you very much," Margaret said. "I really appreciate this Mrs. MacPherson."

"Call me Fiona," she replied. "If you decide to wait until tomorrow just let yourself in. I'll be working."

"What do you do?"

"I'm a nurse in the newborn nursery at the hospital. Never had any of my own but I'm an expert when it comes to babies."

Margaret smiled.

Fiona continued. "I used to be on the medical floor. That's where I met Mr. McGuiness."

"Mr. McGuiness?"

"Yes. This is, was, his house. Anyway, he needed someone to take care of him and he hired me as his housekeeper and nurse. Well, he finally died here two years ago and left me his estate. There was a lot of gossip in town about it, especially after a nephew he hadn't heard from for years, came from Manitoba to contest the will. He claimed I'd taken advantage of a poor old sick man. He ended up with some of the money, what was left of it, but I kept the house. I take in roomers to help with the upkeep. It's quite nice, isn't it."

Margaret nodded. "Is this Mr. McGuiness' room I'm going to live in?"

Fiona said quickly, "You don't mind, do you."

"Do you mean because he died there in the bed?"

"Yes."

"No. I'm not particular. Heaven only knows what's been going on in my bed at the Wellington Arms."

Fiona's eyes crinkled and she laughed. "I'm looking forward to having you here, Margaret. It'll be nice to have another woman in the house."

Chapter Four

WALT CARRIED THE LAST OF her suitcases into the vestibule of the boarding house on Sunday morning. Straightening up, he rubbed his back and asked, "Are you planning to move anywhere else in town?"

Margaret smiled and handed him a ten dollar bill. "No. You're safe for a while anyway. Keep the change, and thank you again."

She unpacked, hanging her clothing in the armoire, filling the drawers of the bureau, appreciating the quality of the furnishings in her new home. Wearily she slid the empty suitcases under the bed and straightened up to rub her aching back. Her side throbbed too and she felt a headache starting as she collapsed in the rocking chair by the window. Later, much to her dismay, she discovered a heavy menstrual flow, unusual because her last period six months earlier had been very light. Now she crawled into bed, greatly alarmed at her situation and wondering what she should do if the bleeding increased.

She was still feeling wretched when Fiona knocked on her door later that afternoon. "Are you getting settled?" she asked.

Too miserable to open the door, Margaret replied, "Yes, thanks."

"Would you like a cup of tea?"

"No, thanks."

"Okay," Fiona said, and went into the kitchen. Sounds of music from a radio and the occasional clatter of dishes drifted across the hall.

Later that evening Margaret stirred from her bed in need of food. She ordered a pizza from a shop listed in the yellow pages, found Fiona's tea bag in the garbage, brewed a weak cup of tea, and managed to eat two large pieces of the pizza until her appetite waned.

A tall young man with a crew cut entered the kitchen and blinked as he saw her sitting at the table. "Hi," he said opening the refrigerator door.

"Hello. I'm Margaret Darwin. I've just moved in across the hall."

He brought out two cans of beer. "I'm Paul Edwards from upstairs."

"Would you like the rest of this pizza? It's still warm."

He grinned. "Sure. Thanks a lot, Mrs. Darwin. John and I are studying for exams. It'll go good with the beer." He bounded upstairs with the box.

Still unwell, Margaret walked to the bank on Monday morning to open an account. Stopping at a grocery store, she bought as much food as she could carry home, and passing the mail order office, went in to purchase a catalogue. Lying in the comfortable bed in the bare room late Sunday evening, she had considered her situation. At least I have a decent place to call my own. And if I'm going to be spending a lot of time in this room what harm can it do to my budget to fix the place up a little? After all, even the Wellington Arms had a calendar and curtains. She spent the rest of Monday lying in bed with the catalogue, planning her decor, and writing out a lengthy order.

When she heard Fiona in the kitchen making supper she put on her old pink chenille robe and went out to give her a cheque for the rent. Fiona studied her new tenant carefully. "Do you drink, Margaret?"

Margaret frowned. "Drink? You mean liquor . . ."

"Yeah."

"No. Not really. Why?"

"You seem so quiet and withdrawn. I just wondered, that's all."

"Oh. I wasn't feeling well yesterday. That time of the month, you know . . ."

"Oh . . . How old are you anyway? I would have thought you'd be all through with that now."

"I'm fifty-seven. I know I look a lot older, and at times, I sure feel like it too."

Fiona passed her a cup of tea. "You've had a rough time, losing your husband and moving and all . . . Well, you're here now and you can get lots of rest. I don't think the boys upstairs will disturb you much. They're a pretty good bunch. I have my room in the attic so I can keep an eye on them. And it's quiet up there too when I'm working the night shift. My hours can be pretty erratic so you might not see much of me either."

Margaret learned that was true. Occasionally a toilet flushed or a faucet ran or the front door closed but she rarely saw the three young men who lived on the second floor. She busied herself that week thoroughly cleaning the room, washing the windows, dusting the blinds and polishing the floor between rest periods. Her menstrual flow diminished. The ache in her side lessened as well. She stocked her larder, and decided on a sunny Sunday afternoon to walk about town and familiarize herself with New Lancaster. Several townspeople nodded to her as she passed by, and when Margaret responded with a pleasant greeting, she realized with some discomfort that several days had passed without her having spoken a single word to another human being.

The delivery van brought the catalogue order the following Monday and she spent several happy hours decorating her room. The ivory walls and blinds were cheered by the deep fluffy comforter covered with sprays of bright pink peonies. A matching pink skirt for the box spring hid her suitcases. The extra pillows and shams made the large bed look cosy with the pink sheets and blankets. Pink chair pads and scatter rugs softened the hard wooden look of the room. She turned back to the catalogue to order matching swags to drape about the bay window and decided to keep her eyes open for a nice picture or two to hang on the wall.

Her physical condition seemed to improve during these quiet days on Oak Terrace. She slept soundly. Afternoon walks about the town piqued her appetite to the point where she began to cook stews and casseroles, filling the hallways with delicious aromas. Sometimes Fiona joined her at the table. Visits to the library stimulated her interest in old habits. She bought a transistor radio to keep in touch with the rest of the world and found a classical music station situated somewhere across the border in Quebec, using the headset when she thought her landlady might be sleeping upstairs.

A solitary church bell rang across the river on Sunday morning. Curious about who had replaced Harry Copse, Margaret dressed and put on her comfortable shoes to walk the ten blocks to St. Jude's. She still sensed an indefinable need to talk to someone, and much to her dismay, discovered that an ascetic student with a slight case of acne was in charge for the summer. He chanted the prayers slightly off key, which set her teeth on edge, and delivered a boring homily which sounded like a nonsensical recitation of some erudite lecture on the impeccability of Jesus Christ. Her fellow worshippers seemed grim as they casually shook hands with each other and fled. Margaret returned home to a quiet house, unwilling and indeed unable to confess her loneliness to this pedantic young man whose view of life and God seemed so academic and impersonal.

The afternoon became quite pleasant and she dragged her rocking chair out to the veranda and watched the traffic on Bridge Street. Drowsing in the warmth of the spring day she finally shook herself awake, and walking over to the railing, noticed a set of stone steps hidden in the overgrowth leading down to the river. Nearby, amid the dead grass and rocks, buds of perennials were struggling to push their way up through the debris of years of neglect. She went out the front door of the house and walked around to descend to a footpath along the riverbank. Sprouts of tiger lilies, peonies and phlox beckoned and she began to pull at the weeds. Tomorrow, I'll get myself some gloves and clean this place up.

Fiona was getting out of her car in the driveway when she returned to the front of the house. Margaret rubbed the dirt from her hands. "Hello there."

"So what are you up to?" Fiona asked.

"I've discovered the rock garden out back," she replied. "Is it all right with you if I clean it up?"

Fiona grinned. "Of course. Mr. McGuiness used to putter around out there but it was too much for him and nobody's touched it since. You'll find some garden tools in the garage, I think. There's a key around here some place." She walked around the corner of the garage and found the key hanging beside the window. She opened the padlock and as they wrested the door open, a musty smell rushed out to greet them.

Margaret wrinkled her nose and ventured inside. Cobwebs hung on the hoe and rakes. Dead flies and dust covered a set of wicker lawn furniture. An old bicycle leaned against the wall.

"I'd forgotten about all this junk," Fiona said. "If you ever feel like riding a bicycle, be my guest."

Margaret squeezed the tires. "There's still some air in them . . . And look at the big carrier. Someone must have had a paper route. This would be great for taking the washing down to the laundromat or bringing home groceries."

"Just be careful you don't fall off that contraption and break your bones. I don't want to lose my new gardener." She closed the door and began walking toward the house. "Would you like a cup of tea, Margaret?"

"That would be nice. I'll make it though. You've been working all day."

They sat at the kitchen table in a comfortable silence until Margaret said "I can't believe I've been here two weeks already. The house is so quiet . . . I don't see much of the boys upstairs."

"They're in the middle of exams. They have a lot of field work to do too because it's an agricultural college. Have you ever seen the place? It's out the north end of town."

Margaret shook her head. "Uh uh."

"It's a big school. John's going home for the summer but Ted and Paul are staying for the next semester. You'll probably see more of them then."

"Would you like to see what I've done to the room?" Margaret asked.

Fiona followed her across the hall and raised her eyebrows. "It's lovely," she said. "Truly lovely. And your choice of colour is just right. The pinks and greens match the colours in the lamp shades. Compared to this room, the rest of the house looks real shabby." She put her arm around Margaret's shoulders. "I hope you decide to stay in New Lancaster for a long time."

Margaret's eyes filled with sudden tears. It had been such a long time since she had felt another's genuine affection. "So do I, Fiona. So do I."

Margaret pushed the bicycle to a garage in the morning to put some more air in the tires before going on to the hardware store. She found the door locked and the store in darkness. Wondering what was wrong, she went into the quiet coffee shop next door to inquire.

The waitress stared at her. "You must be an American," she said. "This is a holiday, Victoria Day. Everything's closed."

Margaret ordered a cup of coffee and a muffin and went over to sit by the window, realizing she had lost all sense of time. It's going on three weeks since I left Toronto, and it just seems like yesterday. The only other customer in the coffee shop, an old man, rose and walked out to an empty street. With nothing else to do, Margaret glanced through a newspaper, finished her muffin and went home to sit on the porch for the rest of the quiet morning.

Thoroughly bored by her own company, she set off after lunch on the bicycle to explore the north side of the river. Children played in the tree-lined street as she pedaled beneath the budding canopy. Lilacs and forsythia bloomed profusely in the yards of the modest homes, and Margaret marveled at the abundance of flowering bulbs. The vibrant colours of tulips, daffodils, narcissus and hyacinths lined the driveways, filled flower beds in front of the homes, and clustered in rock gardens. She rode on into a heavily wooded area and emerged to find herself on the front edge of the golf course where droves of men and women were shedding their rusty habits and swinging into the season. She cycled on further, passed the sprawling agricultural college, crossed over a railroad track and came at last to an intersection of gravel roads.

A twisted sign with the faded word "Thornloe" tilted toward the ground totally confusing the wayfarer. She noticed a spreading grove of lilac trees a short distance from the road and the grey ruins of a wooden shed lying nearby amid old swaths of brown grass. Margaret walked up a rutted clay lane and leaned her bicycle against a crumbling stone foundation next to a flourishing burdock patch. She strolled across the spread of rough ground toward the lilacs and discovered with some surprise an old cemetery. Most of the grave stone slabs had toppled into the grass and she could barely distinguish the moss-encrusted names. One small granite monument belonging to a George Harrison remained upright. The epitaph "Gone But Not Forgotten" was scarcely visible, and she sat upon it to survey the remains of an old churchyard. A tractor was working a field somewhere nearby, and as the noise faded she turned her face up to the cloudless sky where an airplane left a trail of vapour in the blue beyond. A clanging cowbell distracted her and she watched a line of curious cattle appear along the fence boundary. They gazed at the intruder for a time and then swaying nonchalantly, wended their way to greener pastures. She was reminded of Gray's Elegy written in another country churchyard, "*the lowing cattle wends slowly o'er the lea.*"

Margaret rose and walked to the fence as the herd disappeared over the brow of the hill into a panoramic landscape. Sloping gently from her vantage point a wide basin of cultivated fields stretched several miles toward the purple hills and a cumulus cloudbank on the western horizon. The huge sky dwarfed the land. The immensity astonished her, and lingering by the fence, she felt diminished by the awesome scene. After some time she returned to George Harrison's grave to ponder this man's existence. Had he cleared this very land, toiling through drought and pestilence to support a family? Had he prospered and grown rich? Had he failed and become poor? What difference did it make in the long scheme of things? Now his bones lay beneath the soil that had once provided sustenance for the family's existence. And his family, where are they now? Do any of his aged offspring return to this *"moldering heap"* and their father *"in his narrow cell forever laid"*? She gazed across the valley to the distant hills, pondering the length of days, and the other eyes who had watched the same scene, the sunrises and sunsets in succession; those others who once shared their griefs and joys in this present ruin, their hopes and dreams now long forgotten. Ah yes, *"the paths of glory lead but to the grave."*

Closing her eyes against the glare of the spring sun she tilted her face toward the warmth and harkened back to the Sunday over three weeks ago when she had sat in another cemetery.' Gone but not forgotten ' . . . I'll never forget you John and Jane as long as I live. But after I'm gone . . . And who'll remember me?

A robin chirruped in the grove breaking the soft silence, and she roused to walk over and gather a huge bouquet of lilacs. When a cool breeze wafted through the trees, she looked up to see an enormous grey cloud in the west, moving swiftly to obliterate the sun.

With a freshening wind at her back, Margaret headed for home. Raindrops splashed her face as she neared the golf course and she increased her speed. As she reached the entrance gates a car turned out onto the road causing her to swerve sharply onto the gravel shoulder. The front tire hissed and the bicycle wobbled toward the ditch. Staring at the shredded rubber in dismay, she began the long walk home, plodding through the pelting rain with an unruly front wheel.

Hearing a motor behind, she turned slightly to see a pick-up truck slowing down. It pulled alongside and the passenger rolled down the window. His face under an old fishing hat looked vaguely familiar. The driver leaned forward and called, "Hello! Can we give you a lift to town?"

She recognized the father of the bridegroom, Mr. Haskett, immediately. "I'd appreciate it. Thanks."

The doors opened and both men came toward her. Mr. Haskett smiled and said, "You've been stealing lilacs, I see."

"No. I've been gathering."

He frowned.

"I took Herrick's advice."

Mr. Haskett cocked his head to one side. "Who?"

"Herrick, the poet. He wrote 'Gather ye rosebuds while ye may'. It's a commentary on the fleeting of time. Seize the opportunity. Do what you can while you're able . . . You know 'Strike while the iron is hot' . . . 'Make hay while the sun shines.'"

The men were still staring at her and she realized she was babbling. Blushing, she gathered the flowers into her arms and said, "There were so many I don't think they'll be missed." The rain was pouring down now plastering tendrils of hair to her cheeks. Raindrops dripped from the tip of her nose and she couldn't wipe them away because of all the lilacs.

The men swung the bicycle into the back of the truck and the passenger said, "Hop in. We're getting soaked."

He gave her elbow a boost and she wriggled into the middle of the seat as he rolled up the window and took off his dripping hat. It was only then she recognized him as the father of the bride.

As they drove into town the aroma in the cab became overpowering and Mr. Haskett sneezed. "I think I'm allergic to the damn things!"

She turned to him. "Should we get rid of them?"

"Oh no," Midge Lander's father protested. "I love the smell of lilacs." He smiled down at her. "Where are we taking you anyway?"

"Oak Terrace. Fiona MacPherson's? I'm Margaret Darwin and I have a room there. Do you know Fiona?"

"Sure," Mr. Haskett replied. "Everyone knows Fiona. You tell her Ed and Doug came to your rescue. Do you want me to drop the bike off at McGuire's garage tomorrow? It'll save you pushing it over there."

"Thank you very much . . . If you're sure it's not too much trouble . . ."

Mr. Haskett pulled up to the house and Doug helped her out with her armload. A tiny sprig of lilac caught in his wedding ring linking them together. He twisted the snag gently.

"Just snap it off," she suggested.

"It's okay." He managed to free his finger as she thanked them again, and hurrying up to the porch, she watched them drive off.

When Fiona returned from work she found a bouquet of lilacs in an old jam jar on the kitchen table. Margaret came out of her room to tell her about the flat tire and how Mr. Haskett was taking it to the garage to be fixed.

"That Ed has a heart of gold," Fiona said. "You'd never know he's one of the richest guys in town."

"Oh?"

"Yeah. He's a building contractor. Works all over the district. I hear his son, Brian got a raw deal from Midge Landers. They were supposed to get married a couple of weeks ago and he was working day and night to finish the house he was building for her. Then the day of the wedding he found out she was seeing someone else as well, some guy who was in town working with the gang on the pipeline. Well, Brian stood her up. There she was at the church, and he didn't show. I heard Ed sent Brian and the best man away on the honeymoon instead. It'll be a long time before people stop talking about this one."

As Margaret lay in bed that night waiting for sleep, she stroked her abdomen and thought about Ed and Doug, and what sort of relationship they had. Where do their loyalties lie? How can they remain friends after what their children have been through? Brian must have been heartbroken to learn of his fiancee's infidelity. And Midge must be suffering with the humiliation of being jilted at the altar. How can these two men ignore the heartaches of their children and play golf and still hang around together in spite of what happened? Some people I'll never understand!

Two more days of rain prevented Margaret from pursuing her gardening. She went to the library instead and brought home a book of poetry and a new mystery novel to pass the time. When she stopped at the garage to ask about the bicycle, Mr. McGuire came out of the office.

"Yes, Mrs. Darwin . . ."

"Mr. Haskett brought my bicycle in here yesterday. It had a flat tire."

He shook her hand. "Ed was looking at the other tire too. He said we'd better replace them both."

She raised her eyebrows. "How expensive are tires?"

"Ed said to put it on his account."

"He mustn't do that," she protested.

Mr. McGuire leaned toward her. "Look, Mrs. Darwin. I'm just going to do what Ed says. You can take it up with him if you want to later. Your bike will be ready for you tomorrow."

The rain had softened the hard clay on the slope and Margaret was able to pull out the weeds quite easily. Working a few hours each day, and relaxing her sore muscles in a hot bath at night, she had cleaned out the whole rock garden by the end of the week. The perennials rewarded her by growing in leaps and bounds.

Satisfied with her efforts, she rocked on the veranda on Sunday afternoon in the warm sunshine. She had debated the thought of attending the morning service at St. Jude's and decided to go because anything was better than sitting in a quiet house by herself. Clyde Morrow at the organ proved to be a pleasant diversion but when the service itself became a repetition of the previous Sunday, Margaret decided she would definitely not return for another theological lecture. Growing sleepy in the May sunshine she roused herself and set off for the boardwalk along the beach.

The Beachside Patio was packed with diners enjoying the fine weather and the view of the calm blue lake. Margaret rested on a bench, drinking in the panoramic beauty. The heavily forested western shore stretched far down the lake to disappear into the sky, and the southern islands hung suspended over the horizon. The fields above the eastern shore had grown incredibly green. Barefoot children played along the beach, shrieking as they dashed in and out of the cold water. Margaret tilted her face up to the warmth of the sun, realizing during the years of John's illness she had forgotten the intoxicating pleasure of a bright warm afternoon in May.

To dispel any unhappy thoughts of her present circumstance, she stood up and continued her stroll to the far end of the boardwalk. Here she discovered another park with a grandstand and a racetrack. Greenhouses lined the side street and she turned in to look at their colourful bedding plants. Continuing up a long slope at the southern end of town, she stopped at a small tearoom to rest and eat an early supper. Her feet were aching and she lingered over dessert and coffee. When the place was ready to close, she pried her feet back into her shoes, and avoiding the business section of town, came to an intersection with churches on three of the four corners. The United Church was closed. Cars filled the Baptist parking lot and she noticed a number of families walking toward their building. The Presbyterian Church stood closer to the street with a parking lot behind. Several cars lined the curb. Margaret heard an organ playing, and on impulse, she turned and walked inside.

The interior seemed gloomy at first until the evening sun burst through the high pebbled glass windows above the doors and illuminated the front of the sanctuary where a plain wooden cross hung on a painted plaster wall. The stark simplicity contrasted sharply to the wealth of colour at St. Jude's. She sank into a pew halfway down the side aisle behind an elderly couple and slipped off her shoes. Most of the congregation occupied the centre section but craning her neck, Margaret could see a few more worshippers on the far side of the church. The organist was playing a medley of hymns and she settled comfortably into the pew cushion wondering what Presbyterians did in church.

A choir of four women and four men entered the loft and gathered together behind the organ. As a tall balding man, robed and mantled, entered and sat down behind the lectern, the choir stood to sing, their hushed tones so sweet and rich, their voices blending together with the organ so beautifully that Margaret was moved to sudden tears. Noticing Doug among the choristers, she looked around for Deirdre as the minister rose. Mesmerized by the Scotsman's voice, Margaret listened to Angus McKelvie read a Psalm and give a brief sermon. The choir rose to sing, "Abide with me. Fast falls the eventide." Their mellow voices chanted softly as the dying rays of the sun shone upon the cross. "Though darkness deepens, Lord, with me abide."

As the hymn ended the minister prayed above the soft strains from the organ. "Oh Lord, support us all the day long through the troubles of life 'til the shadows lengthen, the evening comes, the busy world is hushed, the fever of life is o'er and our work, done. Then, oh Lord, in thy tender mercy grant us safe lodging, holy rest and peace at last, through Jesus Christ our Lord. Amen."

Margaret remained seated, her eyes closed as a cloud of peace enfolded her. The organ played the postlude. The congregation merged into the aisles, their voices of greeting melding into the background. Unwilling to break the spell she finally slipped out the side door and walked home in the twilight accompanied by an unfamiliar sense of tranquility.

She thought about the peace of God that next week as she pedaled several times to Cook's greenhouses for flowers for the rock garden. Passing the funeral home one day she pulled over to the curb with the rest of the traffic as the cortege entered the street. She watched the faces of the mourners and wondered what personal agonies that family had suffered. Later, rocking on the veranda, she thought about death and what it would be like to die. As one door closes, does another door open? Is it that simple? And what about judgment? Phrases of her Anglican catechism came to mind. "The righteous judge." No. I don't want to think about judgment. She stood up and went inside. She could not permit herself to think of judgment without thinking about Jane. And I won't think about Jane now . . . But I should call Charles and Bruce. They must be wondering about me by now . . . Surely they must . . .

That evening, armed with a pocketful of change, she walked downtown to a pay telephone in the quiet lobby of an office building and prayed she wouldn't have to tell too many lies about her whereabouts. Lying had always been taboo in the Darwin household. She had disciplined her children sharply for their small deceptions, teaching them that one lie always leads to another. And now she found herself guilty of the very thing she so despised in others. She dialled Charles' number first.

Mavis' mother answered the phone. "Margaret? Is that you?"

"Yes, Gertrude. Is Charles home?"

"Oh dear. No, they're out for the evening. I'm here with the children."

"Oh. I thought I'd better call and let Charles know I'm fine. I got here safely and have a very nice place to live. The weather's been lovely."

"What time is it over there in England?"

Margaret gulped. "Almost bedtime. Did Charles and Mavis have a nice time in Bermuda?"

"Oh yes. This call must be costing you a fortune, Margaret. I'd better let you go. I'll tell them you called. Goodbye now."

Dialing Bruce's number, Margaret wondered if this call would be so simple. Jennie answered, pleased to hear that she was all right, surprised at the clarity of her voice, sorry that Bruce had just left to take the boys to a ball game. Margaret agreed that satellite transmission was a wonderful invention, she was sorry to have missed Bruce, and were the children looking forward to summer vacation? Jennie reported a few of their plans and then told Margaret this call must be very expensive and she would tell Bruce his mother had called and she was to take care of herself.

The whole exercise had taken less than five minutes and cost Margaret less than five dollars. She treated herself to a steak dinner that night at the Beachside Patio.

Margaret forsook St. Jude's on Sunday morning and went to St. Paul's United Church instead. Passing St. Andrew's, she was tempted for a moment to turn in to hear Mr. McKelvie again. Her need to talk to someone in the church was becoming fainter now and she attributed it to her reluctance to share her life's experiences, and to her growing conviction that she could and should manage her own affairs as she had in the past. The security of her room at the boarding house and her familiarity with the town and some of its inhabitants added to the increasing stability of her situation, and so her attendance at St. Paul's became more of a social outing than a spiritual quest. A large and friendly congregation filled the clean bright sanctuary, and huge sprays of flowers from a wedding the previous afternoon adorned the front of the church. The minister, Mr Gilmore, tall and dark and handsome, reminded Margaret of her son Charles, as he stood before his flock, reflecting on the aspects of St. Paul's relationship to the community. His affable personality surfaced and laughter was heard in the pews. Margaret quite enjoyed herself and chuckled with the people around her. Several women greeted her warmly and invited her to the strawberry social to be held in two weeks.

Tired of dragging her rocking chair out to the veranda every day, Margaret went around to examine the wicker furniture in the garage. Apart from the dust and dirt, it seemed quite sound, and when Fiona returned home from work that afternoon, Margaret received her permission to give it a coat of paint.

She returned to St. Andrew's for the evening service anticipating another pleasant evening. Sitting in the choir loft, Doug caught her eye and smiled. Margaret scanned the congregation for Deirdre in vain. Angus McKelvie read some inspiring poetry and the sweet mellow voices of the choir touched Margaret so deeply she wished she could sit there and listen to them all night. As the choir filed out after the benediction, Doug smiled at her again. For no apparent reason, Margaret was constrained to bolt out the side door and hurry home.

One of the young men who lived upstairs was unloading a small sailboat from the back of a pick-up truck in the driveway.

"Hello," Margaret called from the sidewalk. "Do you need any help?"

The tall lanky teenager turned to her.

"I'm Margaret," she explained. "I live downstairs from you."

He stuck out his hand. "I'm Ted. I can manage okay, I think. I used to sail this on our pond when I was a kid. My mother's been after me to get it out of the shed so I'm going to try it out on the river. I'll put it around the back of the house."

 She thought immediately of her rock garden. "Let me carry something."

He gave her the paddle and the centerboard. Pulling the boat off the truck, he turned it over, and balancing it on his head, staggered around the side of the house.

"Be careful," she warned. "It's very steep right here . . ."

He slowly wended his way down to the bank and set the boat down on the grass. "Phew!" he said rubbing the top of his head. "That's heavier than I thought." He looked up at her garden. "You've made it very nice out here. I watched you from my window when I was supposed to be studying for exams."

"Thanks," she replied, holding out the paddle and centerboard. "Where do you want these?"

"I'll put them under the boat," he said.

She walked back to the front of the house with him and watched as he stowed the aluminum mast and sail inside the garage. "Say Ted, would you help me carry this furniture over to the house? I want it for the back porch."

He looked at it ruefully. "It's pretty dirty to drag through the house."

She nodded. "Maybe you could hand it to me over the railing."

He took the furniture outside and swept off all the cobwebs with an old broom. She helped him carry it around to the back of the house and went inside to take it from him as he hoisted it onto the veranda.

Monday morning, she scrubbed off the two chairs and the rocker and the table and left them to dry in the sun while she pedaled down to the hardware store for several cans of white spray paint. The breeze blew her newspapers about as she transformed the furniture, and by the time she had finished, the porch floor was a mess. She went back to the hardware store for a half gallon of grey paint and had covered up all her mistakes by the time Fiona came home from work.

Fiona was delighted with Margaret's efforts but Margaret was in pain. Her side was aching so badly she spent the next day in bed recovering from her labours. She often wondered about her solitary state and her health, and what would happen to her when she became debilitated like her husband and whom she could depend on to help her. She knew the tumour in her abdomen was growing, feeling its presence almost constantly. She also knew she was losing weight. Most of her clothes didn't fit properly any more. She cinched in her slacks and skirts with a belt to hold them in place, and folded her blouses in pleats about her waist so they wouldn't look so baggy. The dresses she had worn to Charles' and Bruce's weddings were a smaller size and she felt they were still suitable for church. Since she had no social life or occasion for new clothing anyway, she decided to manage for the present with what she had in the closet.

The next afternoon Margaret rose from her bed to sit on the veranda, and finding the wicker very uncomfortable, she decided to buy some chair pads as well. Ted was out on the river in his little red sailboat. She watched him sailing back and forth progressing slowly toward the harbour. He disappeared from sight for a while before sailing back up the river heading straight for the bank. She walked down as he came in and watched him drop the sail, pull out the centerboard and haul the boat out of the water. He stowed everything underneath and stood up rubbing his back. "Well that's the last time I use that boat," he said.

"What's the matter with it?"

"It's too small for me. The river's too narrow to have a good run on any tack. And the lake's too dangerous. I'd be swamped on a windy day."

"What are you going to do with it then?"

"I'll find some kid who lives in a cottage on one of the smaller lakes around here. Did you ever sail?"

"A couple of times. It was a bigger boat though."

"Why don't you try it then? It might be fun for you if the wind's right. It's not hard to rig. You just drop the mast in this hole here, and put the centerboard in here. This is the rope you haul the sail up with and fasten it here. And this is the rope you hold to control the boom."

"It sounds simple enough. The worst I can do is tip it over."

He glanced at her. "You do know how to swim . . ."

"Oh yes."

"Well, put the lifebelt on anyway, just in case."

They walked up the bank together and Margaret went into the house. If I drowned I wouldn't have anything to worry about, would I? . . . She shook her head to dismiss the very thought of suicide. Euthanasia as a solution to John's suffering, and Jane's too, had come to her in the darkest hours of her nights. A pill, a needle . . . No. The thought was abhorrent to her, and while the phrase "death with dignity" came to her over and over again, she had snuffed it out and decided that "living with dignity" was the better alternative. She had watched the staff at Thornbury care for her husband, change his diapers, treat his pressure areas and she had doubted he still had his "dignity", but somehow she felt as long as she was there as his wife, to hold his hand, to talk to him in his semi-comatose state, then he was still a person who deserved her respect and nurture. But when it would happen to her, she still wondered if it wouldn't be easier to end life quickly when the pain became unbearable. Could one still live with "dignity" while reduced to clinging to one's basic instincts, fighting and clawing for one's last breath?

She went to the bank in the morning to draw out some spending money and noticed Midge Landers behind the teller's counter. As the girl dealt with her customers pleasantly and politely, Margaret failed to see any resemblance to Doug, and decided she didn't look like Deirdre either. She was relieved when her turn came, to transact her business with another teller instead because she was sure Midge would remember her as the observer of the activities in room 306 and maybe St. Jude's vestibule as well.

She bought the seat pads for the wicker furniture and made three trips to Cook's on her bicycle for hanging baskets of fuchsia, bleeding hearts and ivy geraniums for the veranda. The townspeople were becoming used to the sight of this older woman pedaling a rusty contraption along their streets but she remained a mystery in their midst. They knew nothing about this stranger with long strands of pale hair wafting about her head, her eyes hidden by dark glasses, the legs of her slacks fastened securely with antique clips about her ankles.

Walt shared the little he knew of her one afternoon when she pedaled past the barber shop, her blue nylon squall jacket billowing in the breeze. "She came in on the early train one morning. From Toronto, I think."

"Oh?" Russ, the barber, paused, his scissors suspended by a customer's ear.

"Yeah. She was at the Wellington for a while."

Heads turned sharply from the magazines and newspapers with a collective "Oh?"

"Naw. She's not that kind of a woman . . . I don't think so anyway. I moved her over to Fiona's place."

Amid a spate of guffaws, Walt protested, "Fiona's not so bad . . ."

More laughter followed.

"Maybe she likes a little fling now and then, but so what?"

One of the men ventured, "So maybe her new boarder likes a fling now and then too."

Walt folded his newspaper and stood up. "You guys should be ashamed of yourselves."

After he had left the shop, Russ said, "What's with him?"

Another man nodded his head. "Yeah. Everybody knows birds of a feather flock together, so what's the big deal?"

Another man said quietly, "Just a woman's reputation, boys. Just a woman's reputation. And in this town that is a big deal!"

Working several hours each day, Margaret found the slope behind the house a great source of satisfaction as she guarded her petunias and portulaca from the perpetual weeds. Other perennials appeared spontaneously in nooks and crannies along the weedy fringe and she nurtured them carefully, expanding the perimeters of her garden. The cedar hedge along Bridge Street to Oak Terrace afforded her a small amount of privacy, and it became her daily morning ritual to sit on the sunny porch in her bathrobe, sip her coffee, read the folksy humour in the New Lancaster Herald and listen to the radio.

Margaret walked to church the following Sunday morning in a cool drizzle. With some misgivings she had decided to try the other church on the corner and as she turned at the sign "FIRST BAPTIST CHURCH", she wondered if there was a second Baptist church in town that she had missed. And why don't they call themselves St. Something like everybody else? Even the Catholics belong to St. Mary!

Nevertheless, she marched undeterred into the building and was greeted by a smiling couple who asked her name. A pleasant usher showed her to a seat where she was inundated by a barrage of noise! Everyone seemed to be laughing and talking while children scurried up and down the aisles. Margaret tried to compose herself for worship but, distracted by the bustling activities in the pews, she examined the interior of the church instead.

The sanctuary was a mixture of old and new. Arched Gothic beams spanned the ceiling where fans purred quietly. Vertical blinds covered long coloured-glass windows. Artificial ficus trees were potted around the paneled choir loft. A bare wooden cross hung on the wall above an arched window with a maroon velvet curtain. The organist and pianist struggled valiantly to keep together in a lively rendition of the children's hymn "Jesus loves me". As the choir entered the loft, several men came to sit on the dais and took part in leading the congregational singing and reading and praying. Margaret sang the unfamiliar hymns and wondered why the minister didn't do something.

When Mr. Ferguson, a middle-aged man, came to the pulpit, he reminded Margaret of a burly football player who had lost a lot of weight. She immediately became aware of his strength as a preacher and listened avidly to the sermon, the story of Abraham and Isaac on the journey to Mount Moriah. She vaguely remembered hearing it before and had wondered then what was the point. So God wanted to test Abraham's faith. But did God really expect him to kill his own child in cold blood? Now she listened as Mr. Ferguson drew the analogy to the journey of Jesus Christ to Calvary. She learned that Isaac's faith in his father was comparable to Abraham's faith in his God, and Jesus' faith in his heavenly Father. He wound the whole lesson into a message of faith in a God who lovingly treats His children with acts of mercy and loving kindness.

As she shook Reverend Ferguson's hand at the door, he asked her name and said warmly, "Now, Margaret, you'll never be a stranger here again. Come next time as a friend."

She was so receptive to the invitation she returned for the evening service and almost immediately wished she was across the street in St. Andrew's. A small group of musicians sat near the piano and played their drums and horns with gusto as another group of people sang into microphones. The congregation clapped their hands in unison and Margaret longed for Presbyterian peace. She felt it worth all the aggravation just to hear Mr. Ferguson preach again but he remained seated while several of the church members came to the pulpit to tell what Jesus Christ had done for them. In spite of her misgivings, Margaret Darwin learned something that night from the Baptists . . . That if Jesus Christ was the Lord of your life, you could expect Him to help you out of any situation. She thought about it for a long time after she went to bed. An Anglican all her life, she had learned the catechism. She had been confirmed in the faith. She had married in the church, and baptized and raised her children to be good Christians. But could anyone remotely expect God to take a vital interest in every aspect of his or her life? How could God possibly keep track of the minutiae of everyone's lives unless . . . The words of her catechism classes returned to her mind as she drifted into sleep, unless He was really an omniscient, omnipotent and omnipresent God.

She bought a Bible the next week and read some of it as well as the Herald in the morning. Working in her garden and taking solitary walks along the beach occupied her afternoons. An occasional adult swimmer ventured into the water but most of the beach people were mothers with young children, sitting on the sand to visit while their offspring dug huge holes and made castles by the shore. The marina was filling with power boats and sailboats. She spent part of one afternoon watching them lift a large cruiser into the water, and reading the name on the hull, AMY'S AMIE, she wondered if it belonged to Ed Haskett. Mindful of her debt for the bicycle tires, she waited on the pier, hoping he would appear for the launching. She waited in vain and surmised that even if it really belonged to Ed, the man might have more important things to do than supervise the handling of a very expensive boat.

As Margaret sat on her porch on a warm breezy Saturday morning, bored with her own company and her inactivity, she looked down the slope at the little red boat. The invitation to adventure grew strong and at last she said to herself, "Why not," and went inside to change her clothing. She turned the boat over and dragged it down to the water's edge. It took her some time to work through Ted's directions but eventually she put on the lifebelt, pushed the boat out into the river and hoisted the sail. The wind blowing upstream immediately caught the craft and Margaret skimmed up the river under the bridge. The movement across the water was so exhilarating that she laughed exuberantly and wondered why she hadn't done this sooner. Experimenting with the boom, tightening, releasing, discovering the perimeters of speed and safety, she sailed upriver viewing New Lancaster from the back door, the ends of streets and neighbourhoods, the playing fields of the high school. She moved through thickly wooded areas where no houses could be seen. Then an expanse of green fields opened up along the right bank and she steered closer to the shore. A group of golfers was getting ready to tee off again. One of them, wearing an old fishing hat and a yellow shirt, walked over to the bank and shouted, "Do you know how to sail that thing?"

She recognized Doug. "Of course," she laughed. "And it's so much fun!"

"How do you expect to get back?"

She waved gaily as she skimmed by. "I'll manage."

He shook his head and went back to his golf game.

Margaret sailed on out of sight. "What's he talking about, 'How do I get back'? I'll sail back, of course."

The river was becoming narrower and the current seemed stronger.

Perhaps I should go back now. I'll just turn around and head for home.

She pulled on the tiller but the boat refused to turn, and with the sail still full, it was now sliding sideways upstream. She pulled harder but it still wouldn't respond so she propped the tiller with her knee and paddled hard to force the boat to turn. The sail slammed wildly to the other side rocking her fiercely, and now the boat was sailing backwards upstream.

"Now what do I do?" she wailed. "Where am I going?" With visions of rapids and waterfalls around the next bend, she pulled on the tiller again but it wouldn't respond so she paddled furiously again and the sail slammed back to the other side as she continued upriver. "Oh God! I wish I'd never come sailing!" she cried. "How am I going to get home again!"

Considering her plight, she decided to steer for the shore, abandon her voyage and walk cross country to a road and find her way home on foot. When she drew near the bank the sail slackened, the boat slowed and she reconsidered her situation. Carefully, she edged forward and dropped the sail, folding it neatly upon the boom in the bottom of the boat. She pushed off out into current and began to drift downstream. As the river widened, the current slowed, and paddling again, she managed to straighten her course and float home.

Her feet were soaked by the time she hauled the boat up onto the grass and turned it over. "That was fun," she murmured, climbing the slope, "but I'm going to the library next week and get a book to learn how to sail." She poured a cold drink and propped her bare feet up on the railing of the porch when she spied a man in a yellow shirt slowly putt putting up the river in a dingy. She crouched down behind the railing when he noticed the red boat on the grass and turned around to head downstream. Margaret sat up in her chair again. "Doug was looking for me," she mused, unsure whether she should be thankful or flattered at his concern for her safety. "Deirdre's a lucky woman to have a man like him," she decided as she went inside to have a hot bath before supper.

She returned to the Baptists in the morning. Another couple shook her hand at the door and asked her name. She endured the noise and enjoyed another sermon about Abraham. As Mr. Ferguson greeted her afterward, she said she was looking forward to more adventures with Abraham. He laughed and said, "Come back next week."

When evening came, she stood at the corner wondering which church to attend. The musical prelude rocketed out of First Baptist and she headed across the street to St. Andrew's. Doug smiled at her from the choir and Margaret looked around for Deirdre. She wasn't in the sanctuary and Margaret felt disquieted as Doug continued to glance at her through the service. With Mr. McKelvie's final amen, Margaret left through the side door and hurried home.

She asked Mrs. Bowman the librarian if she could recommend a book on sailing. Mrs. Bowman pulled out a small paper back book and said "A gentleman saw this, the other day and laughed so hard, I had to remind him to hush." When Margaret read the title "SAILING" the fine art of getting wet and becoming ill while slowly going nowhere at great expense (a dictionary for landlubbers, old salts and armchair drifters) she burst out laughing and Mrs. Bowman pursed her lips and frowned "You and Mr. Parker would make a good pair with the same sense of humour."

Margaret found several more books on sailing in the library. Studying them, she quickly realized the little red boat wasn't in the same class as a real sailboat. However she managed to pick up several ideas that helped her understand the principles of the sport. One could not sail directly into the wind. A forty-five degree angle to the wind was the bare minimum needed for progress. She learned one must always turn into the wind when changing direction or the mast could be damaged if the boat "jibed". She learned more nautical terms: tacking, broad reach, starboard and port, bow and stern, halyards, lines, boom, mast, tiller, rudder. On a fine day in mid-week she judged herself capable, and bravely tacked her way down to the pier and back. When she told Ted of her adventures he said he was happy she was enjoying the boat but sooner or later she would want a bigger one. She laughed at him in disbelief. But as the summer wore on she discovered he was right.

Slipping on the steps in the garden Saturday afternoon, Margaret twisted her ankle and hobbled back into the house to put a bag of frozen peas on her injury. When Fiona returned from work, she helped her bind the ankle with a tensor bandage. Margaret missed church on Sunday and wondered if Mr. Ferguson might think her insincere. Her ankle improved by the following Sunday but her left side ached so badly she had to stay home from church again. She lay in bed, feeling quite miserable with a bout of menstrual pain and spotting. She was positive that Fiona suspected her to be a hypochondriac until they met in the kitchen one afternoon.

Her landlady smiled over her teacup and asked, "When did you have your last physical examination, Margaret? Going through the change of life is no picnic, so I've heard. Maybe this pain in your side means you're ovulating but it could be something else too. We don't have a gynecologist any more but there are still a few good doctors left in town."

"I'll be all right, Fiona. Don't worry about me. I've seen enough of doctors and hospitals for a while."

"I'm sure you have. Before Mr. McGuiness, when I worked on the medical floor I used to see a lot of patients with Alzheimer's. They were there waiting for a bed in the chronic unit to open up. I always thought the real victim of the disease was the family, especially the spouse. Mr. McGuiness was different. He still had all his faculties right up to the end, but I had had enough of looking after old people. That's why, when I went back to work I asked for the newborn nursery. I'll take a crying baby any day compared to dealing with all the troubles of the elderly. How long was your husband in a hospital?"

Margaret sipped her tea. "Four years. I'd kept him at home for three years after we got the final diagnosis . . . I'd noticed a few little changes in his behaviour but it wasn't until he had his car accident that I really knew something was wrong. Fortunately it was a minor fender-bender, and since he was in the insurance business, the company looked after that part of it."

"I had no idea on our first visit to the doctor of the hell that awaited us. After all the tests, the family was called in for a consultation. We were stunned. At least the children were. By this time I think I knew, but they couldn't accept it. And John . . . poor, dear John. I'll never forget his face as he leaned over and gave me the car keys. He said, "I'm all yours, dear, for better or worse.""

Margaret wiped her eyes. "He accepted his fate so calmly, so stoically. He went to see the accountant, the lawyer. He modified his will and gave me power of attorney. It almost seemed like it was business as usual. He finished up his affairs at the office, said goodbye to his friends. I think they couldn't believe what was happening. But I could see the changes . . . And John did too. After one frustrating afternoon with trying to work the combination on our wall safe and cope with turning the knob he finally broke down and wept in my arms."

Margaret wiped her eyes again. "He confessed his deepest fears, his sorrow for his future and mine. He wondered how I would manage; who would look after him at the end; how the children would deal with his illness. He seemed so vulnerable . . . I think I never loved him more than at that moment. He finally fell asleep and that's when I wept. I knew that I had to be strong for the both of us and I felt utterly inadequate to deal with what I felt lay ahead."

Fiona reached out and touched her arm. "Does it bother you to talk about this now?"

Margaret nodded. "Yes. And thank you for listening, Fiona. I think I'll go back to bed for a while."

She covered her eyes with her arm in a semi-darkened room remembering those mornings when she had hated to get out of bed and face another day. Her frustration levels fluctuated with John's varied endeavours, his bouts of assisting her with "all this housework!" One morning, while she vacuumed the bedrooms upstairs, he had cleaned out the kitchen cupboards and added the partial contents of spice jars to other spice jars "just to fill them up". And that same week, Margaret had a stern conversation with the bank manager after receiving a nasty letter from the utility company about a worthless cheque. She then discovered John had previously strolled into the bank and an unsuspecting teller had permitted him to close their checking account, transferring the money to a new savings account.

She became vigilant over the trash can when she discovered the deed to their house in the waste basket in his study where he spent long hours "just sorting through my files". At that point, she wondered what other documents he may have thrown out.

She knew he missed going to his office everyday, and once, to appease his anxiety, she took him downtown to see his friends. "Never again!" she had decided when he refused adamantly for a half hour to get into the car and return home. A complicated series of locks were added to the entry doors of the house when he began escaping at all hours to roam the neighbourhood.

The final straw to break Margaret's resolve to keep her husband in the family home came after she spent two watchful weeks with him at a cottage in the lake district in the autumn. She had decided she needed a change of scene and felt it would be good for him as well. Shortly after their arrival he had become agitated and she gave him the medication to calm his anxiety. Then he stood for a long time looking through the screen door at the lake. She was busily involved getting settled and didn't notice his tears until he sobbed, "I want to go home." Attempting to distract him as one would a child, she suggested a walk on the beach. They came to the end of the lawn and he refused to walk on the sand saying that his mother didn't want him to get his shoes dirty. For the next two weeks she dealt with his fixations on his shoes and his mother, mostly by ignoring them and at other times trying to convince him his mother wouldn't mind. Even after they returned to their large spacious home in Thorn Hill, he still wanted to go home and she realized he had slipped further into the past and his childhood.

On the day of their return she went to the basement seeking the source of a ghastly smell. To her horror she discovered he had pulled the plug on the freezer before they left on vacation and her summer harvest now lay in a soggy mess along with rotting roasts and steaks and a maggot filled turkey. Retching constantly she cleaned up the slimy contents. In quick order she fumigated the basement, put the house up for sale, gave some of their furniture and goods to their children, auctioned others, and moved the rest to an apartment in Thornbury Village.

John's confusion had mounted within the small confines and he wandered about for days looking for the staircase. There had been an angry confrontation with two men who came to visit his wife, and he drove Charles and Bruce from the apartment, shouting dire threats and forbidding them to return. She gave the car to Bruce after John insisted on driving again. He had shouted, "I want the keys! Now!" The verbal abuse escalated to periods of shoving and pushing, and Margaret often wept in despair as she watched him napping briefly in his chair. Later, John entered a phase where he refused to sit down. He would pace through their small apartment for hours until he collapsed on the sofa, the bed or the floor. She fed him finger foods as he marched. One afternoon, he fell against the wall, breaking the plaster. Fearful that he would break a bone the next time, she finally consented to admit him to the chronic care facility where he was drugged into submission.

He vegetated there for four long years.

Sometimes, late at night when she couldn't sleep, she would sit in the apartment and focus on the fifth window from the end on the third floor of the building where her husband lay barricaded in his bed. Her arms longed to hold him in a loving embrace, She missed the intimacies of marriage so badly in those quiet hours. John had forgotten that aspect of their relationship long ago. There had been those awful first moments when she realized he did not know her as his wife and she had displayed their wedding picture to no avail. Gradually he failed to even recognize her as his loving caretaker. Those solemn vows taken as a young radiant bride now sentenced her to cell 342 as surely as a judge pronounced the penalty on a convicted felon. She had gone willingly, dutifully into exile from life, into a monotonous daily routine that only varied with the weather. She bathed her husband. She fed him. She dressed him in his clothing to push him in a wheelchair about the gardens, morning and afternoon, talking to him about anything and everything as he retreated further into a silent world of his own. When it was too cold or wet, she pushed him about Thornbury Village, through the halls and atrium where dozens of other objects of pity slumped in their chairs, dozing, drooling, driveling. She escaped to the activity centers where therapists worked with the less mindless in music and games. She took John into the cafeteria for tea parties and bought him sweets at the tuck shops. She read the headlines of the newspapers to him, determined, desperately determined to preserve his person, his status as a member of the human race.

She sat by his bed when he could no longer sit in a wheelchair, playing tapes of their favourite music as she knit sweaters and mittens for her family. One afternoon, when she had fed him lunch and darkened the room for his nap, she went to the cafeteria for her own lunch. She returned to find John lying in bed, covered with a mass of yarn he had unravelled from the back of a cable stitch sweater vest she had been knitting for Charles. His eyes lighted up when she entered the room and he held out the remnants of the knitting and said quite distinctly, "There!"

Sometimes, she lay in bed at night wondering about her own insecurities that bound her so tightly, so completely to this person that she could not let him go. She met many other spouses in similar circumstances over the course of John's illness. They remained acquaintances, wearing invisible shells, unwilling and unable to become involved in the others' problems. The staff attempted to interest them in group sessions but this therapy only scratched the surface of their deep underlying sorrow. Margaret felt her survival lay in living one day at a time, waiting until the ordeal ended. And now it had.

A heat wave arrived with the close of the school year and children's voices rang across the neighbourhood from morning until night. The humidity became oppressive and Margaret watered her garden early in the morning or late in the evening to keep her flowers blooming.

The Baptist church was delightfully air-conditioned and Margaret ignored the noise, anticipating Mr. Ferguson's sermon after her two week absence. Reading the church bulletin she then discovered he was on vacation for the month of July. A lively older minister replaced him and eloquently pleaded for the congregation to repent or suffer eternal damnation. Margaret looked around at the people in the pews and wondered how they had all sinned so grievously since Mr. Ferguson's departure. His passionate pleas for sinners to come to the mercy seat lasted through all of the verses of the last hymn, "Just as I am". And when he began on the first verse again, Margaret had enough. The preacher's eyes lit up at the sight of her moving along the pew but she turned and walked out of the church.

With the scorching temperatures Margaret hoped St. Andrew's was also air conditioned but when she arrived on the doorstep that evening, she found the church locked. The Baptists were the only ones open for business. Unwilling to suffer through another service of brimstone and hellfire, she went home to a sweltering house instead. She put on an old loose smock and sat on the porch fanning herself with the Herald. As the evening turned to twilight and the neighbourhood grew quiet, she decided to walk down by the lake to find relief from the heat.

The marina lights twinkled as groups of people sat on their boats enjoying the evening. Their laughter rippled across the water in unison with the tinkling ice-cubes in their glasses. The Beachside Patio was crowded too, and as she passed by, Margaret saw Doug rising from one of the tables and leaning over to kiss an attractive young woman. Shocked, she turned her head and continued on down the boardwalk toward the darkened beach.

The humid night closed around her as she sat on a bench and watched the rising moon cast a long beam across the lake. She was more upset than she wanted to be at Doug's behaviour. He's a married man and he means nothing to me. I scarcely know him, but the few contacts we've had have been pleasant. He seemed so nice . . . But now . . . Like father, like daughter? Is it possible that patterns of behaviour are transmitted through the family's genetic pool? Poor

Midge. Is she at the mercy of her father's philandering DNA? And maybe I did find him charming. And those smiles from the choir . . . Oh what a hypocrite! I'm glad I saw him with that woman tonight. Now I know what he's really like.

She stood up quickly and walked down to the shore where the water gently lapped the edge of the sand. She took off her shoes and waded into the warm shallows. Glancing around at the dark empty beach, she unbuttoned her smock, dropped it on top of her shoes and dashed into the lake. The water closed over her head giving an instant relief from the heat. She surfaced wiping her face, and began to swim out into the moonlight. Her body seemed to gather strength from the light and she felt she could go on forever. Caution drew her back toward shore and she swam along the beach toward the bright lights of the marina. Then she turned and swam back through the glassy surface toward the darkness of the far end of the beach. The pleasure of swimming alone in the moonlight under a starlit sky brought her a quiet happiness. She turned over to float on her back and watched the constellations overhead, Orion with his sword and belt, the big dipper, and the little dipper with Polaris at the hub of the universe. As the moon rose higher, the stars faded and she swam out to meet the light again. Tiring at last, she turned toward shore looking for a landmark to find her clothing. Her eyes scanned the beach and she saw a figure sitting on the sand very close to where she judged her clothes to be. She swam into the shallows keeping herself submerged. Much to her dismay, she recognized the man in the shadows.

"Doug?"

"How's the water?"

"Fine."

"Are you coming out now?"

"No."

"Oh."

"Go away, Doug."

"Not until you come out."

"I'm not coming out until you leave."

"Why not?"

"If you must know, I'm in my underwear . . ."

"Oh . . ." He stood up and carried his socks and shoes over to a bench along the boardwalk and put them on, keeping his back to the water.

She scrambled out, squeezing the bun of hair at the back of her head, and grabbed her smock. Shaking the water from her arms and legs she finally pulled the smock over her head and walked up to the boardwalk to put on her shoes.

Doug turned around then. "Margaret, Margaret. What am I going to do with you? First, you get flat tires, and then you go on wild sailing expeditions, and now here you are swimming all by yourself in a lake in the dark. Don't you know it's against the law in New Lancaster to swim in the dark alone?"

She stared at him. "Against the law? You've got to be kidding."

He smiled. "Well, against my law anyway."

She didn't know whether to be angry with him or ignore him so she bent over and took a long time to tie her shoes. When she finally straightened up he made a deep bow with a flourishing sweep of his arm and said, "And now if Madame will allow, I will accompany her home."

Margaret drew her lips into a thin line. "Look, Doug. I think we'd better get something straight right now. You might call yourself a Christian but I don't think much of a man who cheats on his wife. I saw you kissing some woman as I came past the Patio tonight, and now you're here with me while Deirdre is probably sitting at home right now wondering where the heck you are."

She sat down on the bench again and turned her head away unprepared for the laughter.

"Cheating on my wife . . . Deirdre?" He threw his head back to hoot at the stars and she turned to watch this display of madness. He wiped the corners of his eyes and sat down beside her. "Look, Margaret. I think we'd better get something straight right now. I'm not married. My wife died two years ago. And that woman I was kissing in the restaurant is our daughter, Anne. She's home from Toronto for the weekend and I was saying goodbye to her because she was going off to visit a friend. I saw you go by and decided to join you for a walk. By the time, I paid the bill and got out of the place you were dashing into the lake and I didn't want to leave you here by yourself. So . . ."

"But Deirdre . . . The wedding . . ."

"Deirdre is my wife's cousin. We're just friends. That's all. Deirdre was a bit of a wild flower when she was younger. She broke her parent's heart when she left town and went off to live on a commune with some hippies. A few years later, she came home with a little girl. I doubt if Midge knows who her real father is. Anyway, Deirdre moved back in with her parents and settled down, sort of. Her father's dead now and she asked me if I'd walk Midge down the aisle."

Margaret rubbed her chin. "I guess I owe you an apology then . . . I really misjudged you."

"Accepted," he said and stood up. "Now, will Madame please allow me to accompany her home?"

She smiled and stood up too. "There's just one more thing. I don't know what your last name is if Midge Landers isn't your daughter."

"It's Parker. Douglas James Parker, teacher of history and math at the local high school. I'm almost sixty years old and I've still got my own teeth. Now, what else would you like to know?"

She laughed and they began to walk across the parking lot toward town. "Your daughter. What does she do in Toronto?"

"She's a doctor, doing her residency in Ob/Gyn. She has another year to go and then she can hang out her shingle and stop living off her poor old father."

Margaret smiled. "Do you have any other children?"

"My son, Michael. He's a farmer."

"Oh?"

"They call him an agronomist. He lives in Africa., Kenya."

"Oh?"

"Yes. He's doing some research on bugs, weevils. They lose a lot of grain to their bugs over there. I guess it's an important job."

"I'm sure it is to the Africans."

"Anyway, what about you? What are you doing in New Lancaster?

"I'm on my summer vacation."

"Are you married?"

"I'm a widow. My husband died about five months ago."

"Oh."

"It was Alzheimer's. It seems like he died a long time ago but it just became a reality last March."

"Are you planning to stay in New Lancaster long?"

"I don't know yet . . . It all depends."

"Oh?"

"I haven't made up my mind."

"It's a nice little town. I've been here almost thirty-five years."

"Oh?"

"Yes, I got a job teaching here right after university and I've been here ever since. I met Janet and we married and had the kids . . ."

They had reached Bridge Street and he stopped to say, "How about going for a cup of coffee?"

She shook her wet head and realized under the street lights the outline of her wet bra under the smock was quite visible. "No thanks. I don't want to scare everyone in the shop."

He laughed. "I'll take a rain check then."

They walked on across the bridge and he pointed to the red boat lying in the grass. "So how are you at sailing these days?"

She chuckled. "I got some books at the library. I'm improving."

"I'll take you out sometime and show you the ropes, whoops, lines."

"There's not enough room in there for the two of us."

He smiled. "I have a boat we can fit in. It's tied up in front of my house down across from the pier."

"Oh?"

"It's a nice boat. She handles well. It's easy for me to sail it alone but it's more fun when someone else is aboard. Do you play golf?"

"No. I've never tried. Was it Mark Twain who said playing golf just spoiled a good long walk?"

He laughed and took her elbow as they crossed the street and turned onto Oak Terrace. Approaching the door, she wondered how to say goodnight to a man after all these years but Doug solved her dilemma. He held out his hand and said, "If you decide to go swimming again in the moonlight, give me a call."

She smiled and shook his hand. "Goodnight, Doug. Thanks for the company."

She turned and went into the darkened house, her head and heart in turmoil. When she had moved to New Lancaster she had expected to have some problems, serious problems, but never in her wildest dreams did she imagine something like this. She had spent a pleasant hour in the company of a very amusing, attractive man, and in her heart, she knew it would be quite possible to become interested in him. Their encounter had been a tonic to her soul. And he seemed interested in her too. He had mentioned a rain check for coffee. And she was thirsty, so very thirsty for contact with another human being, for conversation, for companionship that defined her as a woman. The innocent mention of swimming in the moonlight belied the suggestion of another kind of relationship and she knew she mustn't let it happen. The very thought of becoming involved with any man was absurd. She just couldn't afford any more complications to her present situation. It was as simple as that. And as she showered and got ready for bed, she decided to avoid him as much as possible.

The following week, the phone in the kitchen rang several times and Margaret ignored it. Fiona was working the night shift and had disconnected the extension upstairs. Margaret no longer sat on the veranda in the morning because she was afraid he would see her from the bridge or the street. The heat wave continued and she escaped to the farthest point of the beach and spent long afternoons under a tree reading and regularly plunging into the lake to cool off. On Thursday afternoon she was preparing to leave the house when the front doorbell rang. She froze in her room and heard Fiona shuffling down the stairs. She quietly closed her door and hid behind it.

"Good afternoon, Fiona. Did I wake you?"

"You sure did, Doug."

"I'm sorry. I was wondering if Margaret's at home."

"I don't think so. Just a minute."

Margaret heard the footsteps outside her door. The knob turned and the door opened slightly and closed again.

"No. She's out."

"All right. I'm sorry to have troubled you."

The front door closed again and Fiona climbed back upstairs. Margaret went over to sit on her bed. I hope he gives up soon. I can't go on hiding like this forever.

She spent a troubled afternoon at the beach, watching the waves lap the shore. The wind seemed to be strengthening and she wondered if Doug was out on the lake among all the sailboats. The temptation to accept his invitation, the hunger to spend a few hours engaged in pleasant conversation with him almost overcame her resolve and she dived into the breakers repeatedly, swimming furiously as if to exorcise him from her thoughts.

Her long hair was becoming unmanageable, and on the way home, she stopped at Dixon's Salon and made an appointment for a haircut the next day. On Friday afternoon, Sally Dixon smiled as Margaret slid into the chair in front of a counter full of beauty aids. "So you've decided to get rid of your locks, my dear."

Margaret sighed. "I've been swimming a lot lately. It's too much trouble to keep it long. I think if you lop it off below my ears it'll be fine."

Carrying a bag full of conditioners and cosmetics, she left Mrs. Dixon's shop looking like a new woman, her hair tinted light brown, bluntly cut with a bang swept to the side behind her ear. "You look years younger," Sally had said as Margaret paid her account.

Fiona agreed with Sally Dixon. "You look great," she said. "I'll have all the fellows in town ringing my doorbell. Doug Parker was here yesterday looking for you."

"I wonder what he wanted," Margaret murmured as she turned to fill the kettle.

"You," Fiona replied.

On Saturday, Fiona invited Margaret to accompany her to a shopping mall in Englewood, a town thirty miles north of New Lancaster. She needed a new dress for a friend's son's wedding. Margaret was grateful for the invitation. It was another place to hide.

Margaret chose to attend St. Paul's on Sunday morning because she couldn't bear another harangue from the Baptist minister and she didn't want to meet Doug at St. Andrew's. Sitting in the United Church she discovered it was a joint service with the Presbyterians, Mr. McKelvie was in charge, and it was too late now to change her mind. As she rose to sing the first hymn a man stepped into the pew beside her and she knew it was Doug without turning her head. He reached to take one side of the hymn book. "All things bright and beautiful . . ." His rich voice joined hers. "All creatures great and small . . ." She gazed at the front of the church so she couldn't see his brown hand and clean thumb nail on the page. "All things wise and wonderful . . ." The aroma of his shaving lotion wafted near. "The Lord God made them all . . ." She sang the rest of the hymn in a fog of heady sensations. His hand brushed hers as he took the hymn book and she prayed her own prayer as Mr. McKelvie gave the invocation. When he invited everyone to shake hands with the people around them, Doug took her hand. "Hello, Margaret. Welcome to St. Paul's." He leaned over to whisper, "I like your new hairdo." She smiled and turned to shake hands with the woman behind her.

She was so conscious of his presence during the service that she couldn't remember a thing Mr. McKelvie said. Doug was wearing a white summer shirt with a flowered tie and light beige slacks. During the sermon, he turned slightly in the pew, crossed his legs and rested his right forearm against her shoulder. Sometimes his hand crossed over to rest on his knee and she noticed the blond curly hairs on his tanned arm, a gold watch on his left wrist and no wedding ring.

She was wearing a cream coloured sheer dress with long sleeves and a matching long vest with a tiny green fleck. She turned slightly to cross her legs and rested her left hand with her wedding rings very much in evidence on her knee. After the benediction, Doug stepped out into the aisle and allowed her to precede him. She wondered if she could lose him in the crowd but he stayed close behind, and when she reached Mr. McKelvie at the door, Doug laid his hand on her shoulder to introduce her to his pastor. "This is Margaret Darwin, Angus. She's the new girl in town."

Mr. McKelvie smiled. "Good morning, Margaret. I see Doug is taking care of you."

"Not really," she protested, but the two men chuckled and it was time to leave.

Doug took her arm as they went down the steps. "Would you like to go somewhere for lunch?"

She studied the ground for a moment. "I'm afraid not. Fiona and I've made plans for the afternoon."

"Well I'll drive you home then," he said, and guided her to his car in the parking lot. "Been sailing lately?" he asked casually as he climbed in behind the steering wheel.

"No. It's been too hot. There hasn't been enough wind on the river and Tinkerbelle's too small for the lake."

"Tinkerbelle. That's a cute name. How'd you like to come down and see Pretty Lady?"

"That's the name of your boat?" "It suits her too. Do you want to come?"

"Well . . ." she wavered.

"It won't take long. Fiona can wait a few minutes." He turned off Bridge Street onto Oak Terrace, drove several blocks, and pulled into the driveway of a long grey brick bungalow. The cherry red front door matched the colour of the geraniums in the planters across the front windows. A wide chimney rose above the far end of the house.

"There she is," Doug said as he turned off the motor. When he pointed toward the river Margaret realized he was talking about the boat and turned from her admiration of his home. She opened the car door and walked toward the flagstone steps at the side of the garage that descended to the back lawn. Several pines whispered in the breeze at the far end of a wide deck across the rear of the house with glass sliding doors opening onto it. An expanse of lawn ran down to the lake where massive stones were piled along the shore. Weeping willows clustered in the far corner.

"It's lovely here," Margaret said. "You have a wonderful view of the bay." She held her hand above her eyes to gaze at the eastern shore.

"It's home," he said and held out his hand. "Come on and I'll introduce you to the Lady." As he led her across the soft grass toward a wooden jetty, her heels sunk in the soil and she stopped to take off her shoes.

The waves lapped at a dinghy behind the Lady's gleaming white hull. A blue canvas tarp was wrapped around the sail on the boom. Doug squinted in the sunlight at his pride and joy. "I've had her about ten years now. She's a lot of work . . ."

Margaret noticed the fresh varnish and shiny brass fittings. "But she's worth it, isn't she," she finished, touching one of the stays on the mast. "And being a school teacher is ideal for you . . . I mean you can spend a lot of time sailing . . . You have the whole summer . . ."

He nodded. "I keep pretty busy, I guess. Between sailing and playing golf and cutting all this grass, I don't have time to be bored." He took her hand to help her over the railing and she walked around the large cockpit. He unlocked the door to the cabin and she stooped to see its interior.

"It's big," she said with a hint of surprise.

"It's quite comfortable for two. Any more and we have a crowd."

She leaned against the cabin. "You must know you're a fortunate man, Doug. You have it all." She gestured toward the house. "You really love it here, don't you."

"I wouldn't want to live anywhere else," he said. "It's beautiful in the winter too. The lake freezes and covers with snow. On a sunny afternoon with a big blue sky, and snow drifting across the ice, it just seems like heaven."

She cocked her head. "That's odd. I always think of heaven with green grass and flowers."

"Wait until January, Margaret. I'll show you heaven."

She straightened up. "I must be going. Fiona awaits."

He helped her climb back onto the jetty. "Do you want to put your shoes on? Your nylons are turning green."

She laughed. "But my heels get stuck in the soil. I should have worn my deck shoes."

"You can wear them when you come sailing with me. I have to go to Toronto this week but I'll call you when I get back."

As they walked toward the house a small wire-haired terrier galloped across the lawn barking incessantly. Doug bent down to scratch its ears.

"Yours?" she asked.

"Sort of. Hobo adopted the Wilsons, my neighbours, and me last summer. We don't know where he came from but he just made himself at home. He stays at their house most of the time because they're usually around, but if they go away then Hobo and his basket move into my house and he's happy with me too."

She bent down to pat the dog. "He's an awfully cute little mutt."

"Shhh, Margaret. Don't hurt his feelings. Hobo thinks he's a ferocious Doberman. You should see him chase the neighbourhood cats."

They walked up to the house and she put on her shoes. "Tell me how you get geraniums to match your door," she asked as he opened the car door for her.

He went around to get in his side, and backing out of the driveway said, "It was Janet's idea. Several years ago, she bought the flowers at Cook's and went to the hardware store and found paint to match. We've had a standing order every spring with Cook since. If he ever stops growing this variety, I'll have to repaint the door."

He was silent the rest of the way to her house and she jumped out before he had time to open his door. "Goodbye, Doug. Take care of yourself in the big city."

He nodded as she closed the door and hurried into the silent house. An overwhelming sadness flooded her being. She undressed and lay down to mourn the bright future which she could never share with this man or any man. The pain of her loss was so acute that she buried her head in her pillow and cried. The old griefs for John were forgotten. His loss seemed negligible compared to her own now. Every time she saw Doug she was reminded of a life she used to share with a husband. She wanted so much to be held, to be comforted, to be loved violently, tenderly, . . . She wrapped her arms about the pillow tightly desperately wanting to feel those old passions still remembered.

Oh God . . . What a mess I'm in. I never thought I could feel this way again. This is so cruel. How can you do this to me? No . . . I'm doing this to myself. I just can't see Doug any more. I have to take control of myself . . . But look at me. I'm a total wreck, lying here crying over something that never belonged to me in the first place. What am I going to do, God? What am I going to do?

She lay in bed all afternoon more depressed than she had ever been before. When Fiona was making herself a sandwich, Margaret stirred and went into the kitchen. "Do you need any volunteers at the hospital these days?" she asked. "I have to find something to do."

Fiona licked her finger and said, "Funny you should ask that. I was talking with Joan Woods the other day and she said they're really short of drivers for the Meals on Wheels program. It seems everyone wants the summer off."

Margaret shrugged her shoulders. "That's no good for me. I don't have a car."

"Do you know how to drive?"

"I used to but I gave the car away over five years ago and haven't been behind the wheel since."

"So you don't have a license either."

She shook her head.

"Well, get dressed and I'll take you out and you can try driving my car. If you can get your license, you could use the "Meals" car."

Later that evening when Margaret was carefully driving along the road toward the golf course with Fiona at her side, a maroon sedan pulled out on to the road heading back to town. "There's your friend," Fiona said and leaned over to toot the horn. Doug turned his head, and recognizing Margaret at the wheel, tooted his horn in reply.

"He's a nice guy," Fiona remarked. "Could you see yourself dating him?"

Margaret fixed her eyes on the road. "No," she said firmly. "Not Doug, or anybody else."

Her role as a volunteer with the Meals program saved her sanity. Joan Woods welcomed her with open arms the next morning. "You see about getting your license right away," she suggested. "I'll have to take you around this week to show you the ropes anyway and then you can do it yourself. Did you really mean you could help out everyday?"

Margaret brought home a handbook from the license bureau to prepare herself for the exam, and Friday afternoon, Clyde Morrow took her out for her road test. He was very kind and forgiving when she made an error, and when they arrived back at the office, he took her picture and made out her license. She looked at the photo and wondered if this was the staid aging woman who had left Thornbury Village less than three months ago. Her face was thinner, her eyes larger and the haircut had transformed her into someone she didn't recognize.

Mr. McKelvie shook her hand after the church service. "My wife and I are leaving for six weeks in Scotland tomorrow so say goodbye to Doug for me, Margaret. I hear he won't be back until Tuesday."

"Tuesday,' she mused on the walk home. "I've got two more days before I have to deal with him again."

Her volunteer work kept her busy each morning and early afternoon. On Wednesday she headed for the far beach and swam and read until it was time to stop at the tearoom for supper. Ted had left a message on her door. "Some guy called twice and I said you weren't home."

Thursday afternoon she accepted a dinner invitation from Joan Woods and stayed at her home until mid-evening. Fiona had left a message. "Doug called. Here's his number. He wants you to call him. I'm getting an answering machine for this place!"

Wondering how to discourage him, she dialed his number. His machine answered.

"Hi Doug. It's Margaret returning your call. Sorry to have missed you."

Friday she stayed very late at the hospital, straightening her accounts, and getting ready for the next week's deliveries. She ate supper in the cafeteria and went home to bed. She roused to hear Ted on the phone in the kitchen. "Yeah. No. I don't think she's home. Just a minute . . . No, she's out."

Saturday morning, she knew she was going to have to see him sooner or later so she pushed Tinkerbelle into the river and sailed down to the pier. The lonely dinghy rocked beside the jetty. Pretty Lady had gone.

Doug wasn't in church Sunday morning either, and Margaret took a long detour on the way home past his house. The geraniums waved at her in the breeze from the lake but the boat was still away. She walked to the beach in the afternoon and watched a spirited ball game. When the score reached twenty versus three in favour of the home team, she lost interest and watched a horseshoe tournament instead.

The beach was crowded with families swimming and teenagers playing volleyball and throwing frisbees. She sat on a bench and watched as the boats on the lake headed back to the marina. To avoid going home too early, she ate a cheeseburger at one of the booths and watched another ball game.

That night she became violently ill, vomiting and retching until she thought her stomach would come up too. Diarrhea was another agony and she finally lay on the bathroom floor, too weak to go back to bed. By morning, she made her way past the kitchen where the boys were eating breakfast and asked Ted to call Joan Wood at the hospital and tell her she couldn't come to work. He and Paul were so appalled at her appearance the two of them put her to bed.

"Do you want us to call a doctor?" Paul asked.

"No," she whispered. "I'll be all right. Fiona will be home soon. She'll take care of me."

He brought her a glass of water. "You're sure you'll be all right?"

Her side was aching fiercely too and she wondered if she should have called a doctor. Exhausted from the night she lay drowsing, heard the front door open and Fiona going upstairs. The phone disturbed her later but she was too tired to move and she wondered if this was how a person felt as they were dying. She awoke around four o'clock to a tapping on her door. Ted stuck his head inside. "Doug's here. He wants to see you."

"Doug?"

The door opened and Doug stepped inside. "Ted says you're ill."

She shut her eyes and ran her fingers through her hair. "Yes . . . I had a pretty rough night . . ."

He came over and looked down at her. "You didn't call a doctor?"

She closed her eyes again. "No. I think it was the hamburger I had at the beach last night." It suddenly occurred to her that the statement was probably true. She opened her eyes and tried to sit up. Doug reached for another pillow and put it behind her shoulders. She pulled the sheet up to her throat. "I must look a fright," she murmured.

"I've seen you looking better," he agreed. "But don't worry about it. I've seen worse too."

Ted stuck his head in the door. "Would you like a cup of tea?

She nodded. "Thanks."

"Would you like one too, Doug?"

He hesitated. "Sure. Why not."

After Ted left, Doug looked around the bedroom. "This is very nice." He walked over to the window bay. "Nice view." He picked up the rocking chair and carried it over to sit by her bed.

She ran her fingers through her hair again. "So what have you been doing?"

"I was over at Ville Marie this weekend. There's an annual regatta. We have a lot of fun over there. Some of those French sailors are pretty good."

"Ville Marie? I think that's where the radio station is . . ."

Ted brought two mugs into the room. "Do you want milk or sugar?'

"No," they said in unison. "This is fine," they said again. They laughed at each other and Ted left them alone again. Doug continued talking to her about his adventures across the lake as they sipped their tea. He saw she was growing drowsy and leaned over to take her empty mug. "You'd better get some more shut-eye," he said. "I'll call you in the morning."

He replaced the chair and bumped into Fiona at the door. She was in her dressing gown and yawning. "I thought I heard a man's voice," she said. "What are you doing in Margaret's bedroom?"

"Taking care of the sick."

"Sick!" She pushed past him into the room.

Margaret tried to sit up again. "I'm all right now. It was just something I ate yesterday."

Fiona felt her forehead. "You feel warm."

"I don't have a fever. It'll just take some time to get over it. That's all."

When Doug called in the morning Margaret told him she was much better and was going to laze around the house all day. She was sitting on the veranda reading that afternoon when he walked around the corner of the house and handed her a large cold bottle of ginger ale. "Chug-a-lug," he said.

"Will you join me?" she asked.

"Sure." He climbed up over the railing and she went into the house to get some glasses and ice. They sat in a comfortable silence watching the traffic of New Lancaster. "Your flower garden is quite nice," he said at last.

She nodded. "The peonies were gorgeous but now the day lilies are coming along and they're beautiful too."

"Janet used to plant a lot of flowers," he mused. "I can't be bothered with all that work."

"Your geraniums are lovely."

"They're easy though. I just throw some fertilizer on them once in a while and when they start to look tired I chop off their heads."

She smiled. "Do you have a guillotine?"

"Nope. Just a rusty jackknife." He took it out of his pocket and showed it to her. "My father gave that to me when I was eight years old."

"You must have been a good little boy for him to trust you with a knife."

He stood up and walked over to the railing. "I'm still a good little boy. I'd better go along now." He put one leg over the side. "Do you suppose this is how Romeo climbed over Juliet's balcony?"

She smiled. "If you taught English instead of History you'd know that Romeo never climbed up to the balcony. He stayed below in the garden and recited poetry instead."

He grinned. "I'll see you tomorrow."

"I may go back to work."

He raised his eyebrows.

"Meals on Wheels."

"So that's where you've been. I tried to call you several times."

"Oh I keep busy with one thing and another."

Margaret tried very hard to keep their relationship on a casual basis. They sat together in church the following Sunday and he took her to the golf course for lunch. She developed a closer friendship with Fiona, realizing she needed an excuse for empty hours. They went shopping in Englewood again and ate lunch occasionally at quaint tourist traps. The weather remained very warm and she often went swimming in the evenings to stay away from the house. Doug found her one night and walked her home. She shook his hand at the front porch and went inside feeling guilty about treating him so casually.

July turned to August and Mr. Ferguson returned from his holiday. When Margaret told Doug she planned to go the Baptist church in the morning, he joined her there and said later he quite enjoyed Jack Ferguson's sermon and asked if she was planning to become a Baptist someday.

She hesitated. "I'll wait and see who the bishop sends to St. Jude's. Surely that student won't be there forever!"

Before she got out of the car at Oak Terrace he reached for her hand and she wondered how to rebuff this advance. He turned it over to look at her palm. "No calluses. You're not sailing these days."

"I'm too busy," she said. "And it's boring on the river. There's not enough wind."

He chuckled. "I'll take you sailing when I come back."

"You're going away?"

"Yes. For a couple of weeks. With Ed and some of the boys. We're going fishing up on the Abitibi River."

"Where in the world is that?" She realized he was now stroking her arm but she couldn't stop him and she didn't want to either.

"It's half way to James' Bay."

"Can't you find fish closer to home?"

He was winding a lock of her hair around his finger. "It's a man thing, Margaret. We like to think we're voyageurs. Something primal. We wear the same clothes everyday and grow beards and smell awful by the time we come home."

"Couldn't you at least wash or go swimming in the river?"

"Nope. It's against the rules. And besides, the water's about fifty degrees." He slid across the seat toward her and put his arm around her shoulder. "How about if I kiss you goodbye?"

Her mind was tumbling in a dozen different directions. She leaned toward him and sniffed. "You smell pretty good now. Okay." She turned so he could kiss her on the cheek.

He kissed her gently, and from the pressure on her shoulder she knew he didn't intend to stop there. She opened the door and slipped out. "Goodbye Douglas James Parker. Have a safe trip."

The look of disappointment in his eyes was almost more than she could bear but she walked up to the porch and turned to wave as he drove slowly away from the curb.

Margaret missed him terribly, far more than she wanted to admit in those lonely hours in the middle of the night. She knew he would be back and wanting more from her, a word, a touch. But she could not, must not let her guard down for a moment or she would be lost and then it would be disastrous for them both.

Sunday morning, Mr. Ferguson greeted her and asked when Doug would return from his fishing trip. Margaret was rapidly becoming aware of one of the fundamental truths about living in a small town. Everyone knew everyone else's business. She was becoming part of it herself while delivering meals to the elderly who had nothing more to do all day than rock on their porches and talk on their phones. Mr. Ernest Jones told her one day about the young woman who lived next door. "That Midge Landers is pregnant! Oh it's supposed to be a secret but I seen her out in the back yard at the clothesline, and when she lifted up her arms . . . Well I know what I see when I see it!"

The weather turned cool and rainy most of the next week and Margaret wondered about the voyageurs on the Abitibi. Saturday morning dawned bright and warm and she decided to go sailing downriver to the harbour. Cruising by the Pretty Lady, she almost fell out of the boat when Doug's head appeared through the Lady's front hatch.

"Margaret!"

She recovered quickly. "I didn't know you were home," she called, sweeping rapidly past the jetty.

"Turn around! Come back!" he shouted.

She was pleased that she could skillfully manoeuvre Tinkerbelle back to the dock. As she dropped the sail, Doug caught the bow and tied it behind the dinghy. He reached down to help her out of the little boat and it tipped precariously. She laughed as he pulled her up beside him.

"Welcome home. When did you get back?"

"Late last night. I was just checking the bilge. With all this rain . . ."

"Bilge. Let me think. That's down at the bottom of the boat, isn't it."

"You'll make a sailor yet, Margaret." He squinted across the lake. "How'd you like to do some real sailing. Try your hand on the Lady instead."

She shrank. "Oh I couldn't."

"Yes you can. It'll be a piece of cake. I'll just nip up to the house for a minute."

While he was gone she climbed aboard Pretty Lady and sat down to talk to herself. Now look. You're going to be spending some time with this man and you can't run away from any situation you get yourself into, so be careful. Don't get too close to him. Don't encourage him in any way. If you make the wrong move, he's going to be all over you and you won't want him to stop. So watch it!

He returned carrying a cooler chest and a baseball cap. "Here. I don't want you to sunburn that pretty nose."

She groaned inwardly and wondered why she had ever agreed to this adventure.

He moved quickly about the boat, removing the tarp, hauling out the jib and setting it up and checking the halyards on the mainsail as well. He went below and passed her up the tiller and the seat pads. The motor coughed and he made some adjustments with the throttle. Going forward, he brought in the bow fender and cast off the bow line. He came back to the stern, slipped the tiller into the fitting and cast off. Gearing forward, he steered into the current and headed for the outer harbour. The boat rocked about in the choppy waves as he turned off the motor. "Here, you take the tiller while I raise the jib. That's the little sail at the front. Just keep her pointing into the wind."

Margaret swallowed and took the tiller. It seemed to draw to the left and she had to pull hard to point the bow around to the southwest.

Doug pulled in the other fenders as he went forward and hauled up the jib. He came back to the cockpit and steadied the tiller for a moment before slipping a handle into a winch on the gunwale. He began to crank and the line tightened and she felt the boat turning as the jib swelled. "You're doing fine," he said in answer to her silent query. He crossed the cockpit and cranked another winch as the main sail rose majestically overhead. It flapped menacingly and she waited. He came back to crank it in and slip the line into a cleat at the stern. He took the tiller from her and she relaxed with a big sigh.

He smiled and turned the boat onto a starboard tack and looked around, checking the other lines. The hull swished through the chop on the lake as the silence of a summer morning surrounded them. "Here," he said, giving her the tiller again and she felt the power of the craft's movement in her hand.

"Now you're sailing. How about a cup of coffee?"

"Is there a sail-through restaurant out here?" she asked.

"Sure. It's called Doug's Donuts." He rose to go below.

"Don't leave me here alone!"

"I'll just be a minute. You're okay."

He put a kettle on the gas ring and stood in the companionway to watch her progress. In a few minutes the kettle whistled and he disappeared below. Handing her a mug and a doughnut, he said, "Time for your coffee break but you'll have to dunk."

She looked at the stale doughnut.

"Leftovers from the trip," he explained. "I'll take care of the Lady now."

She moved over to sit along the port gunwale and watch the shore shrinking behind them.

After a long silence Margaret felt constrained to say something so she looked up at the mainsail and then across the water. "This is nice. I don't know why anyone would want a powerboat."

He nodded. "When the kids were in their teens they were always after Ed to take them water-skiing. He's had just about every kind of boat there is, and never has time to enjoy them."

"I saw Amy's Amie. Is that his?"

"Yes. Amy's friend cost him a fortune. I'm glad my tastes are simple and affordable."

There was another long silence. She sipped her hot coffee and looked out beyond the bow.

He cleared his throat and said quietly, "Are you happy?"

Startled, she glanced at him and looked away again. "Why do you ask?"

He lifted his cap and ran his fingers through his hair. "Oh I don't know. Sometimes you seem very far away and I wonder what you're thinking about."

She shrugged her shoulders and focused on the bow again. "What do I think about? The usual things, I guess . . . My family, the future." She leaned toward him and said dramatically in a deep voice, "The meaning of life."

"You've never mentioned your family, except that your husband died of Alzheimer's."

"I have two sons. They live in Toronto. They're married and they each have two sons too. I had a daughter . . . But she died . . ."

"When she was a child?"

"No. Jane died two years ago. She had AIDS."

"Good God! That must have been a dagger in your heart. Your husband and your daughter . . ."

She nodded and looked away. "I don't know how I got through those days. I guess just one day at a time . . ."

"Was she married?"

"She was living with a man. They'd met in college." She turned to face him. "Jane was what you might call unconventional. A free spirit. As far as I can understand it, she'd been experimenting with drugs in the dorm, and probably a lot of other stuff as well, and that's when she became infected. She knew her father and I didn't approve of her lifestyle. We had some bad times then . . . Some very bad times . . ." She drew a deep breath. "Eventually she straightened herself around, graduated, got a good job and settled down with Ken.

"Then the roof fell in with John's diagnosis and I fell apart too. It seemed like we couldn't talk any more. It was like the family had come apart at the seams. And it was my fault, I guess. I became so protective of John. I devoted myself to him completely. I felt so devastated, so alone, and yet I had to be strong. I had to take charge . . . Anyway, the damage was done. The children went on with their lives, busy, busy, busy, and we all seemed to manage. I didn't learn of Jane's illness for a long time. I knew she and Ken had split up but l didn't know the reason why. She seemed to draw into herself. She wouldn't talk, and I thought she was depressed because of Ken. It wasn't until she called to say she was in hospital that I learned the nightmare was only beginning."

She rubbed her face and looked away. "I really don't want to talk about it any more, Doug. Do you mind if we change the subject?"

He looked at her with moist eyes. "Okay."

She swung her legs up on the cushion, and leaning against the cabin, looked back at New Lancaster and asked, "So what are you going to do with the rest of your life?"

"I'm planning to retire in January at the end of the semester."

"Oh?"

"Retire or take a sabbatical. I'm going to Italy and study the Etruscans."

She sat up. "The who?"

"The Etruscans in Etruria."

"I've never heard of them . . ."

"They were an ancient civilization . . . About three thousand years ago. No one knows where they came from. They were an agricultural community but then they found metal in the hills and this gave rise to the Iron Age. The Roman civilization came about as a result of Etruscan industry. There's so much more to learn about these advanced people. The Phoenician traders, and later the Greeks became vitally interested in their skills and commerce, and this is when shipping in the Mediterranean became commonplace."

"The Etruscans . . ." she mused.

"They're not a household name," he admitted. "But archaeologists are digging up new treasures everyday and I'd like to go and study ancient history first-hand. If I were a rich man I'd travel all over Europe. I've taught students the exploits of historical figures like Charlemagne and Frederick the Great, but now I'd like to see these lands they conquered. Did you know Charlemagne waged a war against the Saxons for thirty years before adding them to his empire?"

"Was he fighting in England too?"

"No. Saxony."

"But I thought the Saxons were English."

"German. There was a segment of them who emigrated to Britain to help the Angles war against the Picts who were a fierce tribe from the north, modern Scotland. I don't want to bore you with all this . . ."

"Oh no. I find it very interesting. In fact I was planning to go to England myself this summer until . . . Until something came up."

"What did you want to do in England? Visit the Queen like the pussy cat or shop in Harrod's?"

She smiled. "Heavens no! I hate shopping. I was thinking of a walking tour through the Cotswolds."

"Why the Cotswolds?"

"I know this sounds silly but I like the names of those old medieval towns. Elizabethan towns like Bourton on the Water, Stow on the Wold, Moreton in Marsh. Did you ever hear of the Bisley boy?

"The who?"

"The Bisley boy. The boy who became the Queen of England."

He stared at her. "What on earth are you talking about?"

"This is what happened according to some Cotsallers. Henry the Eighth didn't like Elizabeth because she reminded him of her mother Anne Boleyn, so he sent her to live at a place near Bisley. She caught a cold and died. Her guardians were terrified and looked for someone to take her place but they could only find a red-haired boy about the same age who had studied Latin. So he became Elizabeth I."

He stared at her. "I think you're mad to believe this."

She laughed. "But it does explain why she never married and went bald in middle age."

He shook his head.

"Can you imagine Elizabeth reviewing her troops on a spirited steed, chin held high and her wigged hair blowing in the breeze as the Spanish Armada neared the coast? Can you hear these words ringing through the ranks, 'I may have the body of a weak and feeble woman, but I have the heart and stomach of a king!'"

Doug shook his head again. "You aren't serious, surely. Where did you read all this, about the Bisley boy?"

She smiled. "It was an article in a travel magazine."

"I'll give you a history book on Elizabeth to read, if you're interested. I don't think you'd find it boring."

"I might," she admitted. "And I don't know very much about ancient history. I took the children to the museum to look at the Egyptian mummies but they weren't very interesting."

"I agree. But if you could walk through the land of Egypt where those people lived, see their sunrises and sunsets across the shifting desert sands. If you could touch the soil their hands tilled, then these people would become real, very real, just like you and me. Perhaps someday, a thousand years from now, someone will find your rock garden and say, `I wonder what woman created this thing of beauty.'"

She smiled. "I am interested in my roots, my Anglo-Saxon heritage. Several months ago, I was reading about the Tudor Kings and the War of the Roses, and I wondered which of my ancestors had led the charge across the drawbridge to seize the castle, or which of the women in my family had wept over a dying child in a plague or famine."

"You're doing the same thing, Margaret. And when you personalize history, when you put yourself into the scene, then it all comes wonderfully alive."

He reached over to adjust his lines and set the boat on another tack. She could see the traffic on the highway along the western shore. "So where are we going?"

"I thought a run down to Burnt Island and across to Windy Point would be long enough for your first outing. So what made you change your mind about England?"

She rose and walked across to sit on the other side of the cockpit so she could see the cottages along the shore. "Oh . . . several things. I decided not to complicate my life by going too far away. And I remembered New Lancaster."

She told him about their vacation many years ago. He gently prodded her to talk more about herself. "I worked in the same office as John. We met at the water cooler. He was older than I but that didn't matter. We married, and after the babies started, I stayed home to manage the nice house in the suburbs while John worked his way up the corporate ladder. I guess I thought the good life would go on forever but . . . I finally sold the house and we moved into a place called Thornbury Village. Eventually John had to go into the nursing home . . . And now, here I am."

They sailed on in silence as the day grew warmer. She stood up to take off her jacket and glanced at him. He was staring out over the bow. He cleared his throat as she sat down again. "I guess it was easier for me in a way. Janet died of an aneurysm in the brain. One day she was alive and well, and then she was gone. It was an awful shock though. I hit the bottle for a while . . ."

She glanced at him sharply.

He noticed and said quickly, "I laid off the stuff after a bit. I might have a beer with the boys now and then but I don't keep liquor in the house."

She shrugged. "I don't like beer. I think it tastes like soap suds."

He grinned. "A cold one on a hot day goes down easy enough. Anyway, Ed came around quite a bit to keep an eye on me, and Angus McKelvie . . . He got me going to church again, and singing in the choir. It was hard to accept Janet's death, that she was really gone . . . But I think it would be much worse to lose someone you love by degrees."

She stood up and moved across the cockpit. "This is getting morbid, Doug. Let's change the subject again. Tell me about your fishing trip."

He smirked. "There's not much to tell. It was a very long drive to a very hard bed in a very old cabin. The fish weren't biting but the bugs sure were."

"Did you grow a beard?"

"If you could call it that. More like a ragged stubble. I was glad to have a hot shower and shave it off. Ed says he's keeping his until Christmas, but I bet Amy'll change his mind,"

"I'd like to run in to Ed Haskett one of these days and thank him for the new tires he put on my bike."

He laughed. "Ed told me about that. He said you'd been a help to old Harry Copse with that mess at the church."

"I know a bit more about that situation now."

"Oh?"

"When I first came to town I stayed at the Wellington Arms."

He frowned.

"Well I had to go some place and the Beachside was too expensive and all the motels are on the outskirts of town, so Walt took me there. Anyway I got there about two o'clock in the morning and bumped into Midge coming out of the room next to mine. She was there again the next night too, the night before the wedding. You can imagine how shocked I was to discover her the next day in her bridal gown about to marry someone else."

"Yeah. Deirdre has had her hands full with her all right. Midge and Brian went to school together . . . I dunno. It's pretty sad. The house Brian was building is just sitting there almost completed. Ed says he's never gone back to it. Brian's with one of the crews working on the new hangar up at Englewood. I didn't tell Ed this but Deirdre told me that Midge is pregnant. The fellow skipped town and Midge doesn't even know him well enough to want him if he did come back. Look. Here's Burnt Island coming up on the starboard bow."

Margaret sat up to watch him trim the sails and point the bow eastward along the dark thickly wooded shore. "This used to be a great place to pick blueberries," he said. "People would come over here with washtubs and pick berries all day. They'd sleep in the patch among the warm rocks at night and start picking again in the morning."

"How do you know that's true?"

"I read the books on the pioneers who settled here. They came up the lake on a paddle-wheel boat. It wasn't until gold and silver were discovered north of here that the government built the railway and roads. New Lancaster is in the Little Clay Belt. We're an agricultural people, just like the Etruscans."

She smiled. "Then I'd better go home and weed the rock garden so it'll last another thousand years. Would you like me to take the tiller again."

"Sure."

She came over to sit on the other side of the tiller and he remained where he was, silent, so silent she wondered what he was thinking.

Finally he got to his feet. "How about some lunch?"

"Do you have to catch it or pick it?"

He stared at her.

"I'm just kidding," she said. "I meant were you going to catch a fish or pick blueberries?"

He shook his head. "Boy, you sure have a weird sense of humour. I'll go below and make us a sandwich."

"You can steer and I'll make the sandwiches," she offered.

"You're doing fine right where you are."

Some time later, he appeared with a tray of ham sandwiches and pickles, a box of crackers and a chunk of cheese. "The wind's dropping off," he mused, glancing around at the surface of the lake.

They ate slowly and silently as the boat moved sluggishly through the dark water. He went below and returned with two cans of cold tomato juice as they came to the end of Burnt Island.

Margaret scanned the wide expanse of water shimmering in the afternoon sun. "I didn't realize the lake was so big out here."

Doug trimmed the sails again and put his hand over hers on the tiller to push the bow toward Windy Point. He removed it again to point down the lake. "Ville Marie's over there. It's about seven miles, I guess."

As they neared the Point the wind dropped off completely. "Are you sure this isn't Windless Point?" she asked.

He smiled. "You're going to think I'm like the fella who takes his girl for a spin in the old jalopy and runs out of gas."

She laughed. "And you've run out of wind. But we do have a motor."

He cleared his throat. "Yeah, but I'll run out of gas too before we get home. I was in such a hurry to take you sailing I forgot to fill the tank."

"The wind will pick up later, won't it?"

He shrugged. "It could be dark then."

"Don't worry about it," she said. "It's nice out here." The boat was rocking gently on the water. She took off her cap and smoothed her hair before settling it back on her head.

"I told you I like your hair, didn't I."

She nodded. "It's getting grey though."

"How old are you anyway?"

"Don't you know you should never ask a woman her age or her weight?"

"Just thought I'd ask."

"Okay. I'm fifty-seven."

"And I'm going to be sixty in January. We're a couple of old crocks."

"I don't feel old though." She stood up and stretched.

He looked at her and said, "When you do that I don't feel old either."

She blushed and sat down.

He picked up the tray and carried it down to the galley. In a few minutes he came back up with two cans of soda and handed one to her. "I don't want to seem like the wicked villain who has the fair maiden in his clutches but I want to say something to you, Margaret . . . Remember when I asked you if you were happy, and how I said sometimes I felt you were far away from me. I don't want you to be far away . . ." He glanced out across the water before turning back to her. "I didn't know I was a lonely man until I met you. When I saw you standing in the rain with your arms full of lilacs, something happened inside me. I've fallen in love with you."

She covered her face with her hands.

He rushed to sit beside her, his arm around her shoulders. "I know it's too soon for you, losing John, and all the other . . . But can we be friends? More than friends?"

Her shoulders shook convulsively.

"I'm sorry, dearest. I didn't mean to make you cry . . ."

Her throat was so tight with anguish she couldn't speak.

He turned her toward him and held her, stroking her back. "It's all right, Margaret. It's all right."

She sat up at length and wiped her eyes with her hands.

He fumbled in his pocket and gave her his handkerchief.

"It's not your fault, Doug. It's me. I'm sorry . . . You can't love me. You mustn't."

She turned to him and he looked away, his lips drawn in a tight line. She took his hand to hold it against her cheek, the hairs soft against her skin. "I don't want you to be lonely, Doug. I could love you too, but it's not the right time."

The boat rocked gently as he put his arm around her again and said huskily, "We'll work it out somehow. We'll give it time."

The sun seemed to grow very hot as they sat close together in the cockpit, alone with their thoughts. Margaret could feel her shirt sticking to her back and she said at last, "Gosh, it's hot. The sweat's running down my back. I'm going to smell like a polecat before long."

He stirred slightly and rubbed her back. "You smell all right to me." His hand moved up to her shoulders and began stroking the back of her neck.

"Let's go swimming," she suggested.

"I don't think we should. It's pretty deep to drop the anchor."

She sat up. "You do know how to swim, don't you?"

"Sure but . . ."

"Then come on." She kicked off her sneakers, stood up on the seat and jumped off the side of the boat. Surfacing, she cried, "It's wonderful. Come on in."

He stood up and rubbed his chin.

She was paddling around in circles, waiting.

"I don't think I can get you back in the boat."

"What!" she shrieked. "Can't you pull me up?"

"I don't know. Come over here and I'll try."

She swam over and tried futilely to reach the gunwale.

Doug knelt on the seat and grasped her wrists and pulled her up slightly. "Can you hook your foot over the edge?"

She tried. "Ow! I can't do it."

He thought for a moment. "The bow's too high. Come around to the stern and maybe you can stand on the rudder or the motor or something."

She tried again with him pulling on her wrists but she couldn't find a secure footing and scraped her ankle on the motor. "This isn't funny, Doug."

"I don't know why I never got a ladder," he groaned. "If we tie a rope around your waist maybe I could haul you in."

"And maybe you'd fall overboard too."

He looked around again. "If I give you a life jacket and tie a rope to you, I'll start the motor and tow you over to Windy Point. It isn't far. The beach is stony, and I don't know about rocks but you could stand on the bottom."

"Okay. Let's try that."

He pulled a life jacket from below the seat and helped her get it on. Lacing a rope through the armholes at the back, he said, "Now I'm going to let you out on a long lead so you're not near the motor. And I'll go very slowly."

He started the motor and headed for the Point.

"I feel like a whale," she called.

"I'll call you Moby Dick."

As he neared the shore, he could see huge rocks beneath the surface. "I can't go in any further or I'll put a hole in the hull," he said. "We'll mosey along the shore and hope it gets better." He towed her almost half a mile but danger still lurked beneath. He cut the motor and pulled her alongside. "Are you all right?"

"Sure. I'm having the time of my life."

"Well this is it. I'm just about out of gas and I can't pull you home. So, I want you to swim ashore to that cottage. Tell Mrs. Wainwright you're with me and what happened. Get her to call George at the marina to bring me some gas. Can you do that, dear?"

She was drifting in the jacket. "Sure. But let's take this thing off."

"No. Leave it on so you'll be safe."

"It's so heavy I won't be able to swim."

"No, Margaret. Leave it."

She unfastened it and let it float away on the rope. "I'll need my shoes."

Grimly he handed them to her one at a time and muttered so she could hear something about Fletcher Christian and Captain Bligh. She clung to the rudder and put them on. Her green eyes smiled up at him as she pushed off. "Thanks for everything. It's been a lovely day."

He watched anxiously as she paddled toward shore. The bottom of the lake rose up to meet her but it was treacherously slippery and she had to crawl the last hundred yards on her hands and feet. She waved to him from the beach and squeezed the water from her shirt and shorts before heading for the house.

No one was home and the door was locked. She walked around the cottage twice before discovering a loose screen. Rolling a block of firewood below the window, she managed to crawl in across a bed and hoped she didn't leave too much water behind. She found the telephone but no directory so she dialed Walt's number and told him to pick her up at Wainwright's cottage near Windy Point. Crawling back across the bed, she replaced the screen and the firewood. When she returned to the beach to tell Doug, he had drifted out a considerable distance so she waved and walked up to the road to meet the taxi.

"What happened to you?" Walt exclaimed as she spread his newspaper on the front seat of his cab and climbed in.

"I fell in the lake," she said, determined not to add another detail to the story that would be circulating through New Lancaster by supper time. She talked about the weather and asked about every cottage along the road back to town to prevent him from asking any more questions. Running into the house for her purse, she paid him and went in to call George at the marina. The phone rang again as soon as she hung up.

"Margaret. It's Joan Wood. I wonder if you could help me out, or rather my sister. She volunteered to cook at a church camp for a couple of weeks and her assistant has just been admitted to the hospital here with appendicitis. She really needs someone who's capable and I thought of you."

"But I'm doing Meals . . ."

"I can find someone for that if you'll go. It'll probably be fun too. The camp's on Deer Lake about thirty miles west of town."

"How soon does she want me?

"She'll pick you up now if that's all right. The campers arrive tomorrow and she has to get all the food unpacked."

"Well, give me half an hour to get ready."

"You're a dear, Margaret. Thanks."

She knew she looked a fright but there wasn't much time so she changed her clothes, wrote a note to Fiona telling her where she was going, and a note to Ted to tell him where she had left his boat. Packing her suitcase, she thought about the note to Doug.

Dear Captain Ahab

I've been asked to cook for a whole bunch of kids at a camp for two weeks.

I've told Ted where to find his boat.

I hope you got home okay. I love your
Pretty Lady.

M.D.
P.S. That's short for Moby Dick as well as me.

Chapter Five

Joan Wood's sister was a plump jolly woman who greeted Margaret with open arms. "Hi there. I'm Helen Stapleton. What a life saver you are! Are you ready to go? Here, let me take your suitcase. I didn't know what I was going to do when Judy started vomiting this morning. Who would believe that a person sixty years old could get appendicitis! I guess you're never too old, eh?"

Margaret managed to get a few words into the conversation. "Could we stop at my friend's house down the street. I want to leave a note in the door."

Helen talked most of the way to Deer Lake and Margaret was grateful. Physically weary from her afternoon in the lake, she felt emotionally drained as well. She leaned her head against the corner of the seat, threw an occasional "Hmmm" and "Aha" into the conversation and let her mind go to sleep.

As their car pulled in under the tall pine trees beside a long building, Helen's husband, who was also the camp's handyman, came over to help them unload the trunk of fresh vegetables and fruit. He carried Margaret's suitcase into a small room off the kitchen. "Here's your bunk, Maggie."

She cringed at the name but thanked him and went to join Helen who was looking at a mountain of canned goods and groceries in the middle of the kitchen. It was late in the evening before they stowed the last tin, and Margaret was so exhausted she fell asleep on her cot with her clothes on.

Deer Lake Camp was the perfect location for a group of sixty active youngsters. The cabins were arranged in a circle around a parade ground where many of their games were played. The kitchen opened onto a long dining room with windows overlooking the lake. At the far end stood a huge stone fireplace and shelves of books and games. A piano occupied a corner and Margaret guessed this room was where they would spend their rainy days. Fortunately for the cooks and counselors, it only rained once and the most of the days were spent on the magnificent white sandy beach. A dock jutted out into the water with slides and diving boards. Racks of canoes lined the shore beside three rowboats and two small sailboats. A large power boat was moored to a smaller dock near a semi-circle of bleachers overlooking a fire pit and the lake.

The buses from the church in Englewood pulled into the parade ground on Sunday afternoon and the children scattered to find their cabins. Their whooping and hollering shattered the idyllic calm, and the cooks went to work for the next two weeks. After the first pangs of homesickness faded, the campers' appetites became voracious. Helen and Margaret were in the kitchen at sunrise and hung up their aprons at twilight. "You couldn't pay me enough money to do this job," Helen said one night. "I'm only here because the good Lord wants me here. Isn't that right, dear?"

Margaret nodded and wondered if that was why she was there too. She had a fleeting suspicion that for her, Deer Lake Camp was a perfect refuge from Douglas James Parker's attentions. She thought about him in her quiet moments before sleep, or sitting by the lake for an hour in the afternoon while Helen caught forty winks in her cabin.

One afternoon, she heard a young lad pleading with the water sports director to show him how to sail one of the boats. The counselor was explaining that he had too many children to watch in the water and couldn't take his eyes off any of them for a minute.

Margaret rose and walked toward them. "Does he know how to swim?"

Blackie looked at her for a moment. "Why?"

"If he can handle himself in the water I could take him out. I have a boat like this myself."

Blackie turned to the lad. "Do you want Mrs. Darwin to teach you, Jeff?"

"Sure," he said.

This was the beginning of an odd relationship in which Margaret learned far more from Jeff than he learned from her. They spent an hour every afternoon on Deer Lake as she taught him what she knew from the books in the library, and her own experience. He taught her what he knew from growing up in a pastor's home, the eldest son sitting at his father's table.

He called her Dickie. "Every leader in camp has a bird name," he had said on their first afternoon.

"What's a bird name?" she asked.

"It's a pet name. We don't call the leaders Mr. or Mrs. Jones. That's too much like church. So they pick a name like Robin or Jennie for a wren, or Florrie for a nightingale. Something like that. Don't you have a funny name?"

She thought for a moment. "Moby Dick?"

"Naw," he said. "That's a whale. Say! How about the dickie bird?"

By the third day, they were making real progress and she sat up against the mast now out of the way and let him handle the sail and the tiller too. "You're doing very well, Jeff," she said. "Just ease off on the sail a little. We don't want to heel over."

"What's that," he asked.

"If we got going too fast and the wind was pushing the sail hard, we could tip over and Blackie would have to come out and save us."

"I'm saved already," he said. "I asked Jesus to come and live in my heart when I was little and now I'm saved forever."

She cocked her head to one side and asked gently, "How do you know Jesus lives in your heart? Doesn't he live in heaven with God?"

He looked up at her brightly. "But Dickie . . . Jesus is God."

She blinked and didn't know what to say for a moment because he was just a little boy with a childlike faith. "I know he's the son of God . . ."

"But He's God," he said. "He lives everywhere. That's why He can be in heaven and in my heart at the same time."

She didn't want to upset him so she smiled and nodded and suggested he tack to starboard and they could go home.

The next afternoon, he broached the subject. "Dickie . . . I've been thinking about what you said yesterday."

She had too but she didn't admit it.

"When I said Jesus was in my heart maybe I should have said the Holy Spirit instead. But Jesus and God and the Holy Spirit are all God so maybe it doesn't matter who's in there."

Margaret listened to his childish theology and said, "Yesterday I asked you how you know Jesus is in your heart. So if what you say is true, then how do you know the Holy Spirit is in your heart?"

"I just know it, Dickie. I just know it. I talk to God or Jesus or the Holy Spirit and He talks to me too."

Her eyes widened. "He does? How?"

He shifted his bottom. "For sure when I do something wrong. He tells me right away and I have to apologize to Him and whoever I did it to. And then sometimes when I'm scared, He tells me not to worry because He's looking after me and it'll be okay. And when I'm happy and I thank Him for something, I know He's happy too."

Tears came to her eyes and she looked away wishing the hands on the clock of time would stop right then so this dear little kid wouldn't have to grow up and suffer the cruel realities of life. He brought her back again. "What's the matter, Dickie? Did I say something wrong?"

She shook her head. "No, dear. You've said everything right."

Parents came to visit on Sunday afternoon. When she and Jeff went sailing the next day, he said, "I told my Dad about you, Dickie. He was happy I was learning to sail."

She wondered if he had told his father anything else, and was sure he had when he brought up the conversation again. "Jesus has always been God, from way back before there was even a world. I don't know what He called Himself then. He was called Jesus after he was born in Bethlehem because He was born to grow up and save us from our sins. That's why He died on the cross. So He could take our place and die so we don't have to."

"He was a wonderful person," she agreed. "He healed all those people and taught them stories about how we should live. Some men wrote down what he said and we can still read those words today." She hesitated. "But, Jeff, we're all going to die someday . . ."

"Just our bodies die, Dickie. Our spirits live forever and if we get saved then we can live in heaven with Jesus. My Dad said that when we read about Jesus then we know what God is like. And if we know what God is like then we know what He wants us to be like 'cause He wants us to be like Jesus."

Margaret began to read the gospels in earnest that night. The complexities of her religion had been reduced to the simple faith of a freckled nose lad. Rain and wind denied her another lesson on the lake, but she sat in the kitchen as the campers sang and were taught around the fire in the dining room for the next two nights.

One afternoon, as she wiped the tables and set them for the evening meal she listened to Raven's class on survival in the woods. He started by reading a scripture of Moses' encounter with God before approaching Pharaoh.

"'What is that in your hand?' God thundered."

The campers sat up to listen.

"'My staff,' Moses squeaked."

The campers laughed.

Raven walked across the room and whirled around dramatically. "When you are lost in the woods, you must not panic. You must ask yourself what you have in your hand. Turn out your pockets. What is there?"

Raven went on to show them what they could do with a shoelace, a piece of tissue and two sticks of wood. As Margaret moved in and out of the room, she heard Raven's last piece of advice to the campers. "Your very best resource is prayer. You can call on your heavenly Father and He will answer and show you what to do."

When she and Jeff went sailing the next day, she prepared the other boat too. "You're on your own now, Jeff. You've earned your wings or your sails. Off you go. I'll be right behind you."

"You're like Jesus, Dickie. You're letting me go but you're still right there with me, too."

She thought what a wonderful world it would be if all the little boys were like Jeff. He hugged her tightly on Saturday afternoon before the buses pulled away. "Thanks, Dickie. I'll never forget you."

She kissed the top of his head. "And I'll never forget you either."

Chapter Six

Fiona's house seemed cool and quiet after the hot, noisy kitchen at the camp. Margaret went into her room and found a note from Doug with her jacket on her bed. He was leaving for Toronto. Anne had called to say that Michael's father-in-law had died, and Michael and his wife were flying home from Kenya. He would be back in time for school.

Doug rang the doorbell on the Tuesday afternoon after Labour Day, and Margaret invited him out to the veranda for a cold drink. He sank wearily into the rocking chair and loosened his tie. "So how have you been?" he asked. "How was camp?"

"Unforgettable," she replied. "And how was Toronto?"

"Forgettable."

She felt he had something on his mind so she waited quietly while he clinked the ice cubes in his glass, rocked, and stared across the river. After a prolonged comfortable silence, she finally said, "I didn't know your son was married."

"It's been something of a problem." He twisted in the chair and crossed his legs. "I might as well tell you all about it if you care to listen."

"Of course."

"When Michael was a kid, he wanted to be a farmer. After high school he went to the college here. And he was smart enough to realize that he couldn't go into farming himself. We just didn't have enough money to set him up on a place of his own. Most of these boys like Ted and Paul come from farm families and they can go home again.

"So Michael decided to go into research to grow better crops. He went to the university in Guelph, met a girl, fell in love and brought her home to meet us. There was just one thing he didn't tell us. She was black. Well, brown anyway. I'm not a racist, Margaret, but I figure marriage has enough problems without adding our cultural differences to the pot. So needless to say, when we first saw her, Janet and I were shocked to put it mildly. We tried to be nice, to make her feel at home for Michael's sake. And you can just imagine what was said around town. I know the two of them sensed the gossip. Their defenses were raised, and before they left, Michael told us that he and Dorian were planning to be married. Janet was heartbroken. We both were because we now realized Michael felt he could never return to live in New Lancaster with his wife.

"We went to the wedding in Toronto. Dorian's folks were very nice people and I think they felt the same way we did about the marriage. Her father drove a city bus in Toronto while his daughter worked on her PhD in microbiology." He looked out across the river. "The girl is smarter and has more education than anyone here in town." He shrugged and turned back to look at her again. "They finished school and these jobs opened up for them in Africa. Dorian's a professor at the university in Nairobi and Michael works for the UN. He came home for his mother's funeral but Dorian was expecting a baby soon and she remained in Africa.

"So when Anne called to tell me about Dorian's father, I had to go. I saw my granddaughter for the first time." He sighed. "She's a beautiful little girl . . . Looks just like Janet with a good tan. And then I drove them to the airport and said goodbye. They've gone back home, and now I realize what a little part of their lives I share." His eyes drifted to the hanging planter behind her head and he was silent.

She reached out and touched his arm. "You look tired, Doug. You should go home to bed."

He rubbed his face. "I know. It's just that the house holds so many memories."

"But they're good memories, aren't they . . . And it isn't just a house. It's your home. You gotta do a heap of livin' to make your house a home as some hill-billy philosopher once said. So treasure those memories. Guard them carefully . . ."

He studied her earnest face.

"Concentrate on all the good times you've shared. I learned to sing a song at camp that goes like this. 'Count your blessings. Name them one by one. And it will surprise you what the Lord has done.'"

He smiled and stood up. "Are you changing your religion again, Margaret? You've been church hopping a lot this summer."

She walked him to the door. "I'm going to the Baptist church this Sunday. I went to St. Jude's last week and that awful student is still there!"

Shaking Mr. Ferguson's hand after the morning service, she asked, "Could I come and talk to you some day?"

He pulled an appointment book out of his vest pocket. "How about Tuesday afternoon at three?"

That night, Margaret felt disloyal to the Baptists as she slipped into the pew at St. Andrew's. The peace surrounded her, and as the choir sang, she closed her eyes wishing she could stay there forever. Angus McKelvie greeted her after the service like an old friend, and as she asked about his trip to Scotland, Doug came up the aisle to join the conversation. He drove her home later and seemed more like his old self.

"So how's school these days?" she asked as they turned on to Oak Terrace.

He shut off the motor and turned to sit sideways in the seat. "It's hard to believe that this may be my last semester. Retirement used to seem like light years away, and now it's here and I don't think I'll like it after all."

"Why?"

"It's this business of growing old, closing chapters in my book, passing milestones in my life. Maybe I'm afraid of losing my edge . . ."

"What does that mean?"

"I see these old duffers around the nineteenth hole at the golf course and all they want to talk about is the old days . . . The good old days. I think they've forgotten that the good old days weren't all that great. They went through a war and a depression and more wars . . . But that's ancient history to them now. They don't want to bother with the problems our children are facing today. They just want to sit back on their fannies and reminisce . . ."

"So . . ."

He reached for her hand. "So I'm afraid I'll become one of them and sit on my fanny and think about the good old days too."

She looked out at the street ahead. "Was it Kierkegaarde who said 'Reflection is usually the death of passion'?"

He frowned. "I don't know, Margaret. You tell me."

She shifted uneasily. "I think what he was saying was that when you lose your passion for truth and justice, you lose your lust for life."

He watched her carefully.

"I guess the danger lies in accepting the status quo . . . When you don't really care any more . . . When you stop growing as a person . . . When you don't have anything left that you want to learn . . . I don't know, Doug. Does this make any sense?"

He stroked her arm with his finger. "Yes. So maybe I'm staving off the 'death of my passion' by going to study the Etruscans."

She smiled. "And in the meantime, keep thinking about sunny Italy when the winter winds begin to blow."

He looked away to stare down Oak Terrace. "Will you come with me? To sunny Italy?"

She closed her eyes and knew she wasn't going anywhere. The pressure in her abdomen had been increasing lately and she felt a hard lump in her side constantly now. She was spotting intermittently and still losing weight everywhere but her waistbands were growing tighter. "I'm sorry, Doug. I can't . . . I'm truly sorry."

He got out of the car abruptly and came around to open her door. She saw tears in his eyes reflecting the streetlight and she touched his arm. "I can't do this to you, dear. We shouldn't see each other any more."

He pulled her close and hugged her fiercely. "Don't send me away. Please don't send me away."

She stood passively and he quickly released her. "It's all right. I won't push you," he said huskily and went around to get in the car. She stood at the curb and watched the tail lights disappear into the mist of a September evening.

Autumn had arrived in New Lancaster. The yellow birches, orange maples, burnt oaks and silver poplars cast their glories to the ground as Margaret scuffled across the lawn of the church on Tuesday afternoon. Butterflies danced in her stomach as she walked down a hall to stand in front of Mr. Ferguson's secretary.

The woman smiled up at her. "Good afternoon, Mrs. Darwin." She pushed back her chair and stood up. "The pastor will see you now."

Mr. Ferguson rose as she entered his study and shook her hand. He gestured to a comfortable chair. "Please sit down." He walked over to close the door of the office and came back to sit in another comfortable chair across from her. He seemed so informal in his grey slacks and soft blue cardigan that she drew a deep breath and settled back into the chair. He smiled and crossed his legs. "So how are you enjoying New Lancaster?"

"I like it very much. I've never lived in a small town before."

"Where was your home?"

"Toronto."

"Oh I see." He nodded his head. "Well this must be quite a change for you then. I lived in Hamilton for a number of years when it was much smaller than it is now. I come from the Maritimes. Have you ever been to Halifax?"

"No. I've only been as far east as Quebec City."

"So what brings you to New Lancaster? Do you have relatives here?"

"I was here once, a long time ago with my husband and children. I always thought it was a nice little town."

"You're married?"

"I'm a widow. My two sons still live in Toronto. They're married with families."

"You must miss them . . . Living so far away."

She glanced out the window at the leaves fluttering down. "No. I don't miss them at all."

He raised his eyebrows and after a gentle pause said, "I don't want to pry, Margaret, but if you want to talk, I'm here to listen."

She turned to him and said quickly, "Oh it's nothing serious. We haven't quarreled or anything. It's just that I feel I don't really belong in their lives. We're . . . we're sort of disconnected . . ."

He waited for her to go on.

"You see . . . It was my husband. I mean it wasn't his fault he developed Alzheimer's Disease, but he did, and it was my place to take care of him, and the boys were married and they were busy and they didn't know how to talk to him or be around him, and when they were there, John became belligerent because he didn't know who they were. And after they'd leave, usually in a hurry, he'd demand 'Who are those men? What are they doing in my house!' They'd call on the phone but they didn't come to the house very often because of their father's attitude, and so I didn't see much of them. And they had their families to take care of so I felt sort of left out, you see. And I couldn't leave John alone . . . He was sick for over seven years and that's a long time to be away from your kids. I . . . I guess we just grew apart."

He nodded. "But after your husband died did you try to get . . . reconnected?"

She looked soberly into his quiet face. "I could have but . . . I'm going to tell you something Mr. Ferguson that must be held in the strictest confidence."

He leaned forward. "Nothing goes beyond these walls."

"Very well then. The simple fact is this . . . I'm dying."

He uncrossed his legs and sat up straight.

"I found out this spring that I have ovarian cancer. The tests said my prognosis is terminal. On top of everything else we've been through, I didn't want my children to have to deal with the inconvenience of my dying so I decided to go away and die by myself. They think I've gone to England on a long vacation."

He sat back in his chair and rubbed his chin. "Do you think you can carry it off, this charade? They're going to have to know sometime, before or after. What will this do to them? To learn their mother couldn't trust them to care for her in her hour of greatest need?"

She stared out the window again. "I never thought of it that way. I just figured this would be the easiest for them. I never thought about after . . . I don't want them to feel guilty. Perhaps I'll go back to Toronto when I start to get really sick. I'll go back and tell them and they won't have to put up with me for a long time."

He stroked his chin. "It may not be that simple. If you became ill very suddenly you wouldn't have the opportunity. While you're still in relatively good health is the time to put your house in order."

"Put my house in order," she mused. "In a way that's what I've been trying to do. Godwise, I mean."

"Godwise?"

She leaned forward. "My spiritual life has been a wreck for a long time. When John died I didn't even know the name of the rector of my own church. I hadn't gone for years. I couldn't leave John home alone and there was no one to help me. I realize now it was almost as if I had closed the door to a very large part of my own life."

"Surely there were support groups to help spouses in your situation. You didn't avail yourself of any of these?"

She shook her head. "You can call it loyalty or duty. I had promised to stand by him in sickness and in health until death do us part. Even after he was admitted to a chronic care facility I felt I had to be there for him every day. I climbed on to his funeral pyre like an ancient Hindu wife."

"Wifely duty is one thing, Margaret. This sounds more like bondage or guilt."

She stared at him. "Guilt? Perhaps it was guilt. He had been a loving devoted husband. As his illness progressed, his frustrations increased. When he became unable to do the simplest of tasks, my heart ached for him. The cliche in Alzheimer's lingo is that it's the spouse who becomes the victim, it's the spouse who suffers most. But that's not true. John suffered immense torment. I can still see him shaking his head when words failed. And then even his thoughts failed and he'd just groan aloud. I was still alive to the joy of a new grandchild, listening to the first robin's song, waking to the fragrance of the rain washed rose garden. He had lost everything he loved but it was still all mine to enjoy, our home, our books, our music . . . And yes . . . I guess I did feel guilty . . . Very guilty."

"Can you understand that this guilt was misplaced?"

"I'm not sure. My emotions have been riding a roller coaster lately . . . And now I feel guilty because I've forgotten John, the way he used to be. The love has gone and I just remember him with a great pity."

"I think you shouldn't dwell on all this, Margaret. You can ask God to help you lay these feelings of guilt behind you. St. Paul wrote that we should focus on whatever is true and pure and lovely and virtuous . . . And when we do that then the God of peace will be with you."

She smiled and leaned forward again. "You know, that's absolutely true. When I first came to town I went to the Anglican church and met Mr. Copse."

"Oh, Harry . . ."

"Well, the student who replaced him was awful. I thought I was in a seminary lecture. So that night I dropped into St. Andrew's. The music, Mr. McKelvie praying . . . I'd never heard anything like it before. It seemed like God was right there too and I really felt the peace."

"So you've put your house in order . . ."

"Oh no. Not yet. But I've listened to your sermons . . . And I'm learning so much. A young boy at camp told me about asking Jesus into his heart. And how Jesus came to save us from our sins . . ."

"Have you ever asked Jesus to save you from your sins?"

"My sins? Uh . . . No . . . We used to say the confession in church every Sunday. I haven't been doing it lately, but . . ."

"But can you see the difference between the prayer book confession and what your little friend was telling you about asking Jesus for forgiveness on a very personal basis?"

She stared at the carpet. "Is there a difference? A real difference?"

She finally raised her head to look at him and he nodded gravely. He leaned forward and took her hand. "Look, Margaret. I'm not going to give you a crash course in salvation. I sense God is speaking to you and I don't want to run ahead of His plan for your life. I'll give you a little book with some scripture verses in it and you'll see that one of your first steps toward God is repentance. You must realize you are a sinner and need a Saviour. How quickly you take the next step is up to you.

"Your little friend at camp was telling you about 'saving faith'. There are two sides to the coin of faith. On one side is the knowledge of God. Your catechism taught you about the Fall of Man, and the provision God made for our redemption when He sent His Son into the world to die a substitutionary death on the cross. You can know all of that and still not have 'saving faith'. Not until you look at the other side of the coin . . . And that implies belief with a personal trust that God went to these ends just for you. You see, Margaret, God is vitally concerned with your person. He loves you so much He was willing to allow His Son to take the penalty for your sins. You receive your salvation when you believe that you need to repent of all your sins, and trust that God's Words, His promises, are all true."

"I'm not sure I'm a very trusting person . . ."

"What do you mean?"

"I know lots of people but I don't have one real friend in the whole world, someone with whom I can share all my burdens. I haven't trusted anyone with the fact that I'm dying, apart from you."

"Surely you have one friend, my dear. Mrs. MacPherson?"

"Fiona?" She shook her head gravely. "I couldn't tell her. She'd feel sorry for me and hover around and make me go to a doctor. I'm sure

I could trust a doctor to keep a secret, but his nurse? His receptionist? And then it would be all over town. I know how gossip travels."

"What about Doug?"

Margaret hesitated for a moment wondering what Mr. Ferguson thought he knew about her relationship with Doug, and then said slowly, "No. Not Doug either. He suffered enough losing his wife. I wouldn't want him to feel he had some responsibility toward me too. I don't know, Mr. Ferguson . . . I guess I'm just a mess . . . Since John's illness, I've found it hard to even relate to people. I keep everything bottled up inside. There are a lot of secrets inside this head."

He flexed his fingers and said quietly, "I won't probe inside your head, Margaret. I'm not a psychologist. But Jesus is the best person in the world you can talk to, and believe me, my dear, He's always ready to listen to you. Trust Him for that. Tell Him all those secrets."

"I do talk to God . . ."

He nodded. "But did you realize He was really listening?"

She bit her lip. "I don't know . . . I think so."

"He is."

She regarded his serious face.

He leaned forward and patted her hand. "There's a verse in the Bible that says if you truly seek God with your whole heart, you will find Him. And after you find Him, you'll discover that all along He has been faithfully waiting for you to open your heart's door to Him. He's only a prayer away, Margaret. Trust Him to give you that saving faith.

"Now, listening to you today, I suggest one area in your life you should deal with is forgiveness. You may need to forgive your children. I sense a seed of bitterness that they weren't more supportive of you through John's illness. And I do think you need to do something about this secret you're harbouring."

She grasped his hand with both of hers. "I can't tell you how good it is to talk to someone about this. I feel like you're lifting a load off my heart."

He shook his head and smiled. "Jesus is doing that for you. He said, 'Come unto me, all of you who are weary and burdened, and I will give you rest.' Only Jesus can help with your problems, Margaret. I'm just here to point you to Him. Would you like me to pray for you now?"

She nodded and bowed her head.

"Heavenly Father, in the name of Jesus we come before You with all of our problems and our needs. You are the answer . . . The only answer. And now I pray for Margaret. I commit her to You. You alone can ease her burden, erase her guilt. May she soon come to know You as her loving Father who will undertake for her. May she come to know Your Son as her Saviour who will never leave her nor forsake her . . . As the One who will carry her in His arms as a shepherd carries his little lamb. Thank You for hearing us, Father. We love you . . . Amen"

Margaret wiped her eyes as Mr. Ferguson rose and opened his desk drawer. When he handed her a little book she shook his hand and said softly, "Thank you. And God bless you."

She walked home slowly to sit on the porch in her rocking chair as the chill of autumn began to descend upon the river. Sharing her secret with Jack Ferguson had not completely removed the heartache she had borne since that awful day in Dr. Green's office, that moment when her life changed forever. She had not yet released all those fearful feelings of desolation that gripped her soul during the quiet, wakeful hours when sleep failed. But now she realized that just as her future had changed she was in the process of change too. Suddenly, inexplicably, she felt constrained to pray the words of a hymn she had learned to love, *"Spirit of the Living God, fall fresh on me. Melt me, mold me, fill me, use me. Spirit of the Living God, fall fresh on me."* A heavy truck lumbered across the bridge distracting her thoughts, She shivered and went inside to prepare supper.

With the onset of autumn, more volunteers returned to help with the Meals program and Margaret only worked two days a week. She was grateful for the extra time. Her garden needed care, and she wearied easily, toiling up and down the slope carrying bags of mulch she dragged home from the store on her bicycle carrier. Tempted to buy some tulip bulbs she succumbed at last, knowing all the while she wouldn't be there in the spring to see them bloom. She spent the afternoons drowsing in the rocker on the veranda with Mr. Ferguson's book open on her knee and her Bible on her chest.

Doug phoned on Thursday night after supper.

"It's for you," Fiona called.

Unable to escape, Margaret reluctantly picked up the receiver.

His cheerful voice said, "How about coming with me to the school dance tomorrow night? I've been volunteered to chaperone the kids."

"I'm sorry, Doug. I can't make it.'

"You're sure?"

"Yes."

"You know what you've just done, don't you."

She grew alarmed. "No. What?"

"Now I'll have to dance with the coach of the girl's basketball team and Sally's six and a half feet tall!"

She chuckled. "Good for Sally. She's a woman you can look up to."

"So what have you been doing these days?"

"Working mostly in the garden. I'm putting it to sleep for the winter."

"I'm taking the Lady out of the water on Saturday. Do you want to come along?"

She dug down deeply for another excuse. "Well, if it's nice, I thought I'd take Tinkerbelle for a cruise up river. The leaf colours are beautiful and it'll be our last outing this year."

"Okay. Have fun. I'll see you around."

She hung up and said to the wall, "That man handles rejection awfully well."

Late Saturday morning, Margaret dragged Tinkerbelle into the river. The water level had dropped so she took off her shoes, waded aboard and set off upstream. With a following wind, she had a good run as far as the railway bridge. The sumac had exploded into a riot of scarlet along the banks, and as the river narrowed, the tall silver poplars formed a bright canopy overhead. The yellow birches danced among the sumac while the tamarack stood at attention in golden lines. She pulled in to the bank at the mouth of a creek and dropped the sail. Water gurgled over the dark rocks in the shallows, and when a distant jay screamed shrilly a covey of partridges nearby, fluttered into the air. She lay down in the bottom of the boat, resting her head on the stern and watched the branches against the sky as she drifted back out into the current. She had no fear. The river was no threat to her now. Peace and beauty were hers for the taking and she continued to drift sleepily through the autumn afternoon. A flock of wild geese cried overhead as they flew toward the marsh at the end of the bay. She passed the golf course but since Doug was busy with his Lady, she didn't even raise her head. The smell of burning leaves wafted across the river and she sat up to steer herself through New Lancaster. "Thanks, Tinkerbelle," she said softly as they floated under the bridge. "Thanks for the summer."

She carried all the gear up the bank and was washing it off with the hose at the side of the house when Doug pulled up at the curb and came over to see her. She brushed the hair out of her eyes and said, "Just putting her away for the season."

"Are you all right?" he asked.

"Of course. Why?"

"Ed called and said he'd seen you lying in the boat going sideways down the river. He said you looked like you were sleeping."

She laughed and turned off the tap. "I can't get away with anything in this town, can I? If I sneezed right now, six people would call to ask me about my cold! It was such a beautiful afternoon with the colours and all, I just drifted along like the Lady of Shalott."

"Who?"

"I keep forgetting that you history teachers don't know much about poetry. Tennyson wrote a poem about unrequited love. Heartbroken over Sir Lancelot's indifference, the Lady of Shalott set herself adrift in a little boat and died."

He looked at her standing before him in her bare feet with her slacks rolled up to the knees and wondered if there was any hope for his unrequited love. "Do you need some help?"

"I'm all done," she replied. "I'll lean the sail against the house and let it dry. Come on inside and I'll make you a cup of tea. You can tell me about the dance."

They were sitting at the kitchen table when Fiona came home from work. "Jack Ferguson was admitted to the cardiac unit this afternoon. I hear he's pretty sick."

"Oh no!" Margaret cried. "No . . ."

Doug shook his head and frowned. "Poor Jack. That's too bad."

"He was such a kind, gentle man," Margaret said. "We had such a nice talk last Tuesday." She sniffed and went over to get a tissue to wipe her eyes.

"Don't use the past tense," Fiona said. "He's not dead yet."

"He's younger than I am," Doug mused.

Fiona poked his shoulder. "Everybody's younger than you are. I hear you're retiring soon. You're going to Italy?"

He glanced quickly at Margaret. "Who told you that?"

"A friend of mine saw you in the travel office getting brochures."

He stood up. "I see exactly what you mean, Margaret. Well, goodbye ladies. Thanks for the tea."

After he left and Fiona disappeared upstairs Margaret went into her room to lie down. A sense of impending doom hovered nearby. Her mind struggled to shrug off a weighty oppression. Why do You let these things happen to us, God? Why? And Mr. Ferguson's such a good man. He's one of Your own. I'm sure his house is in order. He doesn't need to repent because he hasn't done anything wrong. And I haven't either . . . Not really, except tell a few lies. And they were lies that didn't hurt anyone. In fact, they helped Charles and Bruce. They don't have to worry about me.

She remembered something she had heard Mr. McKelvie say about mocking God. Am I mocking You, God? I can't fool You, can I? I'm a liar, aren't I? And You won't forgive me for my sin of lying if I don't stop doing it. But I can't call Charles and Bruce and tell them the truth. Not yet. Not until I have to. So I can't repent of lying . . . But maybe I have another sin I can repent of instead. I haven't stolen anything. And I haven't cheated anyone.

Doug came immediately to her mind. Oh . . . Yes. I've cheated Doug. He of all people deserves to know the truth. I've cheated him in so many ways. I'm not the friend he wants me to be. And I'm certainly not the lover he wants me to be. Well that's good, isn't it, God? You wouldn't approve of us having an affair. But I think about making love to him, and that's a sin too. Yes. I've cheated Doug. But I can't tell him the truth either. I've got to find something I can repent of to start to put my house in order.

She finally drifted into sleep, an uneasy sleep, and dreamed of Jane, not the sweet little child with a missing front tooth, or the lanky young girl with a mouth full of wire braces. In her dream, Margaret was in the hospice looking for her grown daughter among the dying. Searching through the long rows of sterile white iron beds, she was calling her name, desperately frantic because she couldn't recognize her beloved Jane among the horrific skeletal bodies. All around her raged rampant gluttonous death . . . She had forgotten what Jane looked like and she had to find her . . . She had to . . .

She woke suddenly and sat up, the terror still reeling through her mind. Swinging out of her cosy bed she paced the floor to rid herself of the nightmare. The lights across the river were shining through her window and she sat down in the rocking chair to collect her thoughts. Closing her eyes to the lights she lay her head back on the soft pink cushion. I knew I couldn't bury you in my heart forever, Jane. You were never a quiet child, were you . . . Maybe it was your older brothers' fault. You always had to stand up for yourself against them, didn't you. And now you're standing up again. And what do you want to say? And what do I want to say to you that I haven't already said before? I love you. I've always loved you . . . You knew that, didn't you . . . Didn't you? I know I've made mistakes, oh so many mistakes . . . I hurt you. And I'm sorry. I told you I was sorry and you believed me. You did believe me, didn't you . . . Didn't you?

Vivid scenes came to her mind of old confrontations; Jane's choices of friends, her lifestyle, her habits, the beginning of Jane's intimate relationship with Ken, the end of it, the callous, "I told you so", the unfathomable hurt in Jane's eyes, the insensitive advice, "I know it's hard but you'll get over him and find someone else."

Burdened with her own trials with John, how could she have suspected that Jane was then in the throes of the onset of AIDS? How could she have known that Ken was infected with the virus too, seething with bitter anger and full of death? She and Jane had parted on uneasy terms, Margaret back to cell 342 at Thornbury Village, Jane down into the living hell of AIDS.

Margaret bit her finger as she remembered the morning she had learned the ghastly news of Jane's illness and rushed to her bedside. Even then she had made terrible mistakes, such terrible mistakes. When her daughter told her that she was moving to the hospice to die and she had sold all her furniture, all her belongings, Margaret had said quickly, "Not my china and silver!"

The large eyes in the haggard face had blinked. "But you gave it to me."

"Not to sell!"

Margaret shuddered as she remembered Jane shrinking smaller in the bed. "I had to, Mom. I needed the money."

She put her head in her hands and wept. Oh Jane, Jane . . . Why did I say that! How could I be so cruel! If only I could tell you I understand. Tell you that those material things don't matter. Not any more. If only you had told me before, we could have worked something out. My dear little Jane . . . You were so alone, weren't you? And I was alone. And your brothers. They were alone too in their fears, the fear of catching the virus, the fear of the publicity that their sister had this loathsome disease. The shame of Jane. It sounds like the title of a Victorian novel. You never knew, my darling, they asked me to leave their names out of your obituary. "To protect their children," they said.

Margaret began to rock again. How could they be so cruel, so devoid of compassion? I'm glad you were at the hospice, Jane. Those wonderful people gave you more love than you ever received from your family. And they gave you peace too, didn't they? I remember those days you were dying, drifting in and out of a coma . . . Your nurse put her arms around me and told me not to be sad. She said you had committed your life to God. Oh Jane! Was that true? I didn't know what she was talking about at the time but I do now. I want to commit my life to God too and I'm trying to put my house in order. But it's hard. I've made such a mess of everything. Maybe I can start with you, Jane. I can ask you to forgive me for failing you. And I'll forgive Charles and Bruce for failing me. I'll try to understand what moved them to hurt us so. And if I can't understand, I'll forgive them anyway. Jesus forgave his enemies in spite of everything they did to him. He said, "Father, forgive them. They know not what they do." If he can forgive them for the awful torture they inflicted on him, then surely I can forgive your brothers too. And now I see what Jeff was trying to tell me . . . Jesus showed us how we should live and I'm to become like him. I want to become like him. Help me, God. Please help me.

Margaret entered the sombre, sober sanctuary at First Baptist in the morning to learn that Mr. Ferguson was still gravely ill. The elders and deacons gathered at the front of the church on their knees to pray for the healing of their beloved pastor. Each of them read a portion of scripture to encourage the flock.

As Margaret walked along the boardwalk that afternoon, some of their words echoed in her head. "When you pass through the waters, I will be with you, and through the rivers, they shall not overflow you . . ."

She drew her coat closely about her as the cold wind swept across the lake. The cloudy sky deepened her gloomy mood and she looked out to the drab eastern shore where the autumn colours had faded and more cottages could be seen through the bare trees. She wondered if the Wainwrights ever learned who had dampened their bed, and smiled at the memory of sailing with Doug. *I passed through a lot of water that day, God. And you were with me.* As she thought about other incidents in recent weeks, she saw evidence that God was with her indeed. She remembered her terrifying moments on the river, her experiences at Deer Lake. Walking along the barren shore, she became conscious that she was not alone any more, and felt the same sense of a burden being lifted that she had felt in Mr. Ferguson's office. She stopped and raised her hands to the sky to call, "It's me, God. Margaret. I know my house isn't in order yet, but I just want You to know I love You and I know You're taking care of Mr. Ferguson so I'm not going to worry about him any more."

Fiona returned from work the next afternoon to report that Mr. Ferguson was still in intensive care but the specialist was optimistic for the future. Margaret visited the cardiac unit before she went to work on Wednesday morning and met Jean Ferguson who said her husband was improving and could soon be moved out to the general floor. "The doctor wants to keep Jack in the unit as long as possible though. He doesn't want him to have too many visitors. The waiting room has been crowded ever since he got here."

Margaret touched her hand. "That's quite a tribute to the man, isn't it . . . He's so well-loved by the community . . . And he's been so kind to me."

Jean nodded and her eyes filled with tears. "I was so afraid I'd lose him and I didn't know what I'd do without him."

Margaret put her arm around Jean's shoulders. "I understand. You have to take each day as it comes and trust God to bring you through. I'm just beginning to learn that myself after all this time."

Fiona returned from work on Thursday with a broad smile on her face. As Margaret poured her a cup of tea, Fiona chuckled and said Midge Landers had come in that morning and delivered a baby boy. "It's on the small side but it has a mop of red hair. That baby is the spitting image of Brian Haskett! Deirdre told me she's calling him up to give him a piece of her mind!"

Margaret shook her head. "And I thought life in a small town would be dull."

Fiona returned home on Friday to say that Brian Haskett had been in to see the baby. His mother had come with him and they had stood at the nursery window watching his son and talking for a long time. "This is too good to be true," she chortled. "Let's go to the Fall Fair tonight and see Ed. He'll be there working at the Lions' Booth. I want to tease him about his new grandson."

Margaret was in no mood to watch Fiona gloat and replied, "Not tonight. I'm too tired. 'Meals' is getting more people these days and they all seem to live on the top floor of an apartment house with no elevator."

"Okay then. We can go tomorrow instead."

It rained hard on Saturday morning, washing out the parade. "We'll go later on," Fiona said. "The place will be packed this afternoon."

The curling club building was the main hall for the fair. The skating arena next door was also filled with exhibits, and Margaret and Fiona roamed along aisles viewing jars of preserves, trays of extraordinary vegetables, tempting assortments of pies and cakes and cookies, and exquisite quilts and samplers of crewel and embroidery. They teetered along planks laid over the mud into the curling arena, passing displays of vacuum cleaners and aluminum siding and carpeting and septic systems. At last, Fiona reached the object of her excursion. Ed Haskett was standing beside a shiny blue Buick, wearing his Lions' hat and apron and a benign smile.

"Well hello there Ladies! Are you going to win yourselves a new car? Ten dollars a ticket and you could find yourself in the driver's seat of that sedan. Isn't it a beauty? What do you say, Margaret? Wouldn't you rather drive that car around town than your old bicycle? Come on, Fiona. You need a new car too."

Fiona smiled. "I hear you're a Grampa, Ed."

He grinned. "Yeah. Isn't that something! He's a cute little nipper. Looks just like Brian when he was a baby. Amy and Deirdre have been over at the house all day fixing it up."

"Oh?"

128

"Yep. Brian and Midge have decided to put the past behind them and start all over again. He's taking her home tomorrow."

Fiona threw her hands in the air. "Well if that doesn't take the cake!"

Margaret said, "I'm happy for them. I hope they can forgive and forget."

Ed nodded soberly. "I hope so too. They have a lot to forgive. I'm not sure about the forgetting. When that baby's the captain of the football team, there'll still be people in this town who'll remember . . . So come on and buy a ticket."

Margaret shook her head and opened her purse. "No, but I do want to pay you for those tires."

He punched her shoulder lightly. "I'll tell you what I'm gonna do. You give me ten dollars for the tires and I'll write your name on a ticket."

She gave him the money and he handed her a stub. "If you don't win the car, the second prize is a trip for two to the Bahamas. You could take Doug and the two of you could really go sailing."

She blushed at the reference to Doug and frowned slightly, wondering what discussions those two cronies had had about her. Ed realized his blunder and tucked the bill in his apron. "I'm just kidding you, Margaret. This draw is all for a good cause. The club's sponsoring a seniors' center next door. When I'm a broken-down old geezer I'll have some place to go."

He wrote her name on a ticket and dropped it into a wire cage. She heard music and turned to see an assortment of local musicians on a stage at the end of the building. "Have you heard The Country Gentlemen?" he asked.

"No," she replied.

"They're pretty good. Bobby Mills sings with them and he's good too."

The fiddles were tuning at the piano, and a fellow at the microphone said "Okay folks . . . Get your partners for the first set. And away we go."

The fiddles swung into the melody and Ed took off his hat. "Come on, Margaret. Let's have some fun."

She shrank. "Oh I couldn't. I haven't square danced since high school."

He took off his apron. "It's like riding a bike," he said. "And I bet you didn't do much of that since high school either. Give me your purse and coat and I'll put them over here behind the counter."

He took her elbow to guide her along the booth, past a surprised Doug and out to the floor. Couples were arranging themselves as the caller sang into the mike. "Grab your partners one and more, let's all head for the ol' dance floor. Alymandy left on the corners all, and swing your lady round the hall . . ."

Ed was right. Some of it did come back to her, and she dosie-doed, and dipped and dived in the ocean waves, and when she got turned the wrong way, friendly hands reached out to set her straight. At the end of three dances, she and Ed came back to the booth laughing. Her face was flushed and she pushed the hair out of her eyes wondering where Fiona had gone.

"You're quite a woman, Margaret," Ed said. "No wonder Doug likes you."

She could feel herself blushing again. "Thanks for the dance, Ed. I'd better get my coat and find Fiona."

"Wait a minute. It's my turn," a voice said at her elbow.

Margaret turned to see Doug smiling at her.

"I can't let Ed have all the fun." He reached for her hand.

The Country Gentlemen were playing a waltz as he led her to the floor. She put her hand on his shoulder as he swung her out into the music. Bobby Mills was singing, "It's three o'clock in the morning."

His hand lay lightly on her waist but she could feel the rhythm in his body as he guided her around the floor, holding her closer, moving her away and bringing her back again. "You're a good dancer," she said.

"See what you missed at the high school. And you're not too bad yourself."

"I'm pretty rusty. I haven't danced for years."

He pulled her closer into a swing and said, "Well we can change that."

Bobby Mills crooned into the microphone, "Let me call you sweetheart, I'm in love with you . . .

Margaret found herself dancing closer now, her hair against his cheek, her emotions on the roller coaster again. She was loving every movement they made together, and at the same time praying, "God, get me out of this."

The tempo changed into a quick step as Bobby Mills snapped his fingers to the beat. "You won't find another fool like me, Babe . . ." Doug flung her out to spin around and brought her back again to the refrain, "You know you won't. Who'd sit around all night and wait for you . . ." He held her close as Bobby sang, "And close their eyes to oh so many lies. No one else could love you like I do . . . I want to tell you . . . You won't find another clown like me, Babe . . ." He spun her around again. "No you won't . . . I can't count the times you said you'd leave . . . You know darn well you're foolin' . . . 'cause wherever you may go, you won't find another fool like me." Doug had turned his head and was crooning in her ear along with Bobby. "Sometimes I can't understand what makes me the fool that I am . . . Then you touch my hands . . . And suddenly I know . . . Even though you treat me like you do, Babe . . . You know you do . . . I'm so hooked on you I can't get free . . . Oh but I'll get through the bad times, cause in my heart I know that you won't ever find a fool like me."

The tempo changed again and Bobby sang, "If you were the only girl in the world and I was the only boy . . ." Doug drew her close and tucked their hands next to his chest, humming in her ear, "A garden of roses, just made for two, and nothing to mar our joy . . ." They glided in a world of their own through the other couples, and when the music stopped, they stayed together. Applause from the other dancers broke the spell and Doug led her from the floor.

"I must find Fiona," she said brightly. "I can't imagine where she's gone."

"Stay with me, dear. We can have another dance. I'll take you home."

"Oh no," she said quickly. "I always go home with the feller what brung me." She reached for her coat. "I must go."

"I'm driving to Toronto next weekend. It's Thanksgiving and Anne wants me to come. I could drop you off at your son's place if you'd like."

She shook her head and backed away from him. "Thanks but I guess I'll stay here. Oh there's Fiona. Goodbye, Doug. I loved dancing with you. You're as good as Fred Astaire." She was still backing away and bumped into some teenagers. She turned to excuse herself and fled across the building.

She recognized Fiona's companion as a mechanic from McGuire's garage. "Mike wants to go to the Beachside for a drink. Do you want to come?"

Margaret took her arm as they moved toward the exit. "Thanks but I think I'll walk home. I need some fresh air."

They parted outside and the temptation to run back to Doug was so strong she had to force her feet to walk away through the mist of the cool October night. Her face was wet with tears as she admitted to herself that she lusted for Doug with every fibre of her being. She stopped on the bridge and leaned on the railing. I'm passing through the waters, Lord. The river is flowing. And just when I thought I was getting my house in order too. Now I've got to repent of lust and I don't want to do that either. I'm still a mess. Will you forgive me, God, for being such a hopeless case? She looked down at the water. The railing wasn't very high. It would be so easy to end this agony . . . She straightened her shoulders and marched home.

Another man occupied the pulpit of First Baptist the next morning. Margaret rejoiced with the rest of the congregation that the Lord had answered their prayers for their pastor. After the service she chatted easily to others, waiting in line to speak to Jean Ferguson and when Margaret's turn came, she hugged the woman and asked her to convey her greetings to her husband.

The rain poured down Sunday night and Margaret stayed home from church. Doug called her the next evening. "I missed you last night."

"It was pouring in case you didn't notice."

"I could have picked you up . . ."

"Doug . . . I . . ."

"Look . . . I just called up to see if you'd change your mind about Toronto?"

"No."

"Okay then. I'll see you when I get back."

"Have a safe trip."

"I'll say 'hello' to Anne for you."

"She knows about me?"

"I've mentioned you."

"Doug . . . I . . ."

"Goodnight, Margaret." He hung up abruptly.

She went into her room and sat on the edge of her bed. Her back was aching badly and she had started spotting again. I should pack up and move away from here right now. She lay back and massaged the hard lump in her side, larger than it had been a week ago. I should move away while I still can. She looked around at her room thinking it would be hard to leave all this behind, this wonderful little town and all the acquaintances that she had made . . . Leaving Doug would be the easy part. Staying was torture.

Thanksgiving Monday morning, Fiona called her to the phone. "It's a man," she whispered.

"Doug?"

Fiona shook her head. "I don't know who it is."

She picked up the receiver. "Hello?"

"Margaret Darwin?"

"Yes?"

"It's Don Sutton. Congratulations. You're a winner in the Lions' Club draw."

"The car!"

"No. You won the second prize, a trip for two to the Bahamas. I'm calling to say you can pick up the tickets at Bailey's Travel office. Have fun."

She turned in a daze to Fiona. "How'd you like to go to the Bahamas?"

Later that evening, she called Charles.

"It's good to hear from you, Mother," he said. "How are you?"

"Oh I'm fine," she lied. "How's everybody?"

"They're right here," he said. "It's Thanksgiving. They don't celebrate the holiday in England, do they?"

"They should. We all have a lot to be thankful for."

"So when are you coming home?"

"In a while. I'm going to the Bahamas first though. I met this woman here in New Lancaster and we thought we'd have a holiday together."

"That's great. Do you want to talk to Bruce?"

She thought afterward that she could have told her sons she was going to Outer Mongolia and it wouldn't have mattered. They hadn't noticed her mention of New Lancaster. Or they assumed it was a town in England and didn't really care where she was anyway. Forgive me, Lord. They don't understand I'd like to have more from them. I've let them think all this time that I can manage without them. And, Lord, the sad part is that I can.

Bailey's Travel handled all the details of their vacation. Passports were arranged. Reservations were made. Tickets were bought. She and Fiona were scheduled to leave Englewood on the early morning flight to Toronto. From there they would proceed to Freeport in the Bahamas and fly to Georgetown on Great Exuma that same afternoon.

"I haven't the foggiest idea where we're going," Fiona said. "I wonder if one of the boys has an atlas upstairs."

Paul brought down a map of North America and they managed to find the Bahamas. "Oh well," Fiona said, "I don't care. It's a holiday and it'll get us both out of town for ten days."

There was a message on the answering machine for Margaret when she returned from the hospital Wednesday afternoon. A reporter wanted to come and take her picture for the Saturday newspaper.

Mr. Ferguson greeted Margaret on Sunday morning from the pew behind. "I hear you're taking Fiona off to the Bahamas."

She smiled at his pale thin face. "Perhaps I should have offered to take you instead."

He chuckled. "Jean might have had something to say about that."

Mr. McKelvie shook her hand Sunday evening. "So you're off to the Bahamas."

"Yes," she replied. "Do Presbyterians approve of lotteries?"

"I can't really say . . . I know God doesn't get involved with them though."

She raised her eyebrows.

"It wouldn't be fair. You see, God never gambles because He always wins. He knows the end from the beginning. God wins at everything."

Doug joined them in the vestibule. "How do you know God always wins?"

Angus McKelvie clapped him on the shoulder. "Read the last page of the Book, my boy. We win!"

She walked out to the street with Doug in the soft evening mist of Indian summer. He congratulated her on winning the trip, and asked about her plans. She noticed a change in his manner, an unusual vagueness, and wondered if it was why he hadn't called during the week. On the way home she sat next to the door and asked about Anne.

He gripped the steering wheel and said, "She seems happy. I met the man in her life. I think they're planning to live together."

"Oh?"

"I didn't hear the word 'marriage' though. He's divorced. Has two children who live with their mother."

He pulled up in front of the house and stared down the street. "Anne wants me to move to Toronto after I retire . . ."

She turned to him quickly. "Oh Doug . . . You can't. You wouldn't leave New Lancaster. It's your home."

He glanced at her and looked down the street again. "I think I could. You've ruined this place for me, Margaret."

She frowned and bit her lip.

He gazed out the side window at the halo around the streetlight. "I see you everywhere I go. When I'm on the seventh green I expect you to come sailing by in that silly little boat. You're walking on the beach. The Lady is lonely without you. I sing to you from the choir, "Abide with me, Margaret", when I'm supposed to be singing that to God. And I'll never smell another lilac without seeing your lovely face in the rain." He wrenched open the car door and came around to open hers.

She got out quickly. "I don't know what to say . . ."

"Don't say anything except goodbye." His voice had tightened and she wondered if he might cry. "Maybe I can forget you in the ruins of Etruria."

She touched his arm. "I love you but . . ."

He jerked his arm away. "It's a crazy kind of love, you have then. And it's not enough for me."

She reached out to him again.

He backed away as though stung. "To hell with you, Margaret! I don't know what kind of a damned cat and mouse game you're playing but this mouse isn't going to play any more. Goodnight and goodbye!" He slammed her door and went around to slam the other one too and drove away.

She walked slowly into the house with a leaden heart. At least it was over. Now she could move on. She sat down in her rocking chair and watched the mist rising from the river. I've really done it now, God, haven't I. I've driven a man from his home and all that he's loved . . .

If I leave New Lancaster then maybe he'll stay. That's what I'll do. I'll pack everything when I leave for the Bahamas, and afterward, I'll come back to Toronto and decide what to do. Fiona can send my things when I know where I'm going. She can have all this stuff here for her next roomer. That's the least I can do. And I'll leave a letter for Doug. I owe him an explanation. Fiona can give it to him later.

It took her two days to write the letter.

My dearest Doug,

This is the only love letter I have written to anyone. I'm glad in a way because I can give you a first. A woman my age has so few left to offer. It is the last one too, because by the time you read this, I will be in another place, and maybe another time. I say another time, darling, because I'm dying. Last spring I discovered I had ovarian cancer, and coward that I am, I left Toronto and my family to spare them the inconvenience of the dying process.

And so I came to New Lancaster, the loveliest little town this side of heaven. The loveliest because it is the home of the man whom I love from the bottom of my heart. I respect you, Doug. I admire you. I believe you're the most wonderful, kindest man in the world. And you have so greatly honoured me with your love, a love that I couldn't share. I love you too much, my darling, to allow you to suffer with me through the agony that will lie ahead.

I treasure every moment we've had together. I think I fell in love with you that first night you walked home with me from the beach. I'll carry those precious memories with me always, wherever I go.

I found another love in New Lancaster too, my dearest. I began a journey to find God and learned He was there all the time, waiting for me to want Him. Jesus is with me now, now and forever. And when I step into eternity, He will be there to take my hand.

I wish things were different. I don't want to die. But if this hadn't happened, I'd have never met you, and maybe I wouldn't have been moved to meet Jesus either. I know I've hurt you with my seeming indifference to your love. You'll never know how close I was to giving myself to you the night of the Fair. Please believe me, darling. Your grief would be far greater now if I had.

You were so angry the last time I saw you. Will you forgive me for the mess I've made of your life? And don't leave New Lancaster. I'll become a memory, not a ghost. And when you're sailing some summer day, look up at the blue sky and say you love me still. And when you feel a raindrop on your cheek it's only me saying I miss you.

Goodbye, Douglas James Parker. I pray that you will find the peace that passes understanding. The peace that only God can give to you as He has given it to me.

M.

Chapter Seven

"YOU'RE WORSE THAN A HYPOCRITE," Margaret said to her reflection as she readied herself for their departure early Friday morning and carried her luggage out to the porch. "You've said your farewells from one end of town to the other and no one knows you're actually saying goodbye. Some of these people wanted to be your friends but you wouldn't let them get close to you. They deserve better than that. And they deserve the truth. Just like Doug." She wiped her eyes and looked around her room. All her other luggage remained in a neat row against the wall, the letter to Doug leaning on the lamp beside her bed. I know things aren't important to me now but I do love this room. It's been home. She ran her hand across the back of the rocking chair remembering Doug sitting in it at her bedside when she was ill. She wiped her eyes again and squared her shoulders. Where did I put my sunglasses? I can't go out and face Walt and Fiona looking like this.

Walt drove them to the airport at Englewood. He and Fiona chatted all the way while Margaret sat in the back seat and tried not to think about Doug and their last encounter. She had come out of the drug store on Main St. to see him walking toward her, accompanied by a tall blonde woman in a track suit. "Sally, the basketball coach", she surmised. He seized the woman's arm in a comradely fashion and passed Margaret by without giving her a second glance. She walked slowly home with a dull ache in her heart, hoping he would do nothing foolish to assuage his loneliness.

The Dash 8 took off into the chill of sunrise. The flight was half full, and as the plane droned across the bare harvested fields, she could see New Lancaster beside the silver lake and the dark shadows of Windy Point and Burnt Island. The plane touched down once for more passengers and continued to Toronto in bright sunlight. They flew over a brilliant blue Lake Ontario to circle the CN Tower before landing at the busy airport. It seemed as if every country in the world had a plane parked on the tarmac and Margaret read the names of the airlines as they taxied along the runway toward the terminal.

Fiona chatted to everyone around her as they stood in line at the currency exchange. "Hey! Look at this. A three dollar bill?"

Margaret smiled as she folded her Bahamian money and put it in her waist pouch. She had decided against bringing a hand bag when Mr. Bailey warned them about the purse snatchers, and now she was doubly glad because she had one less thing to carry.

The crowded departure lounge hummed with happy Canadians in a holiday mood. Most of them were dressed casually in sports clothes but there were several men in business suits as well. One of them, a handsome fellow in his mid-forties joined the women in the aisle seat on the plane, and as he and Fiona chatted amicably, Margaret sat by the window, watched the take-off and developed a monstrous headache. The stewardess served her aspirin while Fiona and her new friend Jim, were served cocktails.

Conversations in the cabin became quite animated as more liquid refreshments appeared before lunch. Margaret ate sparingly and listened with aching ears to Fiona's and Jim's conversation over the drone of the engines. She learned Jim was a theatrical agent from Toronto, and his client, a stuntman, was in an action thriller being filmed in the Bahamas. His client wanted to renegotiate his contract because the producer and director decided the script needed more suspense which involved the hero wing-walking over Elizabeth Harbour at Georgetown. The heroine had been taken hostage and was tied up in the cockpit while the villain's accomplice lay dead beside her and the plane was heading out across the Atlantic on automatic pilot. The hero was to jump on to the doomed craft, climb inside and save the fair lady. The stuntman had refused to do it unless they paid him a lot more money.

"Couldn't they do all this with the special effects technology in the studio?" Fiona asked.

"No,' Jim replied." They want to get him with the long shots of Stocking Island and Beacon Hill Monument as well as the close ups of the water and boats."

"But what if your client gets paid his million and falls off the wing?"

"Then I'll have to find a new client."

They were both giggling together over a glass of wine as Margaret listened to the engines change pitch. She sat up and watched the long descent into the kaleidoscope below. Fascinated by the changing colours of the sea, she felt the plane dropping lower and soon they were skimming across green fields near an oil tank farm and then the concrete runway of Freeport International Airport. Retrieving their bags to clear customs, they enjoyed the steel drums playing calypso as they walked through the sprawling new terminal to the Bahamasair Gate for Georgetown.

A blast of heat propelled them across the tarmac to a waiting DC3 and Margaret felt perspiration trickling down her back as she stood in line to climb the steps of the vintage aircraft. Jim looked up at the fuel stained wings and said, "These were great planes. They won the war in the Pacific forty years ago."

Fiona frowned. "This plane isn't that old, is it?"

"Maybe not, but these old workhorses were built to last."

Margaret was almost ill with fatigue by the time the plane took off. She had not slept well the last several days in New Lancaster and now found the heat unbearably oppressive. She turned the air nozzle onto her face and leaned her forehead against the cool window in the back of the cabin to watch the gambling mecca of the Freeport luxury hotels slip beneath the wing. They flew out over the turquoise sea and turned southeast to cross the large island. As the plane climbed into wisps of clouds, the deep blue colour of the water faded into a pale haze.

The sun was sinking lower in the sky as the pitch of the engines changed and they began their approach to Georgetown. Mauve coral reefs glimmered through the blue translucence that became sandy milk near the outlying cays. After the plane rolled to a stop near a windsock hanging limply beside the runway, the passengers spilled into the aisle to reach their bags overhead and waited several more minutes as the temperature in the cabin rose ominously. The doors finally opened and Jim helped them down off the steep steps. "Let's share a cab into town."

Margaret was grateful for his suggestion. Mr. Bailey had warned her about negotiating prices with the locals and Jim seemed to be a capable companion.

A half hour passed before they got their luggage out of the rickety terminal and walked out to where a line of taxis waited on the street. Jim spoke to the driver of a bright blue car. "How much to Georgetown?"

The driver's eyes widened to a friendly grin. "Forty dollar."

Jim shook his head and walked away.

The driver jumped out of the cab. "Thirty dollar, mistuh, for the three. Dat's de rate."

Jim turned back, and the women each pulled out a ten dollar Bahamian bill.

Careening along the Queen's Highway from Mosstown to Georgetown, the cab dodged numerous bicycles and scooters. Several coastal resorts hid behind assorted palms and masses of buttonwood trees. The driver fancied himself a tour guide but his dialect was impossible. They did hear the words 'US Naval Base' as they whizzed past a tangle of old equipment behind a rusting chain link fence. In a short time, they rolled into Georgetown and stopped in front of a two storey pink hotel. Margaret noticed a large white-pillared building nearby in the dusk, and some local people were talking loudly under a huge spreading tree in the center of the square.

Jim got out of the front seat and turned to the women. "If you're not busy tomorrow, meet me here in the bar for lunch."

The driver squeaked, "Where they be goin'? They not stay here?"

Fiona leaned forward. "Our hotel is the Two Turtles Inn."

The driver shifted gears and wheeled around to the other side of the square to stop in front of another two storey building with a small cannon guarding the entrance. He carried their bags into the dark wood-paneled lobby where a large fan whirred softly overhead. Margaret rang the bell at the front desk and soon an attractive Bahamian woman appeared in a crisp white blouse and skirt.

"Yes?"

"You have a reservation for Darwin and MacPherson," she stated.

The woman rolled her dark eyes. "One moment, please," she said and disappeared into the back room.

Shortly, a tall slim Bahamian man appeared.

"Mrs. Darwin? Mrs. MacPherson?"

"Yes."

"I am verree sorree. I have no room."

Margaret stared at him. "What do you mean 'no room'? We have confirmed reservations." She fumbled in her pouch and brought out an envelope. "See. It says right here . . . Twin beds, private bath, air-conditioning, cable TV . . ."

He shrugged his shoulders. "I am verree sorree. They are making theese movee and all the rooms are full . . ."

Fiona bristled. "Now look here. We've paid money for a room and we intend to have one and we're not moving from this desk until you get us one!"

He narrowed his eyes and drummed his fingers on the counter. "Pleese wait," he said at last and disappeared into the back room.

Margaret sagged against the desk. "He's got to find something for us . . ."

"If he doesn't, I'll unpack and put on my pajamas here in the lobby."

"You wouldn't dare."

Fiona grinned. "Of course I would if it'll get me a room."

The desk clerk returned. "Mrs. Darwin and Mrs. MacPherson?"

"Yes?" they said in unison.

"I have found you a bed at the Mermaid. It ees not far from here. It ees not as nice as the Turtles but it ees a bed. I will also geeve you each a scooter to drive while you are here to make up the deeference in the rates."

Fiona narrowed her eyes. "Where ees this Mermaid?"

"Not verree far. It ees near the Ferry. I will drive you there myself and make the arrangements."

Darkness had settled over the island when he pulled up in front of an open restaurant with a weather-beaten picture of a mermaid on the back wall. The aroma of a Bahamian supper filled the air as they went inside and the desk clerk spoke rapidly to the bartender. He turned to the women. "There. It ees all fixed. Henree Rolle ees my friend and he will take care of you. He will geeve you your scooters in the morning. You come and see me if you want anytheeng." He was backing away and flashed out the door.

Henry picked up their suitcases. "Theese way, ladees." He led them across a scrubby lawn and down a dark slope to a corrugated tin shack. Their mouths gaped as he pushed the door with his foot and set the bags down to grope for a string hanging from the ceiling. A single light bulb hung over a double bed and the worn hobnail bedspread couldn't disguise the sagging mattress. Several rusting hangers hung on an iron pipe across one corner. An enamel jug and basin stood on an iron wash stand on the other side of the bed. Fiona walked over to throw back the spread, and found immaculate pillows and sheets with broad bands of lace. Henry said proudly, "My wife. She make everytheeng nice."

Margaret nodded. "Yes. Very nice. Where is the . . . facilities?"

He led her outside to another small building. The single light revealed a large hole in a wooden board, and a stall with a drain in the stone floor and a nozzle on the wall. "You ladees come up for supper. My wife has good food." He nodded his head and disappeared into the night.

Margaret and Fiona looked at each other. "This isn't what we expected," Margaret said with a sigh as they entered the cabin.

Fiona sat down on the creaking bed. "But what can we do about it?"

"Nothing at the moment, I suppose. Do you think we should eat here? Is it safe?"

"I guess we'll have to. There's no place else out here in the boondocks. But I'll tell you one thing . . ."

"What?"

"Tomorrow, let's go back to the Two Turtles and murder the manager!"

Almost too weary to eat, Margaret trailed Fiona up to the Mermaid and a delicious meal that began with a bowl of cold pumpkin soup, followed by a piece of boiled grouper seasoned lightly, and a mixture of peas, tomato, onion and rice. Revived, they enjoyed every morsel and finished the meal off with the guava duff that Henry's plump wife, Mathilde, served herself. When they complimented her on her cuisine, she giggled and waddled back to the kitchen. Exhausted by their long day, the two women climbed into the bed, slid toward the middle and barely moved all night.

Henry gave them the keys to the mopeds as they breakfasted on melon and fresh black bread heaped with guava jelly. Sipping their coffee in the tranquility of a pleasant garden, they reviewed their situation and decided the accommodations could be much worse somewhere else and these would have to do. They went out to examine their transport, and set off to explore the Exumas. The little machines handled easily and the women found it exhilarating to cruise along the Queen's Highway with a fresh breeze blowing off the broad blue Exuma Sound. They came back to Georgetown and putted along the street winding up to the top of the hill and discovered an Anglican church with a bright blue door as well as a spectacular view of Elizabeth Harbour and Stocking Island. The monument was clearly visible across the water. Forests of masts in anchorage surrounded the smaller islands in the harbour. "A sailor's paradise," Margaret murmured. A constant dull ache gnawed at her heart and she suddenly missed Doug so badly she thought she might weep.

Fiona was pointing toward the south and Little Exuma Island. "Isn't it beautiful?" They turned toward the north where rocky headlands, wide bays with deep water, snug coves and long sandy beaches basked in the sun. A small ferry was plowing through the blue water toward the harbour on Stocking Island where several sea planes were moored. Surveying the scene for several minutes, they drove slowly back down the hill to park near the square.

As Margaret bought a wide brimmed hat in the straw market she learned that the huge tree was a very old African fig, and the square was called "the green", a misnomer because very little green could be seen amid the crowded vendor's stalls. Natives and tourists sauntered along the streets and shops. Nearby, a long line of patients waited at the small government clinic. After Fiona found a suitable hat too, she and Margaret walked across the street to the Club Peace and Plenty and met Jim in the Yellow Dog Bar, famous, or infamous, because it was once the kitchen in the slave quarters of a sugar plantation. Movie types and yachts-people jostled each other for space to bend their elbows.

"It's too noisy," Jim said. "Let's catch the shuttle up to the Beach Club for lunch."

Sitting under the umbrella at the lunch table, Margaret looked out across the idyllic scene. This sun-kissed island with its pink coral sand beaches and transparent waters seemed blessed. Calypso music filled the air with echoes of African rhythm in the drums. She watched a couple strolling by, holding hands, and words of an old song came to her mind, "Love is in the air". An orgy of colour spilled from the walls and balconies, bright bougainvillea of red and purple and pink. Hibiscus bloomed with the poinsettia, and vines of coral, orange and blue trailed everywhere. There was no sign of poverty. The native population shared a lower standard of living than one might wish, but even the school children in their uniforms seemed happy, well fed and immaculately clean.

She listened to Jim and Fiona chatting merrily and felt very much like a fifth wheel. When Jim suggested a trip on the ferry to Stocking Island, Margaret yawned and said she thought she might just go home to the Mermaid and have a nap. They urged her to come with them but she recognized the signals and waved goodbye to them as Jim shared Fiona's scooter for the ride down to the dock.

She slept for two hours and wandered down to the beach behind their shack. The water there at low tide was quite shallow and she walked along a jetty to watch the fish. Later, the sun set in a fiery ball plunging into the sea at the last moment and she was surprised to see how quickly the darkness crept over the island. When it was obvious Fiona would not be coming home for supper, Margaret walked up to the empty Mermaid and asked Mathilde for a light meal since lunch had been substantial. She received a huge plate of seasoned rice and chicken and ate more than she should have. A large fruit pudding arrived on the table.

"Thank you, Mathilde. Where is everyone tonight?"

"Dey all go to see de fireworks. De movee people make pictures tonight with boats chasing around under de booms and bangs."

Margaret ate a sizeable portion of the pudding to show her appreciation because she was sure Mathilde would have gone to the fireworks too if she hadn't been there.

She sat under the palm tree watching the waxing moon, missing Doug and wondering what Fiona was doing. She also wondered about herself because she was feeling quite bloated and wanted to blame Mathilde's cooking rather than her own condition. Her swollen abdomen seemed to be enlarging every day. The discomfort almost reminded her of the last stages of pregnancy, and now she wore her shirts hanging over her old slacks, the elastic waist bands stretched to the limit.

Fiona returned before midnight, bubbling with news of her flowering relationship with Jim. "We had such a good day, Margaret. You've got to come with us tomorrow and watch the wing walk!"

Margaret bit her lip and pressed her face into the pillow, afraid she might burst into tears because of her lost love, life's dwindling moments and an overwhelming loneliness.

Spectators packed the harbourfront in the morning. Planes swooped overhead and boats sped across the water but nothing seemed to be happening. Bored by the scene, Margaret left the couple to themselves and followed a group of well-dressed Bahamians up the hill to church. She found it unlike any service she had ever attended in an Anglican church in Toronto. The worshippers sang with gusto, clapping to the beat, swaying with the melody. The Bahamian rector, Mr. Rolle, delivered his sermon with a decidedly British accent, preparing his congregation for the approaching Christmas season and a festival called Junkanoo which she gradually realized must be a celebration akin to Mardi Gras. He urged his flock to set an example of temperance and sobriety and to always bear in mind the one reason for the season, the birth of the Lord and Saviour, Jesus the Christ. A stout matron sang the benediction "Were you there when they crucified my Lord?" Her rendition moved Margaret to tears and she sat there with streaming eyes in a sea of black faces.

She found Fiona and Jim sitting on the seawall in front of the Peace and Plenty. They beckoned her over to join them as several bi-planes swooped and criss-crossed Elizabeth Harbour. "Has he done it yet?" she asked

"No. They're getting the camera's positions first," Jim said. He held up his empty glass to a passing waiter. "Would you like another drink, Fiona? Margaret? How about you?"

She looked up at the waiter. "A glass of ice-water would be nice . . ."

Jim shuddered. "I never drink the stuff. Didn't you know that water rusts pipes?"

Fiona giggled and held up her glass. "I'd better have a beer then too."

After viewing the distant wing walk during lunch, Jim suggested they go back to Stocking Island. "You should come, Margaret," Fiona said. "I never saw a pink beach before. And the shells! You can walk for miles on the ocean side. It's absolutely beautiful."

She declined. "I think I'll write some postcards this afternoon. I'll see you later."

She did send postcards to her sons, but her real reason for not going with them was that she felt ill. By late afternoon her abdomen was becoming so distended that she could only find relief by propping herself up on all the pillows on the bed. She went up to the Mermaid for supper and drank a bowl of soup and a cup of tea. Later she wished she hadn't. Lying in bed that night, waiting for Fiona, she was in such distress with sharp intermittent abdominal pains she decided she must go home. It isn't as though I'm abandoning Fiona. She has Jim to keep her company. She won't even miss me at the rate she's going.

Fiona didn't come back to the shack that night. Downing several aspirin Margaret slept fitfully, wondering . . . At dawn she roused to the sound of a plane circling overhead, annoyed that the filming was starting so early in the morning. Unable to go back to sleep, she eventually got up and was surprised to see a seaplane moored near the jetty, an odd sort of plane with a wide fuselage that floated in the water like the hull of a boat. She walked down to look at it more closely.

A young sun-burned man was taking the cowling off the engine on the port wing. He stopped and watched her approach.

"Good morning," she said. "You've got a problem?"

"Yeah. I think it's the filter on the fuel pump."

"I heard you come in a while ago."

He slapped his hand with the wrench. "Yeah. She'll fly on one engine but with a big load . . . I was lucky the tide was right or I might have been stuck out there." He waved to the shallow bay. "You don't want to get hung up on a sand bar." He turned back to his engine and she walked away.

Later, she carried a cup of Mathilde's coffee down to him. He was pulling out a piece of the motor. "I'll have to buy a new pump. This one's shot."

"Where will you get one?" she asked.

He took off his hat and scratched his head. "I'll try one of the airports, I guess." He seemed discouraged.

"I have a scooter you can use," she said. "I'm not going anywhere today."

He raised the cup of coffee to his lips and drank. "Gee, thanks. That'd be a big help."

She saw him off and went to sit in an old canvas deck chair under a palm tree in the shade. Fiona pulled in on her scooter a little later. She smiled sheepishly as she came over to Margaret. "I . . . I hope you don't mind me leaving you like this. I don't want you to think . . ."

Margaret looked up at her. "I'm not going to judge you, Fiona. I just don't want to see you get hurt. What do you know about Jim?"

Fiona sat down on the grass. "He's divorced. No children. Perhaps there's a girl friend or two in Toronto. A fella like Jim doesn't live like a monk. He just wants a good time . . . And so do I."

"Be careful, Fiona."

She stood up. "I came back to change my clothes. We're going swimming. Jim wants to see the Mystery Cave. There's a lot of blue holes over by Stocking Island." She glanced toward the shack. "Where's your scooter?"

"I lent it to the pilot of the seaplane. He had to get a part for his engine."

"What are you going to do with yourself today then? It's not much fun sitting under a tree."

"Well to tell you the truth, I've got an upset stomach. I think it's this Bahamian food. Anyway, I'm going to take it easy today."

"Are you sure you're all right. I'll stay with you . . ."

"No. No. You go and have a good time. Just be careful you don't go falling in love with a man you can't have."

Doug came immediately to her mind. She closed her eyes, missing him so desperately, wondering if he was missing her too. I'm sorry, darling. I'm so sorry . . .

After Fiona drove away, Margaret went to a pay telephone beside the restaurant to dial Bahamasair. Explaining that she had a ticket for a flight to Freeport on Sunday morning, she wondered if it would be possible to change it and leave tomorrow instead. The young man very kindly told her that all the flights were sold out but she could go on a long waiting list for a cancellation. Disheartened, she went back to the shack and bed, wondering if she should try the government clinic in Georgetown. Lacking her own means of transportation, she waited, bored and restless.

The pilot returned later in the afternoon with a new fuel pump and handed Margaret the keys to the scooter. "So you're all set now," she said.

"I think so. I was supposed to be in Freeport this morning. At the rate I'm going, I'll be lucky if I make it by tomorrow. Well, thanks for the ride."

He walked down to the jetty and started to work.

"Freeport," she mused. "I wonder."

Unable to eat Mathilde's supper, she carried the plate down to the pilot. He crawled down off the wing and wiped his hands on his pants. "Thanks again," he said between bites. "You wouldn't happen to have a flashlight lying around, would you? My batteries are just about gone."

She shook her head. "Henry up at the Mermaid might have one though." She shifted her feet. "I've been wondering if I could catch a ride with you up to Freeport. I'd be happy to pay . . ."

He shook his head. "No Ma'am. I couldn't possibly take you. I'm not licensed for passengers. And my insurance . . ."

He seemed so uncomfortable by her request that she said quickly, "Don't worry about it. I'll get there on Bahamasair."

He handed her the empty plate and walked up to the Mermaid with her. Henry lent him a lantern and he went back to the plane while she lay propped up in bed, massaging her aching abdomen and feeling quite sorry for herself. She could see the lantern in the dark as the pilot worked on his engine, and a thought popped into her mind and wouldn't leave. *I could stowaway in his plane when he takes the lantern back to Henry and he'd never know I was there until we get to Freeport. By that time it'll be too late and it won't matter about his insurance or license. Nobody will have to know. In fact, I could sneak off the plane when he wasn't around and he'd never know either. But I'd have to be crazy to do such a thing . . . And what if he found me aboard? But I can't stand this pain much longer and it'll only get worse. I've got to get back to Toronto and deal with this. I'll leave a note for Fiona and tell her I've gone home. She'll have to take my suitcases though. I can't drag those on the plane. I'll just take some stuff in a plastic bag . . .*

She wrote the note, packed her bags, pulled her nylon squall jacket over her waist pouch and tied her sneakers. Committed to a stealthy departure, she turned off the light in the room and opened the door. From her bed she could see the pilot still working by the light of the lantern. It was almost midnight before he finished and she heard him putting away his tools. She closed her door slightly and watched him carrying Henry's lantern back to the Mermaid. As soon as he disappeared, she sped down to the jetty, afraid she might be seen in the moonlight. Opening the door to the cockpit slowly, she clambered across the seat into the cabin to grope her way over large waist-high bundles packed into the fuselage. She crawled into the tail section and crouched down in the niche. A crumpled tarpaulin lay in a heap. She fashioned it into a pad to cushion the ribbed floor and sat down.

After an interminable length of time, her legs cramped and her stomach was aching so badly she stood up, wishing she could stretch out on top of the cargo. Then she heard the pilot outside loosing the lines. She sat down again quickly and he climbed into his seat and sighed. The door banged shut, and suddenly the interior of the cabin was illuminated by a series of pea bulbs in the ceiling. She could hear him clicking switches and one of the engines sputtered. He adjusted the mixture of gas and oil and soon it was running smoothly.

Margaret looked around in the gloom and saw a handle in the cabin ceiling that she reasoned must belong to a hatch or was part of the cabin door. Thick webbing anchored the plastic covered cargo to the walls and floor. The other engine was running smoothly now and soon she felt the movement of the hull through the water as they left the jetty. With a gentle rocking motion the plane began to taxi out to deeper water for take-off and she hoped the tide was right. This was no time to be marooned in the middle of the bay.

She heard the pilot's voice over the sound of the engines. "Yeah. The engine's okay. Yeah. The weather's good. I'll see you soon. Ten, four." She wondered if there was another control tower nearby since the main airport was at least ten miles away.

The engines burst into full power and the plane began to pick up speed. The floor was vibrating beneath her and she grasped the webbing to steady herself. The whole cabin began shaking as she clung tenaciously to the straps, clenching her teeth to stop from crying out with the agony in her abdomen. The engines were roaring in her ears, and as the plane continued to lift and bounce, she fervently wished she had never begun such an imbecilic venture. The pain became so intense that she was ready to scream when suddenly they were free of the water and she felt the plane climbing, wallowing through the heavy humid air. She sank back on the tarp, her jaw sore, her ears ringing, her arms aching, her abdomen a mass of agony. She swallowed hard, trying to relieve the pressure in her ears as the pilot banked and pushed the plane higher. The interior of the cabin grew cooler, and as the engines changed their pitch at last, she knew they were at a cruising altitude and the flight could only be better from here on. She pulled a corner of the tarp around her shoulders for warmth and wondered how she could escape from the cabin without being discovered.

Suddenly, one of the engines sputtered and stopped. She opened her eyes.

"Dammit!" the pilot exclaimed. "Not again!"

Margaret frantically grabbed the webbing.

"I've lost power on the port engine again. I'm setting down . . . Hog's Cay . . . I don't know . . ."

The other engine stopped and there was a deadly silence. "Jesus! The other one's gone too! I'm going down! Mayday! Mayday!"

The plane tipped forward on a precarious slant. The wind was whistling past the cabin as Margaret realized they were going to crash! She scrambled to her feet, still grasping the webbing and screamed.

The pilot turned to see a dim figure in the tail. His mouth dropped open. "Jesus Christ!" He turned away to fight the controls.

Margaret watched in horror as a moonlit sea rushed up to meet them. They smacked into the water and she was flung violently against the cargo with a searing flame in her belly and a raw jarring in her shoulders. A black abyss sucked her into oblivion.

She awoke to the sound of silence. The little bulbs still shone overhead but water was all around her. Some of the cargo had broken loose and been flung into the niche in the tail where she now sprawled. Turning her head slightly she saw the submerged red lights in the cockpit below glowing eerily. Watching the peaceful scene as from afar she knew she was having a nightmare and closed her eyes. Her head cleared and gradually she realized this was no dream. The plane had crashed. The Atlantic Ocean was outside and inside too. She was trapped! Looking down at the flooded cabin she knew the pilot must have drowned. He was dead! Then she screamed.

The sounds reverberated off the metal walls in the tail and she continued to scream as panic overwhelmed her. Claustrophobia grasped her intellect and she struggled helplessly to sit up in the small space, her shoulders aching savagely. She tried to breathe deeply to calm the fierce pounding in her chest. No. Don't breathe. There's not much air. It won't last long. I'm going to die. Oh God, I'm afraid . . . I'm so afraid. Weeping softly, she lay back to wait for death. Are You here, Jesus? I told Doug You'd be with me all the way. Are You here? Help me to die. Oh please help me die.

Water lapping outside the hull roused her from prayer and the words came to her mind, "When you pass through the waters, I will be with you . . ."

Comforted by the promise of His presence, she closed her eyes and listened to the sounds of water slapping the fuselage. She opened her eyes again. Waves. The plane's in shallow water. We haven't sunk completely. If I can get out of here I might have a chance . . .

Her eyes travelled down to the handle in the ceiling. She rotated her shoulders slowly. The pain was almost numbing and she stretched her arms carefully. Inching her way down the watery slope she reached for the handle but it was beyond her grasp. Taking a big breath, she submerged and pulled herself down to the hatch and twisted the handle. It resisted. She twisted the other way and it yielded slightly. Out of breath, she pushed herself back to the tail to gulp more precious air. She submerged again and wrenched the handle sharply, crying inside with the stabbing spasm in her shoulders. The hatch sprung ajar and she pushed her body upward through the opening into the sea and the dark warm night.

In the pale light from the moon behind a cloud bank she could barely see two feet of the tail section sticking out of the water. She pushed toward it and touched a taut wire. Faint with exhaustion and terror, she hung on the wire and waited for dawn, repeating over and over again, "The rivers shall not flow over me. When I pass through the waters, You will be with me."

As first light crept over the sea, Margaret peered toward the empty horizon. "If I can just hang on here long enough they'll find me. They should be looking for the plane in the morning." She almost dozed as the gentle waves rocked her in the swell. More of the tail appeared with the ebbing tide and she was finally able to straddle the fuselage and keep her head above water.

The sun broke across the cloud bank in the eastern sky. Clinging to the wire, she stood on the tail wing to survey her situation. A little island lay some distance to the west, and as she looked about, she discovered there were more cays even further away. The tide was still receding and she drifted weakly along the plane to sit in chest deep water on the edge of the hatch.

Several gulls skimmed the surface. Their cries comforted her, reminding her of the early mornings at Deer Lake. She remembered Raven teaching the campers about survival in the woods. 'What do you have in your hands?' he had asked.

Margaret looked at her own. "Not much, Raven," she murmured. It suddenly occurred to her that there might be something in the cabin she could use. A life jacket. A flare. The cargo! What was the cargo?

Hanging on to the edge of the hatch, she submerged and dragged a small bundle to the surface. She tried unsuccessfully to break the heavy plastic wrapping with her fingernails. My pouch. My keys. She brought out her key chain and stabbed the plastic. White powder spilled out on to the surface of the water.

"My God," she said softly. "It's cocaine." She stared with disbelieving eyes as the full truth of the situation dawned upon her. She, Margaret Darwin, was sitting on a load of cocaine in a wrecked plane somewhere in the Bahamas and no one would be coming to look for her, no authorities from the airport anyway. If anyone found her, it would be the person the pilot was talking with last night, and he was a drug dealer too, and the life of one woman, her life, would be meaningless. "No wonder he didn't want me on board," she mused.

The hopelessness of her predicament became very evident as the sun rose, hot and relentless over the sea. She sat on the edge of the hatch all morning numbed by the gravity of her situation and the knowledge that a dead man lay beneath her in the cockpit. As the tide was turning she realized she couldn't stay with the plane. The rising waters or the arrival of the drug dealer would mean certain death.

Standing to measure the distance to the nearest cay she reviewed her only option again. "It's now or never," she said and slipped into the water. Sharks. They call them the grey coats. Oh God . . . What if a shark's around here? I wouldn't have long to worry, would I. I'd never know what hit me. And at this point, death might be a sweet relief.

Her senses awakened as the exercise stressed her physical condition, increasing the spasms in her aching abdomen, the fierce throbbing in her shoulders. She swam slowly, breast-stroking her way through the clear water. The cay grew closer and she could see a small stretch of sand among the mangroves. Her hands and knees scraped the hard sea floor and she crawled the last twenty yards to collapse on dry ground. A great white heron wading nearby flapped his wings and fled. She dragged herself further into the shade, closed her eyes and fainted.

Crying gulls roused her later in the afternoon, and in her stupor, she imagined she heard a baby. Her clothing stiff with salt, damp in the creases, her parched mouth reminded her of her situation and she finally sat up to stare across the water at the tail of the plane. "Oh, God," she murmured. "What am I going to do?"

Raven spoke to her. "Look at your resources. What do you have in your hand?"

She glanced around at the patch of sand and the mangroves, wondering if the leaves were poisonous. She reached for a tender leaf and chewing it, quickly spat it out, wanting to rinse away the acrid bitter taste. At last, she rose and waded around the small cay looking for some edible shrub or flower and found instead a large green garbage bag amid a tangle of roots and, wonder of wonders, an old coconut. She shook it, and hearing liquid inside, staggered back to her patch of sand with a fleeting joy.

The shell was impenetrable. Try as she might she could not break it. There was nothing hard enough on the cay to smash it against. As the tide changed at dusk she saw in the shallows a small mound of coral limestone, and crawled toward it carrying her precious coconut. The moon was rising by the time she had crushed the husk. Her shoulders throbbing, she brought the brown stringy nut back to shore and sat down with it between her legs, wondering how to pierce it.

Raven spoke to her again. "What do you have in your hand?"

She opened her pouch and took out her keys. By the time she drank the life-giving fluid, she knew her keys would never open any more doors. Twisted and bent, she stowed them carefully in her pocket and emptied the contents of the pouch by the light of the moon. Passport, tickets and money would never help her now. Her water filled watch was useless. Even time had passed her by. As the warm Bahamian night settled over her world she pulled her hood out of her collar and tied it closely around her face. Stepping into the plastic bag, she drew it up to her waist and lay down to spend a restless night among the mosquitoes and other insects. She tried to pray but words failed her. The enormity of the peril surrounding her was too great, and because she knew she would eventually die, she wept, "Father . . . Into Thy hands I commit my spirit."

The screaming gulls wakened her to a rosy sunrise with the promise of another hot day. Margaret stretched and felt a sudden gnawing ache in her abdomen. She probed gently and discovered the hard lump had disappeared leaving a very tender area on her left side. She frowned, wondering if the impact of the crash had ruptured her ovary and what consequences would arise. Hemorrhage? The cancer spreading more quickly? Shock? Death? She quickly realized that she had indeed been in a state of shock since the crash. With the duress of the previous day, staying alive had been her only concern. Now she had survived, but death was close by and inevitable.

She went back to the marl at low tide and cracked the coconut. Using her keys to pry the meat out of the shell she ravenously ate every morsel and licked the inside for the last drop of moisture.

The day became murderously hot and she moved often to escape the sun's searing rays, her only shade the mangroves that drooped into the water. The tail of the plane was barely visible at high tide and the dull grey colour blended into the haze on the empty horizon. Somewhere in the depths was the body of the nameless pilot. Lying under the mangroves, Margaret wondered about the young man and what had motivated him to turn to a life of crime. Greed? Friends? . . . No friends are here to help you now. Your body's lying out there in a plane loaded with a cargo of death. You're a murderer just like the pushers on the street, and yet the last word you uttered was the name, Jesus Christ. Have you come face to face with Him yet? I think I read somewhere in the Bible that at death, everyone bows down before You, Jesus. I know I will. I'll gladly bow before You. I'll even bow down now before I die.

Margaret got up on her knees and lay her forehead on the sand. I don't know what to do now, Lord. I don't know what to say except I'm sorry I didn't get my house in order . . . And I know I'm still a sinner but Mr. Ferguson said You're the Saviour so will You take me just the way I am?

She began to weep and her tears ran down into the sand. I mustn't cry. I can't afford to lose any water. She sat up on the sand again and stared at the plane. Moved to pray for the young man's immortal soul she could not remember a single prayer for the dead from the prayer book. A poem and an old movie provided her with the words, "They that go down to the sea in ships . . . I commit this body to the eternal deep and this soul to his eternal rest."

I don't think I got that right, Lord, but You know what I mean. I should pray that for myself too. There won't be anybody around to pray for me when I die. I don't feel like crying now. It's as though a part of me has already died. Maybe I am dead and I'm having an out-of-the-body experience. I don't think that really, Lord. Maybe I'm saying all these crazy things because I'm so thirsty. How long does it take a person to die of thirst, especially in this heat?

A hermit crab scuttled across the sand at her feet and she shuddered at the thought of creatures running over and through her decaying body. She lay down again and let her mind drift across the shallows out to where a phantom ship rose on the empty horizon. I'll swim toward it . . . And if I drown then I won't have to think about the crabs . . . She saw herself on board, drawing closer to the shore where John and Jane were waiting on the edge of eternity.

She rubbed her eyes to dispel the fantasy. They'll never add the date of my death to the stone in Fairlawn Cemetery. No one will ever know what's happened to me. Fiona will think I stayed in Toronto. Charles and Bruce won't know where to find me. They don't know where I was going in the Bahamas or who I was going with. But the post cards . . . And maybe when Doug reads the letter . . . Fiona might wonder when I don't send for my clothes. She and Doug might both wonder. He knows I have two sons in Toronto but he doesn't know their first names. And would he even want to bother looking for me anyway? Do any of them of them really care enough to try? Charles and Bruce will have to if I'm to be declared legally dead so they can inherit. And by the time they get around to it, if they do, I'll be long dead . . . A pile of bones on a beach. She gathered her wallet and papers and stuffed them back into her pouch. And if anyone finds my bones, they can identify me with this stuff . . . unless it's rotted too. Oh Doug . . . I've made such a mess of my life. If I had only listened to my heart we'd be together. I miss you so much, darling. Do you still love me enough to look for me . . .

Thunderclouds were forming in the eastern sky late in the afternoon and hope of rain revived her dwindling spirit for a brief time. The sun set behind the clouds as they moved south of her island and she could almost smell the moisture.

"Oh God! Send a few drops my way, please? Just a few drops?" Her voice echoed across the desolate sea and she sank to her knees, sobbing uncontrollably. The mosquitoes attacked her furiously that calm humid night adding to her misery of an aching parched body and a raging thirst. She slept little, praying at intervals, "Dear sweet Jesus, please help me to live until You let me die."

At dawn, a breeze fanned her face as she lay in stupor under the mangroves. Distant thunder echoed across the horizon and shards of lightning pierced the heavy grey sky as long breakers rolled in across the shallows. The wind blasted warm rain against her plastic and nylon encased body and she sat with up-turned face and held the pieces of the coconut shell to gather the precious water cascading out of the heavens. With renewed energy she used the shell to scoop out a wide shallow hole in the sand, and washing the inside of the plastic bag, she lined the cavity and watched the puddle grow. The rain continued to pour down and she took off all her clothing to wash the salt from her skin and hair. She draped her clothing over the mangroves and stood naked in the drenching shower as she drank copiously from the puddle.

The rain stopped as suddenly as it began and the sun soon emerged from behind the clouds. The burning rays scorched her body and she covered herself with her nylon jacket and wondered how to stop her puddle from evaporating. Raven spoke to her again and she broke branches from the mangroves to provide a cover for the pool. Her clothing dried quickly and she dressed and sat down on the sand to rationally consider the hopelessness of her plight. She had no resources. She had nothing to use to catch a fish or a bird. No more coconuts appeared. The distant cays seemed infinitesimally smaller than her own and she judged them to be as equally destitute.

Raven spoke to her again. "Your best resource is prayer."

She almost smiled. It's my only resource, Raven . . . All right, God. I'll talk to You. What should I ask You for? A helicopter overhead? A fishing boat trolling by? You could even send an angel if You wanted to. You sent one to Elijah . . . No. It was ravens that brought him bread, wasn't it? But You sent angels to Jesus after He was in the wilderness for forty days. You really could send an angel, couldn't You, if You wanted to . . . But maybe You don't want to . . . I don't know why You let this happen to me. No. I'm sorry, Lord. I did this to myself. I can't blame You for this. And thank You for sending the rain. You've been awfully good to me, You know. I could have been killed but I wasn't. And You gave me a plastic bag and a coconut too. I remember Mr. McKelvie talking about prayer. He said sometimes we didn't have to say anything. We could just sit quietly and let You talk to us. So I think I'll do that now, Lord. It's Your turn to talk to me.

She sat in the shade waiting for words from on high. She waited patiently. She had nothing else to do. I can sit here all night, Lord. You take Your time and when You have something to say to me, I'll listen.

She tried to remember what else Mr. McKelvie had said about prayer. They had sung the hymn "Sweet hour of prayer" after his sermon. She hummed the tune because she knew few of the words. Other hymns came to mind and she sang the words she remembered and hummed the rest. Then she thought about the Bible verses she had learned recently, those verses in Mr. Ferguson's book. She tried to remember all she had read in the gospels about Jesus and that took her into the evening.

A bird skimmed the shallows, restlessly flying to and fro'. Margaret watched its reluctance to settle on the cay because of her presence. Mindful of the story of Noah sending forth a dove who found no resting place, she held out her hand to the bird. "Come little bird," she whispered. "Come to me and I will give you rest." The bird disappeared in the dusk. As darkness fell across the island, she drank more water and curled up in a ball to try to sleep. "I'm like Noah's dove, Lord. I need a resting place too. My wings are so weak and weary. I'm ready to die now, Lord. When You think it's best, Jesus, stretch out Your hand and bring me into Your ark."

The chugging motor awakened her. A bright beam pierced the darkness and swept on across her island to the sea. She heard a man's muffled voice across the water. "There it is!"

She sat up quickly as chains rattled, anchors splashed and the engine stopped. Their voices carried plainly across the water.

"Christ! Billy sure did an effing number on himself."

"Yeah. It's too bad. Jesus! What a mess!"

"Hey . . . The hatch is open. Maybe he got out . . . Maybe he's around here somewhere."

Margaret shrank beneath the mangroves.

"Put the tank on and go down and see."

She waited with bated breath, not knowing what she could expect if they found her. Several minutes later, she heard, "Naw. He's down there still strapped in his seat. The window's busted. The impact must have popped the hatch. Come on. Let's get to work."

The bright search light illuminated the area, and from her shelter, Margaret could see them entering the plane and carrying the bags of cocaine to a dive platform at the stern, their progress slowed by the scuba gear. She watched and considered the possibility of finding a hiding place on board that boat. If only she could get close to some settlement on an island then she would at least have a chance to live. She drank deeply from her reserves in the puddle and waded into the water.

Stealthily crossing the dark channel, she reached the bow and hung on the anchor chain waiting for an opportunity to get on board. The dive platform was now full of the bags and one man climbed out of the water to move them into the boat. When he finished, he lit a cigarette as his partner surfaced. "For God's sake, man! Come on. We haven't got all night!"

A minute later, he tossed the glowing butt into the water and jumped in after it. As Margaret heard them swimming back to the plane she floated down to the platform and heaved herself on board.

The dirty old scow reeked with oil fumes. She slipped inside the wheelhouse and walked around the pile of cocaine. A broad shelf stretched the width of the cabin in front of the helm. Underneath was a small door. She opened it and found bilge water that smelled deadly. She closed the door again and crouched in the shadows as more cocaine was coming on board. After the men left, she climbed out the large window on the side of the cabin away from the plane and crept forward to the bow, tripping over piles of rope, desperately seeking a locker, a box, a hole, a hiding place.

An old wooden life boat lay on top of the wheelhouse, secured by two leather straps. She unbuckled one and raised the boat slightly to see if there was enough room for her. Relief flooded her mind. The two men surfaced and she froze in the shadows. Unable to see far in the dark through their masks they deposited more bags and swam away again. She quickly assessed the situation and decided to look for something to eat in the next interval. Slipping through the window again, she helped herself to two snack packs of crackers and cheese, two oranges from a bag and a can of beer from the cooler on the floor. She moved outside with the booty and was undoing the other leather strapping when the men surfaced again.

"Do you wanna beer?"

"No. Let's finish up and get out of here."

Margaret went back to the cabin to find something to cushion her body against the hard roof. Among a pile of junk she found a filthy old woolen jacket. It seemed better than nothing and she retreated to her hiding place, climbed underneath and threaded the leather straps through the buckles on the cabin roof. She ate one of the packages of crackers and an orange, saving the rind to chew on later.

The sun was rising as the last of the cocaine came on board. Margaret had dozed off in her wet clothing, and when the engine choked and sputtered, she woke with a start. The men weighed anchor and the boat turned sluggishly in the water. She watched through the gap between the roof and the gunwale as the tail of the plane disappeared from view.

Well Lord . . . Are You going to get me out of this mess after all? She knew she was still in peril, very real danger in the form of two criminals below where she lay. In spite of this threat, she was comforted, knowing that if she did die she would not die alone on some forsaken island. Forgive me, Lord. That was not a forsaken island. You were there with me, helping me through it all. Thank You again for all of that. I know You're with me now, and somehow, You're going to get me off this boat.

The scow wallowed through the sea with its deadly load, a fortunate stroke of circumstance, for Margaret's abdomen and shoulders still ached and she would have been a mass of bruises had the boat plunged heavily into the waves. She never saw any land for all the miles they travelled that day. Dozing amid the noise of the engine, the roll of the sea, she thought about the addicts who would suffer from the effects of the drugs below, young people, old people and even babies. Had Jane tried cocaine? What drugs had she used? Had she become infected with the virus through a shared needle? The consequences of drug use weighed heavily on her mind as she nibbled the remaining crackers. The warm beer did little to quench her thirst. As the twilight turned to an inky blackness, she ate the other orange and chewed on the peel. Her head throbbed with the noise from the stinking engine and she prayed for sleep. Bunching the jacket up into a ball she found an old box of wooden matches in the pocket, stuffed it in her own pocket and finally fell asleep.

She awoke to silence and a muffled voice saying, "We're here. Come and get it." The anchor chains rattled monotonously, and as the boat rocked in the swell she peered through the dark night. An occasional light blinked along a distant shore. She watched, wondering if she could swim that far. A small blue light flashed across the water and soon she heard the roar of a powerful engine. Minutes later, the speedboat cut its power and drifted toward the scow. The men grabbed the lines and lashed the boats together. They climbed aboard the speed boat, and as Margaret unbuckled the straps and slipped out from her hiding place, she heard them describing the crash site and the fate of the pilot.

The lights on shore seemed brighter from the deck and she prayed for an incoming tide to carry her toward land. Soon the men would be moving about and unloading the cocaine. Now was the time to go. She crept toward the bow, glad to leave this stinking barge. Her hand rested on the box of matches in her pocket and suddenly she knew what she would do. She had seen the same trick in an old movie. Striking a match, she stuck it upright in the end of the box and leaned in the window to place it in a heap of oily rags. Then she moved to the bow, and inched her way over the gunwale, to drop into the water.

A wave caught and tossed her forward. No gentle lagoon this, the might of the Atlantic Ocean held her in its grasp. She fought to stay afloat, kicking her way upward in the swell. The waves surged behind her, bearing her away in the dark, cresting beside her. Several minutes later, as a billow lifted her high she turned her head to see the old scow burning fiercely. Slipping down into the trough she struggled to keep her head above the water, and on the crest of another wave, she heard an explosion as the speedboat burst into a giant ball of flame.

She drifted slowly toward land on the tide, saving her dwindling energy. Ahead in the darkness she heard the muffled roar of breakers on the shore. The current dragged her sideways, and as a wave hurled her into the foaming sand, she swam hard along the beach against the ebb tide pulling her back into the sea. Sandy water filled her mouth and her ears and eyes. As she fought for another breath, buffeted by the rip tide, she knew her strength was almost gone. An eddy caught and pulled her around toward shore again and she swam furiously until her feet touched the bottom. She was free at last. Collapsing, she crawled up to the beach and fainted with exhaustion.

The sun shining in her eyes woke her. Too tired to move, Margaret rolled her tongue around her dry mouth over gritty teeth. Her matted hair was stiff with seaweed. She finally turned over onto her stomach to escape the rays and saw a little corrugated tin shack on the slope above the beach. Mustering her strength, she staggered up to the weather-beaten porch and called out faintly, "Is anybody home?" Flies buzzed on a window. A rain barrel stood at one corner and she rushed over to rinse her mouth and drink the rusty water.

She found the door of the house unlocked and stepped into a tidy room with a double bed in one corner, a table and two chairs along one wall and several enamel cabinets along another. She drank again from the pail of water beside a dry sink and found a jar of tea leaves and a half loaf of bread in the cupboard. After setting the kettle to boil on a gas ring on the counter, she took a pail and a bar of laundry soap from under the sink and went outside to the rain barrel again. Here, she washed her clothing and hung it on the line to dry. She bathed herself too, washing the seaweed from her hair with the laundry soap. A dressing gown of her ample absent hostess was hanging on the wall by the bed and Margaret wrapped herself in it to sit down to her first meal in almost a week.

Waiting for her clothing to dry, along with the contents of her pouch, she looked longingly at the bed and the clean white sheets and pillows. If I lie my head down on that pillow now I'll fall asleep like Goldilocks and won't wake up 'til Mama Bear comes home and says, 'Who's that sleeping in my bed?'

By noon, she had dressed and tucked her passport, plane ticket, and wallet back into her pouch. Leaving the place as she found it, she slipped thirty Bahamian dollars under the tea jar, and walked up a sandy lane to a road. Still having no idea where she was, she walked some distance along the tarmac before an old car pulled alongside and a woman drawled, "You wanna ride into Freeport, Ma'am?"

"Please." Margaret climbed inside and sat down beside a black woman wearing a white blouse, flowered skirt and a pink straw hat. "Thank you very much."

"Where are you off to?"

"Home, to Toronto." Margaret replied numbly.

"I'll drop you at the Straw Market then. You can catch a bus there. I've been out to Bootle Bay Village, covering a story about a big explosion last night. There's three men under guard in the hospital in Freeport, but they aren't talkin'. My boss sent me out to dig up something from the local constable."

"And did you?"

"No. Nobody knows what happened."

"And the men . . . Were they hurt?"

"Some burns. Bad enough to be in the hospital but they're not dyin'. By the way, my name's Shirley Rolle."

"Oh . . . Do you have relatives in Georgetown? I met a bartender there, Henry Rolle, and there was an Anglican rector too."

Shirley laughed. "Just about everybody in Georgetown is named Rolle. A long time ago, Lord John Rolle freed all his slaves and divided his plantation among them. He must have been a good man because many of them took his last name."

As they passed through the quaint villages of Martin's Town and Eight Mile Rock, Margaret learned Shirley had been a reporter for the newspaper in Freeport for several years. She leaned her head back against the corner of the open window and watched the woman navigating among the pot-holes in the road. *Shirley sure has a lot to learn about investigative reporting. She could have the scoop of the year if she took the time to wonder why an old Canadian woman, looking like the wrath of God, is out here trudging through the heat of the noonday sun in wrinkled damp clothing, her hair sticking out in all directions, her face sunburned and peeling . . . Of course I wouldn't tell her what happened but if she was worth her salt she could at least ask.*

Margaret said goodbye to Shirley in front of the straw market, bought a green woven coconut frond hat to hide the unsightly mess of hair and took a cab to the airport. Along the way, she thought about the explosions and the fact that the authorities had no information to make a case against the drug dealers. When she reached the airport she found a phone booth, looked up the number for the Freeport Police and dialed. Attempting to disguise her voice, she said, "About de explosions last night at Bootle Bay Veellage? You weel find de body of de pilot of de drug plane in low water near Hog's Cay. He was at de Mermaid near Georgetown. Hees name ees Beelly." She hung up quickly, hoping the Freeport Police didn't have a tracing service on their incoming calls.

The air-line agent raised his eyebrows as she appeared at his desk, showing him her water-bleached ticket for the next day and explaining that due to an emergency she would like to return to Toronto as soon as possible. When he asked the reason, she said simply that she had been in accident. He noticed she had no luggage and seemed in dire straits. His supervisor was equally sympathetic and Margaret found herself on the next flight out that evening. Her senses dulled by the stress of her ordeal, she flew away from those emerald islands in the golden sunshine of the Gulf Stream, away from her little mangrove cay, and a wrecked plane still harbouring the body of a young pilot whom she had befriended.

Chapter Eight

COLD RAIN SLASHED ACROSS THE runway as the jet touched down in Toronto at midnight. The customs officer frowned at Margaret and looked at her passport again. "And no luggage?"

"No luggage," she replied firmly, too tired to offer an explanation.

Headlights gleamed on the wet pavement of the freeway as Margaret huddled in the back seat of the cab, rubbing her arms in a desperate attempt to warm herself. She dashed through the chilly November night into the lobby of the hotel. The front desk clerk assessed this shivering apparition with no luggage and an odd hat, and because her credit card was in order, he granted her asylum on the top floor.

Margaret turned up the thermostat, stripped off her clothing and fell into the bed and a dead sleep. Early in the morning she awoke perspiring, struggling, frightened from a dream where she was trapped in a hot dark tunnel with no way of escape. She rushed into the bathroom and vomited the meal eaten earlier on the airplane. Cold and shivering, she drew a warm bath and submerged, seeking relief from the pain in her abdomen and shoulders, and the pounding in her head. Later, she turned down the thermostat and crawled into bed, weak with exhaustion.

In mid-morning she awoke to escape another nightmare. She had been back in the hospice looking for Jane amid numerous beds of burn victims, gross stinking monsters swathed in putrid bandages. Billy the pilot sat strapped in Jane's bed, his pale vacant eyes sunken in his white bloated face, his red mouth wide open and screaming, his bony fingers reaching and clawing for Jane as she huddled at the end of the bed.

Margaret sprang from her bed to pace the floor, wrapped in a sheet and rubbing her eyes to rid her mind of the horror. As her heart ceased pounding, she walked to the window and watched the tiny figures below, scurrying through the rain across the parking lot. Calm at last, she ordered a bowl of oatmeal and a carafe of orange juice from room service, hoping she would not vomit again.

Eventually, she lay her aching body down again to sleep and awoke in the early evening in the midst of another dream. She and Doug were in the sea, deluged by mountainous waves, clutching, clinging to each other. A giant wave tore her from his grasp and she was swept away into the seething darkness, crying, calling, reaching out for him. She was drowning, kicking and fighting the overwhelming oceanic surge. She had to find Doug. She had to save him. She had to . . .

Her arms and legs flailing, Margaret struggled and tore at the sheets, crying out in the dark, "Doug! Where are you . . . Oh God, Let us live! Let me live!"

Waking, she knew it was only a dream but it had seemed so very real. She sat in the middle of her bed, trembling, and unable to stop the tears streaming down her cheeks. Life had become so precious now. In spite of her apparent acquiescence to death over the past several months, she had struggled to preserve herself from it through the most extraordinary circumstances. And now she wept not for the past, but for her future. She knew above all else that she could not go gently into that good night. No. She would rage against the dying of the light. She would do whatever she must to protect and preserve and prolong her life. Her life was a gift from God and she must not throw it away. As long as He chose to permit her to draw a breath she would use that breath to praise Him. She would return to her doctor and accept whatever therapy he prescribed no matter what the consequences.

She sobbed into the pillow, muffling the wrenching memories of the terrors of the past week and the submissive tears of acceptance for her uncertain future. At last, her shaking hands reached into the drawer beside the bed for the Gideon Bible and she opened it to the twenty-third Psalm. ". . . though I walk through the valley of the shadow of death, I will fear no evil . . . Surely goodness and mercy shall follow me all the days of my life, and I will dwell in the house of the Lord forever." The words comforted her as she read them over and over again, and as she slipped into a deep sleep, the book slid to the floor.

Wakening to a grey November dawn, she ordered a substantial hot breakfast, watched the morning news on the TV, and waited resignedly until nine o-clock when the medical clinic would open. Her fingers trembled as she dialed the number. "Hello, Betty. It's Margaret Darwin. I'd like to see Dr. Green today, please."

"Mrs. Darwin! Is this an emergency?"

She hesitated. "I must see the doctor as soon as possible."

After a long pause Betty said, "I'll squeeze you in before the afternoon's appointments. Can you be here at one-thirty?"

"Yes. Thank you very much."

Clamping the palm frond hat on her head she waited for the elevator beside an impeccably dressed business man who cast dubious glances in her direction. By the time they reached the lobby in a very crowded elevator, Margaret had jammed her clenched fists into the pockets of her jacket and was breathing rapidly. Panic stricken, she fled to a quiet corner of the lobby, struggling determinedly to overcome her irrational fear of small confined places.

Catching a taxi to the nearest large mall, Margaret noticed the driver watching her in the mirror. It's the hat . . . No wonder. Who'd wear this in November? She left it in the back seat when she got out of the cab in front of the large department store. The operator of the beauty salon was opening the door as Margaret came by and turned in. The woman studied her new client's hair and peeling face and smiled. "Where do you want me to start?"

Margaret sighed. "Wherever you think you should. I've just come home from the Bahamas . . ."

During the next two hours she suffered the exquisite pleasure of being pampered. Her hair was conditioned, cut, coloured and curled; her face, masqued, massaged and made-up; her hands, manicured. She left the beauty salon with a bag of cosmetics and a considerable sum added to her credit card.

Riding the escalator to the women's department on the third floor, Margaret noticed the magnificent displays of Christmas decorations throughout the store, and walked into a holiday extravaganza of beautiful clothing. When she saw the coat she knew it was hers, a soft mohair dark green wrap with a wide belt. She wore it out of the store an hour later covering a creamy silk blouse, a beige cashmere skirt, with brown pumps and a matching shoulder bag. All of her other clothing remained behind in the trash container in the ladies' room.

She caught a cab across the city to the clinic and presented herself at Betty's desk. The receptionist didn't recognize this straight, tanned, well-groomed woman who said, "I have an appointment with Dr. Green for one-thirty."

"Mrs. Darwin?" she gulped.

"Yes."

When Dr. Green's nurse appeared in the doorway to usher Margaret into the examining room, she too stared at her patient. Clutching the chart, Mrs. Waters frowned and said brusquely, "Come this way, Mrs. Darwin."

Margaret followed her into the examining room.

"The doctor will be with you in a moment," she said curtly and closed the door.

Too restless to sit, Margaret walked to the window and stared pensively at the leaden November skies. She turned as the door opened and Dr. Green entered. He closed the door quietly and raised his eyes to see an attractive woman walking toward him. "Mrs. Darwin?"

She held out her hand and he shook it mechanically, dazedly sinking down to the edge of his desk.

"Is it too late for me to begin treatment?"

He continued to stare at her. "Treatment?"

"Yes . . . Surgery. Radiation. Chemo . . . Whatever you think best . . ."

His gaze penetrated her mask of serenity.

"I know you have every right to be angry with me," she began. "You had been so kind. You had tried so hard, making all the arrangements for the surgery. But I couldn't face all of that . . . And so I decided to go away and . . ."

He cleared his throat. "And now you've changed your mind?"

"Yes. I realize how precious life is . . ."

"We've wasted so much time, Mrs. Darwin . . ."

"I know. But something's happened to the tumour. It's gone . . ."

"Gone?" Dr. Green ran his fingers through his short wiry hair and turned from her anxious face to open her chart. He pressed his lips tightly together and looked at her again. "I'll have to examine you. Slip your coat off and I'll send the nurse in to help you get ready."

Several minutes later, he asked quietly, "Do you feel any pain here?"

"Yes."

"Here?"

"Yes."

"Here?"

"Yes. It's a little tender . . . Yes."

Some time later, he pulled off his latex gloves and helped Margaret to sit up on the side of the examining table. She watched his grey eyes regard her steadily. "Well," he said at last, picking up her chart. "You can put your clothes on now. I'll be back in a few minutes."

She was waiting by the window again when he returned, waiting with a dreadful anticipation . . . Oh God, let me be anywhere but here . . .

Laying her chart on his desk, he said quietly, "Please sit down."

An icy fear churned her stomach as she sank to the chair and awaited the verdict. He rubbed his hands as he sat down in front of her. "I don't know how to tell you this . . ."

She closed her eyes.

"You've been done a grave injustice."

She bit her lip.

"This should never have happened. Never. I can only say I'm terribly sorry to have caused you so much grief. You aren't dying, Mrs. Darwin."

Her eyes flew open.

He picked up a piece of paper. "This lab report was mistakenly ascribed to you. I've just spoken to the head of the haematology lab and the records indicate two serum CA 125 screening tests were done on this date. One was negative, and this is the other. I've checked the other patient's file and learned that she died two months ago of metastatic ovarian cancer. In other words, the cancer had spread throughout her entire body. The lab obviously has made a monumental error."

Dr. Green's face swam before her eyes.

"I can't prove it but you probably had an ovarian cyst that ruptured. I can't feel anything on the ovary at all. You're still guarding in that area but the healing process has begun."

Margaret's shoulders heaved as she burst into tears. Dr. Green leaned over and wordlessly patted her arm. He reached for a box of tissues and stuffed a large wad into her hand. She covered her eyes and sobbed convulsively.

He patted her shoulder. "There, there, Mrs. Darwin."

"I'm not dying," she gulped.

"No. We've made a terrible mistake."

"Oh God!" she sobbed. "I can't believe this. I can't . . ."

He handed her some more tissues.

"I'm not going to die . . ."

"We all die someday," he murmured. "But you're not dying now." He grasped her hand. "I can't guarantee my patients anything. I try to do my best but the verdicts of life and death aren't mine to make. Judging from your appearance, I think you could live to be a hundred, but if there's a truck out there on Markdale St. with your name on the bumper . . ."

She wiped her eyes and smiled faintly.

He cleared his throat. "I'm sure your family, two sons, isn't it . . . I'm sure they'll have some questions. Would you like me to explain it to them?"

She shook her head. "That won't be necessary."

"I'll talk to Dr. Carson. He's at a conference this week. I know he'll want to see you." He shuffled through the papers. "There was some abnormality in the bowel . . ."

She caught her breath.

"Don't worry! Please don't worry . . . You've been under enough stress. I couldn't find anything in the bowel when I examined you. A colonoscopy will clear up any doubts. If you roll up your sleeve, I'll take another blood sample for the record."

She wiped her eyes again and watched quietly.

He bent her forearm back and filled out a requisition before turning to her again. "Now then . . . I've done a uterine biopsy as well as a Pap smear, and we have a blood sample so we'll wait for those results. I'd like to do another ultra-sound on the ovary when it's completely healed. I'll talk to Dr. Carson about the colonoscopy. He may want to repeat the mammogram and do some other tests as well. But apart from all that, I feel safe in telling you to get on with your life."

She sighed deeply. "I still can't believe this is happening . . ."

He folded his hands on his chest. "I can't begin to imagine what you've been through these past months. If you'd had the surgery, we'd have discovered the truth then, and all you would have now is a scar. I'm sorry you've had all this worry."

She nodded. "I've learned a lot from this. A lot about myself . . . And I've found God . . ."

"Most of my cancer patients find Him," he mused. "I wonder why we leave it until the end."

"When do you want to see me again?"

He rose from his chair. "I'll call you next week when I have the results of the tests and I've spoken to Dr. Carson."

"I've moved. Perhaps it would be better if I called you."

"Make it Tuesday about this time," he suggested.

She reached for her coat. "All right. And thank you, Dr. Green. Thank you so much."

He stood in the doorway of the examining room and watched her hurry up the hall. Rubbing his chin, he mused, "And when the thankful Mrs. Darwin tells her sons about this mess, I may be spending a lot of time with my lawyer." He sighed and turned to meet his next patient.

Light of heart and step, Margaret stopped in the lobby restroom to repair her make-up and gazed at her reflection. "Today is the first day of the rest of your life," she whispered, "and you know exactly how you want to spend it." Thoughts of Douglas James Parker swam through her mind and she felt her heart might burst with the joy of seeing him again and explaining her new found lease on life.

She danced out onto Markdale St. and crossed over to the bus stop, mindful of Dr. Green's admonition about trucks. That would be the ultimate irony wouldn't it . . . What was the name of that movie where Alec Guinness received a similar reprieve from his doctor and then got killed by a train on his way home. Please, God . . . Don't let anything happen to me now. I've got to see Doug again.

Margaret floated off the bus and into her bank to make a withdrawal because the Toronto taxis had made considerable inroads into her supply of cash. Glancing at the clock, she realized she had several hours to spare and decided to go up to Bill Davidson's office and say hello.

The receptionist frowned and said that Mr. Davidson Sr. wasn't in the office today but Mr. Davidson Jr. could see her in a few minutes if she cared to wait. When the office door opened, Margaret rose to greet the son of her husband's old friend.

"Mrs. Darwin." He held out his hand. "I'm sorry Dad isn't in today. He hasn't been feeling well lately."

"Oh dear," she murmured. "I hope it's nothing serious."

"They're doing some tests," he replied evasively, leading her into the office and seating her beside the desk. He drew her file from a cabinet in the corner. "Now, let me see. You've been out of the country . . ."

Margaret caught her breath thinking that if Bill Davidson had been in the office she would have been trapped in her web of lies. Thank You, God. It's time to put my house in order. It's time to get things straight. She became aware that Jim Davidson was still talking to her.

"And . . . Yes . . . The life insurance claims on your husband's policies have been paid . . . And I see Father has invested them, at a very good rate of interest, I might add."

She raised her eyebrows. "Policies? I thought there was only the one for a hundred thousand."

He peered at her over his reading glasses. "You weren't aware of the other? Let me see . . . Your husband took that one out almost forty years ago . . ."

"That was before I met him. Before we were married . . ."

"It was a twenty-pay-life. In other words, the principal was paid twenty years ago and the interest has been compounding ever since. After taxes, you've received in excess of four hundred and fifty thousand dollars in insurance claims alone."

Margaret stared at him. Words failed her as she leaned across the desk to take the form from his hand. Blinking her blurry eyes, she tried to read the words and figures and finally handed it back to him. "Thank you, Jim," she said softly. "And please thank your father for taking such good care of me all these years."

The elevator descended to the lobby and Margaret had to make a conscious effort to push herself into the bustling crowd. Pinch yourself. Wake up. She flowed toward the entrance in the stream of shoppers and found herself out on the street in a world that had never looked more beautiful in spite of the lowering skies and the swarms of grim-faced people bundled up against the sharp wind. "Thank You again, God. It really is time to put my house in order," she murmured, and wrapping her coat tightly, hurried down the street towards Charles' office.

The pretty receptionist smiled up at her.

"I'd like to see Charles. Mr. Darwin, please."

"Do you have an appointment?"

"No. I just want to see him for a minute. I'm his mother."

The girl blinked perceptibly and pressed the intercom. "Mr. Darwin's mother is here to see him."

The office door opened and Charles' secretary emerged. "Please come in, Mrs. Darwin. He's with a client but he won't be long."

Margaret seated herself by the window aware of the secretary's covert glances, and more aware that she was now to bare her soul to her elder son. After several minutes the door to the inner office opened and Charles accompanied a business man toward the reception area. Margaret watched her son's practised courtesy and wondered if he ever tired of soliciting people.

Turning back toward his office he noticed a woman sitting by the window. She stood up to greet him. "Charles . . ."

"Mother! You're looking wonderfully well!" He put his arm around her to usher her toward his office. "You must have had a great holiday. Come and tell me all about it."

She glanced about the attractively furnished room as he motioned her to a comfortable chair. "It's so good to see you, dear. And how are Mavis and the boys?"

"They're all fine. Did I tell you that Mavis' mother is living with us now?"

"Yes. And how is Gertrude?"

"She's . . . . fine. We built a granny flat for her behind the garage."

"That's nice."

"So how are you? Have you decided what you're going to do?"

"Well . . ."

"Bruce and I were talking just the other day. He was wondering if you might want to live with them. He's looking at a bigger house."

"I don't know about that . . ." she began.

"Well, it's something to consider anyway, Mother. We wouldn't want you to feel as though you were all alone, now that Dad's gone."

She resisted the impulse to stand up and scream at him that she had been all alone for years. I'm sorry, Lord. I've forgiven my children for all that, haven't I . . . She uncrossed her legs and moved toward the edge of her chair. "Charles, there's something I want to tell you. I haven't been honest with you and Bruce for the last several months."

He frowned. "What do you mean?"

She drew a big breath. "Last spring, after your father died, I wasn't feeling well and had some tests at the hospital. That was where I got the idea about going to England, reading those magazines in waiting rooms. And then I made a horrible mistake. I thought I had a terminal cancer and very foolishly decided to go away by myself to die."

Charles half rose to his feet. "Mother!"

She held up her hand. "It's all right. I've just come from the doctor's and he's assured me that I'll live to be a hundred . . ."

"But why? Why did you feel that you had to go away?"

She sighed. "Call me a foolish old woman. I'd been through a bad time with your father and Jane . . . And I know it was hard on you and Bruce and your families too. I thought I'd spare you more grief . . ."

"But Mother . . ."

"I know I shouldn't have lied to you. That's one of the reasons why I'm here now. I want to ask for your forgiveness."

"But Mother . . ."

"Please forgive me for not trusting you, Charles. For not having enough faith in you to believe that you loved me and would care for me."

The intercom buzzed and he glanced at it.

"So instead of going to England, I went up north to a small town called New Lancaster. Do you remember a long time ago when we went fishing on the Montreal River and it rained and your father and I took you kids to see Mary Poppins? That's New Lancaster."

The intercom buzzed again.

"So what did you do? Where did you stay?"

The secretary opened the door. "It's Mr. Ramsay . . ."

Charles picked up the phone. "Just a minute, please."

"That my dear, is a very long story." She reached for her shoulder bag. "I'm going to run along now. I want to see Bruce too." She kissed his cheek and left him to his business.

Chapter Nine

THE ONTARIO NORTHLAND HAD GATHERED speed as it left the city behind and plunged into the dark November night. The passengers were scattered sparsely through the quiet coach, and with the lights now dimmed, Margaret felt herself quite alone. Leaning her head against the cold pane she watched a solitary light disappear in the distance across barren wind-swept fields. The whistle wailed as they flashed past red lights where a truck waited at a crossing. She closed her eyes, reliving the extraordinary events of the day that were still tumbling in her mind, Dr. Green, Jim Davidson, Charles, Bruce . . . Dear Bruce.

She had caught him at his factory, embroiled in a friendly argument with his foreman. He had come quickly to greet her, dismissing his employee with a smile, and had led her into his office to give her a hug and a kiss. He had wept when he learned of her ordeal, her lonely summer and the anticipation of her death. Wiping his eyes, he had asked, "And now what are you going to do, Mom?"

"I'm going back to New Lancaster," she replied. "I met a man there whom I love very much. I hurt him badly keeping the truth from him when he was so good, so kind to me. I want to ask him to forgive me too. And if he'll still have me, I'll marry him and live happily ever after."

"Come home with me now," Bruce said. "Jennie and the kids will want to see you. You're looking like a million bucks, Mom."

She laughed. "A half million anyway."

He raised his eyebrows.

She looked at his clock. "If you drive me to the subway, dear, I'll be able to catch the evening train."

She had hurried into Union Station with just enough time to buy her ticket and call Fiona. The answering machine had clicked on.

"Fiona. It's Margaret. Will you leave the front door open tonight? I'm coming in on the early train and don't have my keys. Thanks."

The train rushed northward through the cold blustery night, bearing her home to her dearest love, and as she gazed out at the bleak landscape, her ardent anticipation of seeing Doug again cooled to apprehension instead. Remembering the scenes of their last encounters, Doug's anger masking his pain, she sighed. *He pushed me away so bitterly, so completely . . . Oh God, please let him still love me.* The grim consequences of the situation if he didn't love her rose in her mind. *What if he doesn't want me . . .* She caught her breath. *What if he never wants to see me again . . . What if he's met someone else . . .* The memory of the attractive blonde Sally in the jogging suit stirred her anxiety. *No. He couldn't. He wouldn't fall in love with someone in two weeks! But he said he fell in love with me the first time we met. No. He couldn't fall out of love with me and in love with someone else in two weeks. Not unless he was desperately lonely, and he was! Oh God! Please don't let him love anyone else . . . If he doesn't want me then I won't stay in New Lancaster. I'll have to go away and start all over again by myself. Forgive me, Lord. I won't be by myself. You'll be with me so I won't be alone. Thank You, Jesus, for being here now.*

I've got so much to thank You for, Lord. I told Dr. Green I'd learned a lot, a lot about myself. But I'm learning a lot about You too. You've always been there with me, haven't You . . . I always thought that poem about You being the Hound of Heaven was sort of sacrilegious. The idea of You being a dog didn't seem right . . . But the rest of it is true. I've run away from You all my life, God . . . "I fled from You down the nights and down the days, down the arches of the years, down the labyrinthine ways of my own mind". But I couldn't get away from Your boundless love. And now I ask myself why was I so afraid of You? You've shown me nothing but mercy and grace. You gave me a good marriage to a good man. You gave me children to love. You showered me with so many material things and I never stopped to thank You for any of them, not even the food on the table. Even through the bad times, You were there in the shadows. I can see this so clearly now. It's like You have this plan for my life. You wanted me to find You but I was too mixed up with all my problems to listen or look for You. I was relying on me, my own strength, my own pride and self-confidence. And so You had to get me away from everything, and strip me down to nothing before I'd turn to You, to trust You, to believe that You alone are my source, the answer to every problem in my life . . . *"All which You took from me, You did but not for my harms, But just that I might seek it in Your arms."* You wanted me to learn that everything I have comes from You, even the air that I breathe. And I've learned it, God . . ." Thou art my way; I wander if Thou fly. Thou art my light; if hid, how blind am I. Thou art my life; if Thou withdraw I die . . .

I've been sitting here worrying about Doug when I should have been talking to You about him. Be patient with me, God. I still have a long way to go. Is Doug in Your plan for my life? If he is then I'll thank You for that . . . And if he isn't, then I'll try to thank You for that too. If he doesn't want me then I'll try to understand why . . . Maybe You want me to realize that You alone are my happiness, my joy . . . That I'll find solace in Your arms alone.

The train stopped for a half hour to shunt cars onto a siding and she drank a cup of coffee to clear her head and plan for her meeting with Doug. I can't call him first thing in the morning. Not before school. It'll take a while to explain all this and I can't do it over the telephone. I'll have to tell him face to face. Maybe I should walk over and meet him as he's leaving the school. We could sit in the car . . . Oh darling Doug . . . I've missed you so much . . .

More passengers appeared in the coach and among them, Peter Spencer stopped in the aisle by her seat. Nodding to the empty seat, he said, "Mrs. Darwin, how nice to see you again. May I join you?"

Margaret smiled up at him and moved her purse onto her lap. "Of course. Are you on your way to New Lancaster?"

He crossed his bony knees and replied, "Yes. I'm on my way to fetch John and take him to his son's place in Ottawa. The poor old fellow isn't well and I didn't want him to make the trip alone."

Margaret murmured, "I wondered about him He hasn't been at the church all summer. I wondered if he had stayed in Ottawa."

Peter shook his head. "He told the bishop he wouldn't leave his people behind with a student filling the pulpit. I guess he has spent the time sitting at home resting his tired heart. Poor old fellow. Tell me, Margaret, have you met many of the folk at St. Judes?"

She swallowed the dregs of her coffee. "As a matter of fact I've met the Hasketts and another man who is very nice."

Peter Spencer raised his eyebrows in unfeigned curiosity. "Has this man become very special to you?"

Margaret felt herself blushing. "Yes" she replied. "Doug is a good man and a good friend. I've been praying about marrying him."

Peter Spencer sat up straighter and rose to his feet. "Well here we are already."

When the train glided into the station, Margaret wrapped her coat tightly, swung her bag over her shoulder and stepped down to the platform. Peter took her elbow. Ice crystals swirled about her feet as she hurried toward the parking lot, hoping Walt was there in his cab. A figure stepped out of the shadows of the darkened ticket office, his arm outstretched as if to bar her way. "Margaret . . ."

She turned toward him, her face breaking into a radiant smile. "Doug . . ."

He drew closer and she stepped into the arc of his arm and kissed his cheek.

"I got your letter . . . Fiona . . ."

She kissed his cheek again.

He put his other arm around her. "I love you." His voice quavered and he knew he was going to cry. "Won't you trust me to love you all the way?"

She tilted her head back to see his eyes filled with tears. Clasping his face in her hands, she said, "I'm not dying, Doug. It was all a terrible mistake. I saw the doctor this afternoon and I'm going to live to be a hundred." Peter Spencer stood quietly listening to their conversation, wondering.

His fragile grief shattered and he felt himself falling apart in her arms. Clinging to her, he poured out the anguish of the past agonizing hours, sobbing into the fragrance of her hair.

She stroked the back of his head. "It's all right, darling. It's all right."

His mind was racing, faltering, falling.

"I love you so much," she whispered, her lips brushing his ear, his cheek.

He hugged her fiercely, kissing her hungrily, starving for her love.

She drew away from him breathlessly. "Take me home now, darling. I have so much to tell you . . . So much more to share. Doug, I want to introduce you to Peter Spencer. He's a friend to Harry Copse."

Peter stretched out his hand. "I don't want to interrupt anything here so I'll be on my way to find the taxi. He left them standing shivering in each other's arms. Doug drew her across the platform into the car. Margaret shivered violently. "I'm sooooo cold."

Doug turned on the ignition and drew her close. "Now you can tell me all about it when we get home."

As the car rolled across the parking lot, they spied Peter Spencer huddled around the corner out of the sharp wind. "Oh dear, Doug? Do you suppose we could give him a lift over to the rectory?"

Early Monday morning, Walt squeezed his paunch into the booth at the coffee shop, drank a swig of the fresh brew and opened the Herald to the classified section to scan the obituaries and announcements. His round face broke into a broad grin. "Well what do you know!" he said softly.

> *Margaret Elizabeth Darwin and Douglas James*
> *Parker were married Saturday November 9*
> *at St, Andrew's Presbyterian Church, the Rev.*
> *Angus McKelvie officiating. Fiona MacPherson*
> *and Edwin Haskett attended. A dinner reception*
> *at the Country Club followed the ceremony. Mr.*
> *and Mrs. Parker plan to visit family in Nairobi,*
> *Kenya before going on to vacation in Italy. Their*
> *friends and neighbours wish them every happiness.*

THE END